Legends of Florence

Collected from the People

And Re-told

by

Charles Godfrey Leland

(*Hans Breitmann*)

First Series

NEW YORK
MACMILLAN AND CO
1895

PREFACE

THIS book consists almost entirely of legends or traditions of a varied character, referring to places and buildings in Florence, such as the Cathedral and Campanile, the Signoria, the Bargello, the different city gates, ancient towers and bridges, palaces, crosses, and fountains, noted corners, odd by-ways, and many churches. To all of these there are tales, or at least anecdotes attached, which will be found as entertaining to the general reader as they will be interesting, not to say valuable, to the folk-lorist and the student of social history; but here I must leave the work to speak for itself.

I originally intended that this should be entirely a collection of relics of ancient mythology, with superstitions and sorceries, witchcraft and incantations, or what may be called occult folk-lore, of which my work on " Etruscan-Roman Remains in Popular Tradition " consists, and of which I have enough additional material to make a large volume. But having resolved to add to it local legends, and give them the preference, I found that the latter so abounded, and were so easily collected by an expert, that I was obliged to cast out my occult folk-lore, piece by piece, if I ever hoped to get into the port of publication, according to terms with the underwriters, following the principle laid down by the illustrious Poggio,

that in a storm the heaviest things must go overboard first, he illustrating the idea with the story of the Florentine, who, having heard this from the captain when at sea in a tempest, at once threw his wife into the raging billows— -perche non haveva cosa piii grave di lei —because there was nought on earth which weighed on him so heavily.

There are several very excellent and pleasant works on Old Florence, such as that portion devoted to it in the "Cities of Central Italy," by A. J. C. Hare; the "Walks about Florence," by the Sisters Horner; " Florentine Life," by Scaife; and the more recent and admirable book by Leader Scott, which are all—I say it advisedly— indispensable for those who would really know something about a place which is unusually opulent in ancient, adventurous, or artistic associations. My book is, however, entirely different from these, and all which are exclusively taken from authentic records and books. My tales are, with a few exceptions, derived directly or indirectly from the people themselves—having been recorded in the local dialect—the exceptions being a few anecdotes racy of the soil, taken from antique jest-books and such bygone halfpenny literature as belonged to the multitude, and had its origin among them. These I could not, indeed, well omit, as they every one refer to some peculiar place in Florence. To these I must add several which remained obscurely in my memory, but which I did not record at the time of hearing or reading, not having then the intention of publishing such a book.

It has been well observed by Wordsworth that minor local legends sink more deeply into the soul than greater

histories, as is proved by the fact that romantic folk-lore spreads far and wide over the world, completely distancing in the race the records of mighty men and their deeds. The magic of Washington Irving has cast over the Catskills and the Hudson, by means of such tales, an indescribable fascination, even as Scott made of all Scotland a fairyland; for it is indisputable that a strange story, or one of wild or quaint adventure, or even of humour, goes further to fix a place in our memory than anything else can do. Therefore I have great hope that these fairy-tales of Florence, and strange fables of its fountains, palaces, and public places—as they are truly gathered from old wives, and bear in themselves unmistakable evidences of antiquity — will be of real use in impressing on many memories much which is worth retaining, and which would otherwise have been forgotten.

The manner in which these stories were collected was as follows:—In the year 1886 I made the acquaintance in Florence of a woman who was not only skilled in fortune-telling, but who inherited as a family gift from generations, skill in witchcraft—that is, a knowledge of mystical cures, the relieving people who were bewitched, the making amulets, and who had withal a memory stocked with a literally incredible number of tales and names of spirits, with the invocations to them, and strange rites and charms. She was a native of the Romagna Toscana, where there still lurks in the recesses of the mountains much antique Etrusco-Roman heathenism, though it is disappearing very rapidly. Maddalena—such was her name—soon began to communicate to me all her lore.

She could read and write, but beyond this never gave the least indication of having opened a book of any kind; albeit she had an immense library of folk-lore in her brain. When she could not recall a tale or incantation, she would go about among her extensive number of friends, and being perfectly familiar with every dialect, whether Neapolitan, Bolognese, Florentine, or Venetian, and the ways and manners of the poor, and especially of witches, who are the great repositories of legends, became in time wonderfully well skilled as a collector. Now, as the proverb says, "Take a thief to catch a thief," so I found that to take a witch to catch witches, or detect their secrets, was an infallible means to acquire the arcana of sorcery. It was in this manner that I gathered a great part of the lore given in my " Etruscan-Roman Remains." I however collected enough, in all conscience, from other sources, and verified it all sufficiently from classic writers, to fully test the honesty of my authorities.

The witches in Italy form a class who are the repositories of all the folk-lore ; but, what is not at all generally known, they also keep as strict secrets an immense number of legends of their own, which have nothing in common with the nursery or popular tales, such as are commonly collected and published. The real witch-story is very often only a frame, so to speak, the real picture within it being the arcanum of a long scongiurazione or incantation, and what ingredients were used to work the charm. I have given numbers of these real witch-tales in my " Etruscan-Roman Remains," and a few, such as " Orpheus and Eurydice," " Intialo," and " Il Moschone," in this work.

Lady Vere de Vere, who has investigated witchcraft as

PREFACE

IX

it exists in the Italian Tyrol, in an admirable article in La Rivista of Rome (June 1894)—which article has the only demerit of being too brief—tells us that " the Community of Italian Witches is regulated by laws, traditions, and customs of the most secret kind, possessing special recipes for sorcery," which is perfectly true. Having been free of the community for years, I can speak from experience. The more occult and singular of their secrets are naturally not of a nature to be published, any more than are those of the Voodoos. Some of the milder sort may be found in the story of the " Moscone, or Great Fly," in this work. The great secret for scholars is, however, that these pagans and heretics, who are the last who cling to a heathen creed out-worn in Europe—these outcast children of the Cainites, Ultra-Taborites, and similar ancient worshippers of the devil, are really the ones who possess the most valuable stores of folk-lore, that is to say, such as illustrate the first origins of the religious Idea, its development, and specially the evolution of the Opposition or Protestant principle.

As regards the many legends in this book which do not illustrate such serious research, it is but natural that witches, who love and live in the Curious, should have preserved more even of them than other people, and it was accordingly among her colleagues of the mystic spell that Maddalena found tales which would have been long sought for elsewhere, of which this book is a most convincing proof in itself; for while I had resolved on second thought to make it one of simple local tales, there still hangs over most—even of these—a dim, unholy air of sorcery, a witch aura, a lurid light, a something eerie

and uncanny, a restless hankering for the broom and the supernatural. Those tales are Maddalena's every line—I pray thee, reader, not to make them mine. The spirit will always speak.

Very different, indeed, from these are the contributions of Marietta Pery, the improvvisatrice, though even she in good faith, and not for fun, had a horseshoe for luck; which, however, being of an artistic turn, she had elegantly gilded, and also, like a true Italian, wore an amulet. She, too, knew many fairy tales, but they were chiefly such as may be found among the Racconti delle Fate, and the variants which are now so liberally published. She had, however, a rare, I may almost say a refined, taste in these, as the poems which I have given indicate.

I must also express my obligations to Miss Roma Lister, a lady born in Italy of English parentage, who is an accomplished folk-lorist and collector, as was shown by her paper on the Legends of the Castelli Romani, read at the first meeting of the Italian Folk-Lore Society, founded by Count Angelo de Gubernatis, the learned and accomplished Oriental scholar, and editor of La Rivista. I would here say that her researches in the vicinity of Rome have gone far to corroborate what I published in the " Etruscan-Roman Remains." I must also thank Miss Teresa Wyndham for sundry kind assistances, when I was ill in Siena.

There is no city in the world where, within such narrow limit, Art, Nature, and History have done so much to make a place beautiful and interesting as Florence. It is one where we feel that there has been vivid and varied life —life such as was led by Benvenuto Cellini and a

thousand like him—and we long more than elsewhere to enter into it, and know how those men in quaint and picturesque garb thought and felt four hundred years ago. Now, as at the present day politics and news do not enter into our habits of thought more than goblins, spirits of fountains and bridges, legends of palaces and towers, and quaint jests of friar or squire, did into those of the olden time, I cannot help believing that this book will be not only entertaining, but useful to all who would study the spirit of history thoroughly. The folk-lore of the future has a far higher mission than has as yet been dreamed for it; it is destined to revive for us the inner sentiment or habitual and peculiar life of man as he was in the olden time more perfectly than it has been achieved by fiction. This will be done by bringing before the reader the facts or phenomena of that life itself in more vivid and familiar form. Admitting this, the reader can hardly fail to see that the writer who gathers up with pains whatever he can collect of such materials as this book contains does at least some slight service to Science.

And to conclude—with the thing to which I would specially call attention—I distinctly state that (as will be very evident to the critical reader) there are in this book, especially in the second series, which I hope to bring out later, certain tales, or anecdotes, or jests, which are either based on a very slight foundation of tradition—often a mere hint—or have been so "written up " by a runaway pen—and mine is an " awful bolter " —that the second-rate folk-lorist, whose forte consists not in finding facts but faults, may say in truth, as one of his kind did in America: " Mr. Leland is throughout

inaccurate." In these numerous instances, which are only " folk-lore" run wild, as Rip Van Winkle, Sleepy Hollow, and Heine's Gods in Exile are legend, I have, 1 hope, preserved a certain spirit of truth, though I have sans mercy sacrificed the letter, even as the redcap goblins, which haunt old houses, are said to be the ghosts of infants sacrificed by witches, or slain by their mothers, in order to make/6>//^#z or imps of them.

Now as for this reconstructing Hercules from a foot, instead of giving the fragment, at which few would have glanced, the success consists in the skill attained, and the approbation of the reader. And with this frank admission, that in a certain number of these tales the utmost liberty has been taken, I conclude.

CHARLES GODFREY LELAND.

FLORENCE, April 6, 1894.

CONTENTS

	PAGE
THE THREE HORNS OF MESSER GUICCIARDINI	1
THE PILLS OF THE MEDICI	6
FURICCHIA, OR THE EGG-WOMAN OF THE MERCATO VECCHIO	11
THE LANTERNS OF THE STROZZI PALACE	17
THE GOBLIN OF LA VIA DEL CORNO	21
FRATE GIOCONDO, THE MONK OF SANTA MARIA NOVELLA	26
THE LEGEND OF THE CROCE AL TREBBIO	31
THE TWO FAIRIES OF THE WELL	36
THE STORY OF THE VIA DELLE SERVE SMARRITE	41
THE BRONZE BOAR OF THE MERCATO NUOVO	47
THE FAIRY OF THE CAMPANILE, OR THE TOWER OF GIOTTO	51
THE GOBLIN OF THE TOWER DELLA TRINITA, OR THE PORTA SAN NICCOLO	54
THE GHOST OF MICHEL ANGELO	59
THE APPARITION OF DANTE	62
LEGENDS OF LA CERTOSA	66
LEGENDS OF THE BRIDGES IN FLORENCE	74
THE BASHFUL LOVER	85
LA FORTUNA	87
THE STORY OF THE UNFINISHED PALACE	91
THE DEVIL OF THE MERCATO VECCHIO	98
SEEING THAT ALL WAS RIGHT	107
THE ENCHANTED COW OF LA VIA VACCHERECCIA	109

PAGE
THE WITCH OF THE PORTA ALLA CROCK 114
THE COLUMN OF COSIMO, OR DELLA SANTA TRINITA ..118
LEGENDS OF OR' SAN MICHELE 122
THE WITCH OF THE ARNO 132
STORIES OF SAN MINIATO 141
THE FRIAR'S HEAD OF SANTA MARIA MAGGIORE — THE LADY WHO CONFESSED FOR EVERYBODY — HOLY RELICS ..149
BIANCONE, THE GIANT STATUE IN THE SIGNORIA ...152
THE RED GOBLIN OF THE BARGELLO 160
LEGENDS OF SAN LORENZO 167
LEGEND OF THE PIAZZA SAN BIAGIO.......... 174
THE SPIRIT OF THE PORTA SAN GALLO 176
STORY OF THE PODESTA WHO WAS LONG ON HIS JOURNEY 179
LEGENDS OF THE BOBOLI GARDENS : THE OLD GARDENER, AND THE TWO STATUES AND THE FAIRY 184
How LA VIA DELLA MOSCA GOT ITS NAME 188
THE ROMAN VASE 194
THE UNFORTUNATE PRIEST 201
THE MYSTERIOUS FIG-TREE 205
IL PALAZZO FERONI 211
LA VIA DELLE BELLE DONNE .219
THE WIZARD WITH RED TEETH 221
ORPHEUS AND EURYDICE 225
INTIALO: THE SPIRIT OF THE HAUNTING SHADOW...237
CAIN AND HIS WORSHIPPERS 254

LEGENDS OF FLORENCE

THE THREE HORNS OF MESSER GUICCIARDINI

" More plenty than the fabled horn Thrice emptied could pour forth at banqueting."
— KEATS, The Earlier Version of " Hyperion"

"Prosperity is often our worst enemy, making us vicious, frivolous, and insolent, so that to bear it well is a better test of a man than to endure adversity."— GUICCIARDINI, Maxims, No. 64.

I DID not know when I first read and translated the following story, which was obtained for me and written out by Maddalena, that it had any reference to the celebrated historian and moralist, Guicciardini. How I did so forms the subject of a somewhat singular little incident, which I will subsequently relate.

LE TRE CORNE.

"There was an elderly man, a very good, kind-hearted, wise person, who was gentle and gay with every one, and much beloved by his servants, because they always found him buono ed allegro —pleasant and jolly. And often when with them while they were at their work, he would say, 'Felice voi poveri!' —'Oh, how lucky you are to be poor!' And they would reply to him, singing in the old Tuscan fashion, because they knew it pleased him :

"' O caro Signor, you have gold in store,

With all to divert yourself; Your bees make honey, you've plenty of money,

And victuals upon the shelf: A palace you have, and rich attire, And everything to your heart's desire.'

A

" Then he would reply merrily :

"' My dear good folk, because you are poor You are my friends, and all the more, For the poor are polite to all they see, And therefore blessed be Poverty '.'

" Then a second servant sang :

" ' Oh bello gentile mio Signor',

Your praise of poverty 'd soon be o'er If you yourself for a time were poor ; For nothing to eat, and water to drink, Isn't so nice as you seem to think, And a lord who lives in luxury Don't know the pressure of poverty.'

" Then all would laugh, and the jolly old lord would sing in his turn:

" ' O charo servitor',

Tu parli tanto bene, Ma il tuo parlar

A me non mi conviene.' . . .

" ' My boy, you answer well, But with false implication ; For what to me you tell Has no true application ; How oft I heard you say (You know 'tis true, you sinner !) " I am half-starved to-day, How I'll enjoy my dinner !" Your hunger gives you health And causes great delight, While I with all my wealth Have not an appetite.'

" Then another servant sang, laughing:

" 'Dear master, proverbs say,

I have heard them from my birth, That of all frightful beasts

Which walk upon the earth, Until we reach the bier,

Wherever man may be, There's nothing which we fear

So much as poverty.'

"And so one evening as they were merrily improvising and throwing stornelli at one another in this fashion, the Signore went to his street-door, and there beheld three ladies of stately form; for though they were veiled and dressed in the plainest black long robes, it was evident that they were of high rank. Therefore the old lord saluted them courteously, and seeing that they were strangers, asked them whither they were going. But he had first of all had them politely escorted by his servants into his best reception-room. 1

"And the one who appeared to be the chief replied: "'Truly we know not where we shall lodge, for in all Florence there is, I trow, not a soul who, knowing who we are, would receive us.'

"'And who art thou, lady?' asked the Signore. And she replied:

"'Io mi chiamo, e sono, La Poverta in persona, E queste due donzelle, Sono le mie sorelle, Chi voi non conoscete La Fame e la Sete!'

"'I am one whom all throw curse on. I am Poverty in person; Of these ladies here, the younger Is my sister, known as Hunger, And the third, who's not the worst, Is dreaded still by all as Thirst.'

"'Blessed be the hour in which ye entered my house!' cried the Signore, delighted. 'Make yourselves at home, rest and be at ease as long as you like — sempre sarei benglieto?

"'And why are you so well disposed towards me?' inquired Poverty.

"'Because, lady, I am, I trust, sufficiently wise with years and experience to know that everything must not be judged from the surface. Great and good art thou, since but for thee the devil a beggar in the world would ever move a finger to do the least work, and we should all be in mouldy green misery. Well hath it been said that 'Need makes the old woman trot,' 2 and likewise that Poverta non guastagentilezza — 'Poverty doth not degrade true nobility,' as I can perceive by thy manner, O noble lady. Thou, Poverty, art the mother of Industry, and grandmother of Wealth, Health, and Art; thou makest all men work; but for thee there would be no harvests, yea, all the fine things in the world are due to Want.'

1 Net miglio salotto di recevimento. This is all an accurate picture of old Florentine customs.

2 Nccessita fa la vecchia trottare. On which proverb Matteo Villani comments as follows: "And thus he truly verified the saying of Valerius Maximus, that 'the wants caused by human weakness are a common bond of security,' all of which is briefly expressed in the French proverb, 'Need makes the old woman (or old age) bestir herself.'" Valerius Maximus was the prototype of Guicciardini.

LEGENDS OF FLORENCE

"'And I?' said Dame Hunger. 'Dost thou also love me?'" "'Si, Dio ti benedicha I' replied the Signore. 'La fame ghastiga il ghiotto' —' Hunger corrects gluttony.

"'Hunger causes our delight, For it gives us appetite; For dainties without hunger sent Form a double punishment.'

'Hunger is the best sauce.' Thou makest men bold, for chane cijfamato non prezza bastone—z. hungry dog fears no stick. Thou makest the happiness of every feast.'

"'Ed to, Signore?' said Thirst. 'Hast thou also a good word for me?'

"'A Dio, grazie! God be praised that thou art. For without thee I should have no wine. Nor do men speak in pity of any one when they say in a wine-shop, "He is thirsty enough to drink up the Arno." I remember a Venetian who once said, coming to a feast, "I would not take five gold zecchini for this thirst which I now have." And to sum it all up, I find that poverty with want to urge it is better than wealth without power to enjoy, and, taking one with another, the poor are honester and have better hearts than the rich.'

"'Truly thou art great,' replied Poverty. 'Gentile, buono, e galantiiomo a parlare — gentle, good, and noble in thy speech. In such wise thou wilt ever be rich, for as thou art rich thou art good and charitable. And thou hast well said that Plenty comes from us, and it is we who truly own the horn of plenty; and therefore take from me this horn as a gift, and while thou livest be as rich as thou art good and wise!'

" 'And I,' said Hunger, 'give thee another, and while it is thine thou shalt never want either a good appetite nor the means to gratify it. For thou hast seen the truth that I was not created to starve men to death, but to keep them from starving.'

"'And I,' said Thirst, 'give thee a third horn of plenty; that is, plenty of wine and temperate desire— e buon pro vi faccia. Much good may it do you !'

" Saying this they vanished, and he would have thought it all a dream but for the three horns which they left behind them. So he had a long life and a happy, and in gratitude to his benefactresses he placed on his shield three horns, as men may see them to this day."

When I received this legend, I did not know that the three horns on a shield form the coat of arms of Messer Guicciardini, the historian, nor had I ever seen them. It happened by pure chance I went one day with my wife and Miss Roma Lister, who is devoted to folk-lore, to make my first visit to Sir John Edgar at his home, the celebrated old mediaeval palazzo, the Villa Guicciardini, Via Montugli.

On the way we passed the Church of the Annunciata, and while driving by I remarked that there were on its wall, among many shields, several which had on them a single hunting-horn, but that I had never seen three together, but had heard of such a device, and was very anxious to find it, and learn to what family it belonged.

What was my astonishment, on arriving at the villa or palazzo, at beholding on the wall in the court a large shield bearing the three horns. Sir John Edgar informed me that it was the shield of the Guicciardini family, who at one time inhabited the mansion. I related to him the story, and he said, " I should think that tale had been invented by some one who knew Guicciardini, the author, very well, for it is perfectly inspired with the spirit of his writings. It depicts the man himself as I have conceived him."

Then we went into the library, where my host showed me Fenton's translation of the "History" of Guicciardini and his " Maxims " in Italian, remarking that the one which I have placed as motto to this chapter was in fact an epitome of the whole legend.

I should observe, what did not before occur to me, that the family palace of the Guicciardini is in the Via Guicciardini, nearly opposite to the house of Machiavelli, and that it is there that the fairies probably called, if it was in the winter-time.

THE PILLS OF THE MEDICI

" When I upon a time was somewhat ill, Then every man did press on me a cure ; And when my wife departed, all of them Came crowding round, commending me a spouse ; But now my ass is dead, not one of them Has offered me another—devil a one ! "— Spanish Jests.

" Tu vai cercando il ma, come fanno i Medici" — "Thou goest about seeking evil, even as the Medici do, and of thee and of them it may be said, Anagyram coniuoves." — Italian Proverbs, A.D. 1618.

THE higher a tree grows, the more do petty animals burrow into its roots, and displace the dirt to show how it grew in lowly earth; and so it is with great families, who never want for such investigators, as appears by the following tale, which refers to the origin of the Medicis, yet which is withal rather merry than malicious.

D'UNO MEDICO CHE CURAVA GLI ASINI.

" It was long ago—so long, Signore Carlo, that the oldest olive-tree in Tuscany had not been planted, and when wolves sometimes came across the Ponte Vecchio into the town to look into the shop-windows, and ghosts and witches were as common by night as Christians by day, that there was a man in Florence who hated work, and who had observed, early as the age was, that those who laboured the least were the best paid. And he was always repeating to himself:

" ' Con arte e con inganno, Si vive mezzo l'anno, C«n inganno, e con arle, Si vive l'altra parte.'

" Or in English :

" ' With tricks and cleverness, 'tis clear, A man can live six months i' the year, And then with cleverness and tricks He'll live as well the other six.' 6

" Now having come across a recipe for making pills which were guaranteed to cure everything, he resolved to set up for an universal doctor, and that with nothing but the pills to aid. So he went forth from Florence, wandering from one village to another, selling his pills, curing some people, and getting, as often happens, fame far beyond his deserts, so that the peasants began to believe he could remedy all earthly ills.

"And at last one day a stupid contadino, who had lost his ass, went to the doctor and asked him whether by his art and learning he could recover for him the missing animal. Whereupon the doctor gave him six pills at a quattrino (a farthing) each, and bade him wander forth thinking intently all the time on the delinquent donkey, and, to perfect the spell, to walk in all the devious ways and little travelled tracks, solitary by-paths, and lonely sentieri, ever repeating solemnly, ' Asino mio ! asino mio ! Tu che amo come tin zio !'

" ' Oh my ass ! my ass ! my ass ! Whom I loved like an uncle, Alas ! alas!'

" And having done this for three days, it came to pass, and no great wonder either, that he found Signore Somaro (or Don Key) comfortably feasting in a dark lane on thistles. After which he praised to the skies the virtue of the wonderful pills, by means of which one could find strayed cattle. And from this dated the doctor's success, so that he grew rich and founded the family of the Medici, who, in commemoration of this their great ancestor, put the six pills into their shield, as you may see all over Florence to this day."

There is given in the " Facezie " a story which may be intended as a jest on this family. It is as follows :

" It happened once that a certain doctor or medico, who was by no means wanting in temerita or bold self-conceit, was sent as ambassador to Giovanna la Superba, or Joanna the Proud, Queen of Naples. And this Florentine Medico having heard many tales of the gallantries of the royal lady, thought he would try the chance, and thereby greatly please himself, and also the better advance his political aims. Therefore, at the first interview, he told her that he was charged with a secret mission, which could only be confided to her ' between

four eyes,' or in private. So he was taken by her into a room, where he bluntly made a proposal of love. 1

"Then the Queen, not in the least discomposed, looking straight at him, asked if that was one of the questions or demands with which he had been charged by the Florentines. At which he blushed like a beet and had no more to say, having learned that a bold beggar deserves a stern refusal."

The name of the Medici naturally gave rise to many jests, and one of these is narrated of Gonella, a famous farceur. It is as follows :

" One morning, at the table of the Grand Duke Lorenzo, there was a discussion as to the number and proportion of those who followed different trades and callings, one declaring that there were more clothmakers, another more priests than any others, till at last the host asked Gonella his opinion.

"'I am sure,' said Gonella, 'that there are more doctors than any other kind of people— e non accade dubitarne —and there is no use in doubting it.'

"'Little do you know about it,' replied the Duke, 'if you do not know that in all this city there are only two or three accredited physicians.'

"' With how little knowledge,' answered Gonella, ' can a state be governed. It seems, O Excellency, that you have so much to do that you do not know what is in your city, nor what the citizens do.' And the result of the debate was a bet, and Gonella took every bet offered, his stakes being small and the others great— A quattrino e quattrino si fa il fiorino — Farthings to farthings one by one make a pound when all is done.

"The next morning Gonella, having well wrapped up his throat and face in woollen stuff, stood, looking pitifully enough, at the door of the Duomo, and every one who passed asked him what was the matter, to which he replied, 'All my teeth ache terribly.' And everybody offered him an infallible remedy, which he noted down, and with it the name of him who gave it. And then going about town, he made out during the day a list of three hundred prescribers, with as many prescriptions.

1 " Chiese alia regina di dormir seco." Which was certainly very plain blunt speaking, even for the time.

"And last of all he went to the palace at the hour of supper, and the Grand Duke seeing him so wrapped up, asked the cause, and hearing that it was toothache, also prescribed a sovereign remedy, and Gonella put it with the name of the Duke at the head of the list. And going home, he had the whole fairly engrossed, and the next day, returning to the palace, was reminded of his bets. Whereupon he produced the paper, and great was the laughter which it caused, since it appeared by it that all the first citizens and nobles of Florence were physicians, and that the Grand Duke himself was their first Medico. So it was generally admitted that Gonella had won, and they paid him the money, with which he made merry for many days."

This tale has been retold by many a writer, but by none better than by an American feuilletoniste, who improved it by giving a number of the prescriptions commended. Truly it has been well said that at forty years of age every man is either a fool or a physician.

I have another legend of the Medici, in which it is declared that their armorial symbol is a key, and in which they are spoken of as wicked and cruel. It is as follows:

I MEDICI.

" The Palazzo Medici is situated in the Borgo degli Albizzi, and this palace is called by the people / Visacchi (i.e., figures or faces), because there are to be seen in it many figures of people who were when alive all witches and wizards, but who now live a life in death in stone.

" The arms of the Medici bear a great key, and it is said that this was a sorcerer's or magic key, which belonged to the master of all the wizards or to the queen of the witches.

" And being ever evil at heart and cruelly wicked, the old Medici sought restlessly every opportunity to do wrong, which was greatly aided by the queen of the witches herself, who entered the family, and allied herself to one of it; others say she was its first ancestress. And that being on her death-bed, she called her husband, or son, or the family, and said:

"' Take this key, and when I am dead, open a certain door in the cellar, which, through secret passages, leads to an

enchanted garden, in which you will find all the books and apparatus needed to acquire great skill in sorcery, and thus thou canst do all the evil and enjoy all the crime that a great ruler can desire; spare not man in thy vengeance, nor woman in thy passion; he lives best who wishes for most and gets what he wants.'

" Thus it came to pass that the Medici became such villains, and why they bear a key."

Villains they may have been, but they were not so deficient in moral dignity as a friend of mine, who, observing that one of the pills in their scutcheon is blue, remarked that they were the first to take a blue pill.

Since the above was written I have collected many more, and indeed far more interesting and amusing legends of the Medici; especially several referring to Lorenzo the Magnificent, which are not given by any writer that I am aware of. These will appear, I trust, in a second series.

"A race which was the reflex of an age So strange, so flashed with glory, so bestarrcd With splendid deeds, so flushed with rainbow hues, That one forgot the dark abyss of night Which covered it at last when all was o'er. Take all that's evil and unto it add All that is glorious, and the result Will be, in one brief word, the Mèdici."

FURICCHIA, OR TPIE EGG-WOMAN OF THE MERCATO VECCHIO

" Est anus inferno, vel formidanda barathro, Saga diu magicis usa magisteriis, Haec inhians ova gallina matre creatis. Obsipat assueto pharmaca mixta cibo, Pharmaca queis qusecunque semel gallina voratis, Ova deceni pariat bis deciesque decem."

STEUCCIUS, cited by P. GOLDSCHMIDT, Verworffeiier Hexen und Zauberadvocat. Hamburg, 1705.

" E un figliuolo della" gallina bianca,"— Old Proverb.

THE Mercato Vecchio was fertile in local traditions, and one of these is as follows :

LEGEND OF THE LANTERNS.

" There was in the Old Market of Florence an old house with a small shop in it, and over the door was the figure or bas-relief of a pretty hen, to show that eggs were sold there.

"All the neighbours were puzzled to know how the woman who kept this shop could sell so many eggs as she did, or whence she obtained them, for she was never seen in the market buying any, nor were they brought to her ; whence they concluded that she was a witch and an egg-maker, and this scandal was especially spread by her rivals in business. But others found her a very good person, of kindly manner, and it was noted in time that she not only did a great deal of good in charity, and that her eggs were not only always fresh and warm, but that many persons who had drunk them when ill had been at once relieved, and recovered in consequence. And the name of this egg-wife was Furicchia.

" Now there was an old lady who had gone down in the world or become poor, and she too had set up a shop to sell eggs, but did not succeed, chiefly because everybody went to Furicchia. And this made the former more intent than ever to discover the secret, and she at once went to work to find it out.

" Every morning early, when Furicchia rose, she went out of doors, and then the hen carved over the door came down as a beautiful white fowl, who told her all the slanders and gossip which people spread about her, and what effort was being made to discover her secret. And one day it said:

"' There is the Signora who was once rich and who is now poor, and who has sworn to find out thy secret how thou canst have so many eggs to sell, since no one sees thee buy any, and how it comes that invalids and bewitched children are at once cured by the virtue of those eggs. So she hopes to bring thee to death, and to get all thy trade.

"' But, dear Furicchia, this shall never be, because I will save thee. I well remember how, when I was a little chicken, and the poultry dealer had bought me, and was about to wring my neck—b'r'r'r !—I shudder when I think of it!—when thou didst save my life, and I will ever be grateful to thee, and care for thy fortune.

" 'Now I will tell thee what to do. Thou shalt to-morrow take a pot and fill it with good wine and certain drugs, and boil them well, and leave it all hot in thy room, and then go forth, and for the rest I will provide. Addio, Furicchia!' And saying this, the hen went back into her accustomed place.

" So the next morning, Furicchia, having left the wine boiling, went forth at ten o'clock, and she was hardly gone ere the Signora, her rival, entered the place and called for the mistress, but got no answer. Then she went into the house, but saw nothing more than a vast quantity of eggs, and all the while she heard the hen singing or clucking :

"' Coccodc! Dear me !

Where can Furicchia be ? Coccodi! Furicchia mine ! Bring me quick some warm red wine ! Coccodc'! Three eggs I have laid ! Coccode! Now six for your trade. Coccode'! Now there are nine, Bring me quickly the warm red wine ! Coccode ! Take them away ; Many more for thee will I lay, And thou wilt be a lady grand, As fine as any in all the land ; And should it happen that any one Drinks of this wine as I have done, Eggs like me she will surely lay ; That is the secret, that is the way. Coccode ! Coccode !'

" Now the Signora heard all this, and knew not whence the song came, but she found the pot of hot wine and drank it nearly all, but had not time to finish it nor to escape before Furicchia returned. And the latter began to scold her visitor for taking such liberty, to which the Signora replied, ' Furicchia, I came in here to buy an egg, and being shivering with cold, and seeing this hot wine, I drank it, meaning indeed to pay for it.' But Furicchia replied, ' Get thee gone; thou hast only come here to spy out my secret, and much good may it do thee !'

"The Signora went home, when she begun to feel great pain, and also, in spite of herself, to cluck like a hen, to the amazement of everybody, and then sang :

" ' Coccode'! Che mal di corpo ! Coccode! Voglio fa Fuovo 1 E se 1'uova non faro, Di dolore moriro.'

" ' Coccode! What a pain in my leg! Coccode'! I must lay an egg! And if my eggs I cannot lay, I shall surely die to-day.'

" Then she began to lay eggs indeed— tante, tante —till they nearly filled all the room, and truly her friends were aghast at such a sight, never having heard of such a thing before; but she replied, ' Keep quiet; it is a secret. I have found out how Furicchia gets her eggs, and we shall be as rich as she.' And having laid her eggs, nothing would do but she must needs hatch them, and all the time for many days she sat and sat, clucking like a hen— coccode! coccode! —and pecking at crusts like a hen, for she would not eat in any other way. And so she sat and shrivelled up until she became a hen indeed, and was never anything else, and died one. But when the eggs hatched, there came from them not chicks, but mice, which ran away into the cellar, and so ends the story."

This story greatly resembles one given by Peter Gold-schmidt in " The Witches' and Sorcerers' Advocate Overthrown," published at Hamburg in 1705, and to the same as sung in Latin song by a certain Steuccius. The Italian tale is, however, far better told in every respect, the only point in common being that a certain witch laid

eggs by means of a potion, which produced the same effect on a man. It is the well-managed play of curiosity, gratitude, and character which make Furicchia so entertaining, and there is nothing in the heavy German tale like the "Song of the Hen," or Coccode, which is a masterpiece of a juvenile lyric. The clucking and pecking at crusts of the old woman, as she gradually passes into a hen, is well imagined, and also the finale of the chickens turned to mice, who all run away. One could make of it a play for the nursery or the stage.

The Mercato Vecchio, in which the egg-wife dwelt, was a place of common resort in the olden time, " when there was giving and taking of talk on topics temporal: "

" Where the good news fleetly flew, And the bad news ever true, Softly whispered, loudly told, Scalding hot or freezing cold." 1

This place is recalled by a story which is indeed to be found in the facetiae of the Florentine Poggio, yet which holds its own to this day in popular tale-telling. It is as follows:

"It happened once when Florence was at war with the Duke of Milan, that a law was passed making it death for any one to speak in any way of peace. Now there was a certain Bernardo Manetti, a man di ingegno vivadssimo, or an extremely ready wit, who being one day in the Mercato Vecchio to buy something or other (it being the custom of the Florentines of those times to go in person to purchase their daily food), was much annoyed by one of those begging friars who go about the roads, alia queslua, collecting alms, and who stand at street-corners imploring charity. And this brazen beggar, accosting Bernardo, said to him :

1 " Le cattive nove volano, Le male son sempre vere ; Prima l'annunzio, poi malanno, Chi me ne da una calda, e chi una fredda."

— Italian Proverb.

" ' Pax vobiscum ! Peace be unto you !'

" (A chi parlasti dipace ? —How darest thou speak to me of peace, thou traitor and enemy to Florence ?' cried Bernardo in well-assumed anger. ' Dost thou not know that by public decree thou may'st lose thy shaven head for mentioning the word? And thou darest ask me for alms here in the open market-place, thou traitor to thy country and thy God ! Apage, Satanas — avaunt!—begone ! lest I be seen talking to thee and taken for a conspirator myself! Pax indeed— pack off with you, ere I hand you over to the torturers !'

"And so he rid himself of that importunate beggar."

Apropos of the egg-wife, if chickens are apropos to eggs, there is a merry tale of a certain priest, which will, I think, amuse the reader. Like all good folk, the Florentines make fun of their neighbours, among whom are of course included the people of Arezzo, and tell of them this story:

"Long long ago, a certain Bishop Angelico convoked a Synod at Arezzo, summoning every priest in his diocese to be present; and knowing that many had slipped into very slovenly habits as regarded the sacerdotal uniform, made it a stern and strict order that every one should appear in cappa e cotta, 1 or in cloak and robe.

" Now there was a priest who, though he kept a well-filled cellar, and a pretty servant-maid, and a fine poultry-yard, had none of these clerical vestments, and knew not where to borrow them for the occasion; so he was in great distress and stavasi molto afflitto in casa sua — sat in deep affliction in his home. And his maid, who was a bright and clever girl, seeing him so cast down, asked him the cause of his grief, to which he replied that the Bishop had summoned him to appear at the Synod in cappa e cotta.

" ' Oh, nonsense !' replied the good girl. ' Is that all ? My dear master, you do not pronounce the words quite correctly, or else they have been badly reported to you. It is not cappa e cotta which the Bishop requires, for assuredly he has plenty of such clothes, but capponi cotti, ' good roast capons,' such as all bishops love, and which he knows he can get better from

1 The cappa is a cloak with a hood or "capuchin ;" a cotta is the stole worn by Catholic priests.

the country priests than from anybody. And grazie a Dio ! there is nobody in all Tuscany has better poultry than ours, and I will take good care that you give the Bishop of the very best.'

"Now the priest being persuaded by the maid, really made his appearance at the Council bearing in a dish well covered with a napkin four of the finest roasted capons ever seen. And with these he advanced in plena concilo, in full assembly before the Bishop. The great man looked severely at the priest, and said:

"'Where are thy cappa e cotta?'

"'Excellenza, behold them!' said the good man, uncovering the dish. 'And though I say it, no better capponi cotte can be had in all our country.'

"The Bishop and all round him gazed with breathless admiration on the fowls, so plump, so delicious, so exquisitely roasted, with lemons ranged round them. It was just the hungry time of day, and, in short, the priest had made a blessed happy blunder, and one which was greatly admired. There was general applause.

iii Figlio miff/' said the Bishop with a smile, 'take my blessing! Thou alone of all the ministers of our diocese didst rightly understand the spirit and meaning of an episcopal edict.'"

THE LANTERNS OF THE STROZZI PALACE

" And what this man did was, as the proverb says, mostrare altitii hicdole per laterne — made him believe that fire-flies were lanterns—which means to deceive any one."— Italian Proverbs.

As all visitors to Florence will have their attention called to the Strozzi Palace, and its rings and lanterns, the following will probably prove to them to be of interest:

"The campanelle, or great iron rings, which are on the Strozzi Palace, were the result of rivalry with the Pitti family.

" The Strozzi built their palace first, and then the Pitti said that it would only fill a corner of their own far greater building. And when the latter was finished, the Strozzi, to be even with them, placed those magnificent campanelle at the four corners, and then the great lanterns which are so exquisitely worked, and these were made by Niccolo il Grosso, a very ingenious but also very poor man, who, having begun the work, could not finish it for want of money.

"One morning when this Niccolo was sitting on the stone bench of the palace, there came by an old man who was carrying some onions, and the artist begged a few of these to eat with his bread, telling him he had no money. But the old man said, ' Take them, and welcome, for a free gift, Niccolo. Truly, it pains me to see an excellent artist like thee starving for want of proper patronage. Now I will lend thee a round sum, which thou canst repay me when thou art in better luck.'

"'But tell me,' inquired Niccolo, greatly amazed, ' how dost thou know who I am?'

" The old man replied, ' I know thee, and that thou hast great genius (una gran testa), and I find thee utterly poor, and unable to finish the Strozzi lanterns.

"'Now I wish to do thee a service. Go, with these onions in thine hand, and stand there in the street till the Lords Strozzi go forth, and see thee with the vegetables, and then they will ask thee why thou dost not finish the lanterns. And then thou shall reply, "Signori, because I must sell onions, not being able otherwise to finish the lanterns, for truly all my art does not give me bread." Then they will give thee money, and after that return to me.'

" So it happened as the old man said: the Signori Strozzi, when they came forth, found Niccolb their artist selling onions, and gave him a good sum of money, and with that he went back to the old man. And they gave him a great sum indeed, for he was to make the lanterns all of solid gold, so that the palace might be far finer than the Pitti.

" The old man said, ' Never mind paying me, but put an onion in your pocket and study it.' And this he did, hence it comes that the tops of the lanterns are like onion sprouts. And Niccolb seeing that he lived in a hard and cruel world, in order to be even with it, made the lanterns of iron, though the work which he put upon it was like jewellery, so fine was it, and then gilded the iron and passed the lanterns off on the Signori Strozzi for solid gold, and was soon heard off as being very far away from Florence, in company with the good old man who had put him up to the little game (bel giuoco).

" But people say that after all the Strozzi were not so badly cheated, for those onion-top lanterns could not have been bought even in their time for their weight in gold, and that they are worth much more now."

It is needless to say that this ingenious tale owes its origin to the iron lanterns having been at one time gilt. These famous works of art have been copied far and wide: had the Strozzi family taken out and renewed the copyright for design on them, they might have found that the gold was a very good investment, especially in these times, when a thing of beauty brings in cash for ever. One of the latest and prettiest devices, to be seen in many shops, is a small iron night-lamp in imitation of these Strozzi lanterns.

The im-moral, or at least the concluding sentence of the tale is, " E cost Niccolb se nefuggi a taschepiene —And so Niccoló fled with his pockets full of money." I spare the reader reflections on the history of many bankers in

Florence and Rome, who during the past two years followed his example.

What is extremely interesting and original in this legend is the declaration that Niccoló took the idea of the long and very singular points on the lanterns from an onion. It recalls the story of the acanthus leaf and the basket which suggested the Ionic capital. It was understood by the narrator that the old man who gave " the tips " to Niccolo was a wizard.

There was much more meaning attached to the lanterns and rings, such as Niccolo made, than is generally known, as appears by the following extract:

"Among the striking features of the Florentine palaces are the handsome ornaments of bronze or wrought-iron which adorn the facades of many of them. These were called fanah or lumiere, and were not, as one would naturally suppose, ornaments that a man might place on his house according to his individual taste, but they were the visible testimony of the public recognition of great deeds. On festive occasions, these fanali were provided with great pitch torches, whose crackling flames gave a merry aspect to the whole neighbourhood. Amerigo Vespucci addressed the account of one of his voyages to the Gonfaloniere Piero Soderini, with whom he had formerly been on intimate terms, and the latter procured a decree of the Republic, in accordance with which fanali were sent to the family palace of the Vespucci, and kept burning day and night for three days.

"The most beautiful of all the Florentine fanali. . . are those which adorn the corners of the famous Strozzi Palace. They are of wrought-iron, and were made by a smith who enjoyed a local celebrity, not only on account of his masterly work, but also because he carried on his business on a strictly cash basis; nay, went further, and refused to work for any one who did not prepay, in part at least, for his order. Thus he received the name of Caparra, or Earnest-money."
— Florentine Life, by W. B. Scaife, p. 58.

There is one thing in this legend which alone would seem to guarantee its being an authentic or old tradition.

In it Niccolo appears as a man who is eminently grasping, and who takes care to get his money in advance. And he was in reality so noted for this, that, as Scaife declares, he went further than dealing on a cash basis—and so got the nickname of Caparra, or the Pledge—so well did he know the value of cash. // niartel d'argento ronipe le porte di ferro, or—

" A hammer of silver, as we see, Breaks the iron gates of poverty."

THE GOBLIN OF LA VIA DEL CORNO

" Oh for one blast of that dread horn, On Fontarabian echoes borne, When Roland brave and Olivier, And every paladin and peer

At Roncesvalles died."— Waller Scott.

" The Korrigan who ever wears a horn."

THE Via del Corno is a narrow street passing from the Via del Leone. I have found the following story in reference to the origin of its name, which, if not authentic, is at least amusing and original:

LA VIA DEL CORNO.

"There was in what is now known as the Via del Corno an ancient palace, which a long time ago was inhabited only by a certain gentleman and a goblin. 1

" Nor had he any servants, because of all who came, none remained more than one day for fear of the folletto. And as this spread far and wide, people kept away from the Via del Corno after dark ; but as this also kept away thieves, and the goblin did all the house-work, the master was all the better pleased. Only on one point did the two differ, and that was the point of morality. Here the goblin was extremely strict, and drew the line distinctly. Several times, as was the custom in those wicked days, the Signore attempted to introduce a lady-friend to the palazzo, but the goblin all night long, when not busied in pulling the sheets from the fair sinner, was industriously occupied in strewing nettles or burrs under her, or tickling the soles of her feet with a pen; and then anon,

1 Folletto. This, which meant originally an airy tricksy sprite, is now applied not only to fairies and goblins in general, but also to every kind of supernatural apparition. I have a book in which even comets are described as foHettt.

when, sinking to sleep, she hoped for some remission of the tease, he would begin to play interminable airs on a horn. It is true that he played beautifully, like no earthly musician, but even enchanting airs may be annoying when they prevent sleep.

" Nor did the lord fare the better, even when, inspired by higher motives, he 'would a-wooing go.' For one lady or another had heard of the goblin, and when they had not, it always happened that by some mysterious means or other the match was broken off.

" Meantime the life led by the Signore was rather peculiar, as he slept nearly all day, sallied forth for an hour or two to exercise, go to a barber's, make his small purchases, or hear the news, supped at a tratforia, and then returning home, sat all night listening to the goblin as he played divinely on the horn, or blew it himself, which he did extremely well, toped and hob-nobbed with his familiar, who was a great critic of wine, and, as the proverb says, ' Buon vino fiaba lunga —Good wine, long tales'—they told one another no end of merry and marvellous stories ; and as il vin fa cantare, it makes man sing, they also sang duets, solos, and glees. And when the weather was ill, or chilly, or rainy, or too hot, they cured it with Chianti, according to a medical prescription laid down in sundry rare old works :

" Nebbia, nebbia, mattutina, Che ti levi la mattina? Questa tazza di buon vino, Fatta d'una marzamina, Contra te sia medecina !'

" ' Cloudy sl<y i' the morning early, What will make you vanish fairly ? Ah ! this goblet of good wine, Essence of the blessed vine, Shall be for thee a medicine !'

"Then they played chess, cards, cribbage, drole, ecarte, Pope Joan, bo, brag, casino, thirty-one, put, snip-snap-snorem, lift-em-up, tear-the-rag, smoke, blind-hookey, bless-your-grand-mother, Polish-bank, seven-up, beggar-my-neighbour, patience, old-maid, fright, baccarat, belle-en-chemise, bang-up, howling-Moses, bluff, swindle-Dick, go-it-rags, ombre or keep-dark, morelles, go-bang, goose, dominoes, loto, nwrra or push-pin. And when extra hands were wanted they came, but all that came were only fairy hands, short at the wrist, the goblin

remarking that it saved wine not to have mouths, et cetera. Then they had long and curious and exceedingly weighty debates as to the laws of the games and fair play, not forgetting meanwhile to sample all the various wines ever sung by Redi.[1] So they got on, the Signore realising that one near friend is worth a hundred distant relations.

" Now it befell one night that the goblin, having seen the Signore take off a pint of good old strong Barolo very neatly and carefully, without taking breath or winking, exclaimed with a long, deep sigh :

" ' Thou art a gallant fellow, a right true boon companion, and it grieves me to the heart to think that thou art doomed to be drowned to-morrow.'

" ' Oh you be—doctored !' replied the Signore. ' There isn't water enough in the Arno now to drown a duck, unless she held her head under in a half-pint puddle.'

" The goblin went to the window, took a look at the stars, whistled and said :

"' As I expected, it is written that you are to be drowned to-morrow, unless you carry this horn of mine hung to your neck all day.

" ' Quando ti trovi nel pericolo, Suona questo corno piccolo, E tu sarai salvato, Non sarai affogato !'

" ' If thou find'st thyself forlorn, Blow aloud this little horn, And thou wilt be safe and sound, For with it thou'lt not be drowned.'

" Saying this, he solemnly handed the horn to the cavalier, drank off a goblet of muscato, wiped his lips, bowed a ceremonious good-night, and, as was his wont, vanished with dignity up the chimney.

" The gentleman was more troubled by this prediction than he liked to admit. I need not say that the next day he did not go near the Arno, though it was as dry as a bone; nay, he kept out of a bath, and was almost afraid to wash his face.

" At last he got the fancy that some enemies or villains would burst into his lonely house, bind him hand and foot, carry him far away, and drown him in some lonely stream, or

[1] Redi's Bacco in Toscana is known to the most ignorant in Florence, there being very cheap editions of it constantly sold.

perhaps in the sea. He remembered just such a case. We all remember just such cases when we don't want to. That was it, decidedly.

" Then he had a happy thought. There was a little hiding-chamber, centuries old, in the palazzo, known only to himself, with a concealed door. He would go and hide there. He shouted for joy, and when he entered the room, he leaped with a great bound from the threshold of the door, down and over three or four steps, into the middle of the little room.

" Now he did not know that in the cantina or cellar below this hiding-place there was an immense tino, or vat, containing hundreds of barrels of wine, such as are used to hold the rough wine ere it is drawn off and ' made ;' nor that the floor was extremely decayed, so that when he came down on it with a bounce, it gave way, and he found himself in the cellar over head and ears in wine.

" And, truly, for a minute he deemed that he was drowning in earnest. And the sides of the vat were so high that he could not climb out. But while swimming and struggling for life, he caught between his thumb and finger at a nail in the side, and to this he held, crying as loud as he could shout for aid. But no one came, and he was just beginning to despair, when he thought of the horn !

" It still hung from his neck, and pouring out the wine, he blew on it, and there came forth such a tremendous, appalling, and unearthly blast as he of himself could never have blown. It rang far and wide all over Florence, it was heard beyond Fiesole, it wakened the dead in old Etrurian graves, for an instant, to think they had been called by Tinia to meet the eleven gods; it caused all the folletti, fafe, diavoli, strege, and maliardi to stop for an instant their deviltries or delights. For it was the Great Blast of the Horn of the Fairies, which only plays second fiddle to the last trump. 1

" And at that sound all Florence came running to see what was the matter. The Grand Duke and his household came; the Council of the Eight burst their bonds, and left the Palazzo Vecchio; everybody came, and they fished out the Signore, and listened with awe to his tale. The priests said that the goblin was San Zenobio, the more liberal swore it was Crescenzio, the people held to plain San Antonino. The Signore became a great man.

1 "Can a horn play second fiddle?" inquires Flaxius. "This comes of trying to improve on the simple Italian text."

"' My son,' said the goblin to him in confidence the following evening, as they sat over their wine (here I follow the text of Maddalena), 'this is our last night together. Thou art saved, and I have fulfilled my duty to thee. Once I, too, was a man like thee, and in that life thou didst save mine by rescuing me from assassins. And I swore to watch over thee in every peril, and bring thee to a happy end.'

" ' II momento e arrivato ; Addio, Via del Corno ! Addio, palazzo, addio ! Addio, padrone, nel altro mondo! '

" ' The final hour has come for me ; Street of the Horn, farewell to thee ! Farewell, O palace, farewell, O street ! My lord, in another world we'll meet.'

" Then the goblin told the Signore that he would ere long contract a happy marriage, and that it was for this that he had hitherto kept him from forming alliances which would have prevented it; and that if in future he should ever be in great need of assistance, to sound the horn, and he would come to him, but that this must always be in the palace alone after midnight. And having said this he vanished.

"The Signore grieved for a long time at the loss of his goblin friend, but he married happily, as had been predicted, and his life was long and prosperous. So he put the horn in his shield, and you may see it to this day on the Church of Santa Maria Novella. And so it was that the Via del Corno got its name."

"From which we may learn," saith Flaxius, "that wherever a man is appointed to be on a certain day, there will the man be found. Therefore do thou, O reader, so manage it that wherever thou art appointed to be, thou canst get well out of it. For even Fate smiles when it desires to do so."

FRATE GIOCONDO, THE MONK OF SANTA MARIA NOVELLA

11 In illo tempore —no— in diebus illis, che i frati sogliono percorrere il contado delle terre e delle citta per far proviste alia barba degli scimuniti d'ogni genere pappatorio, vale dir di grano, formentone, legumi, mosto, cacio, olio, canape, lino, uova et cetera—un certo fra Zeffiro, se ne gira alia volta d'un villagio e tenevagli compagnia il suo ciucarello che carica gia a doppio sacchetto."— L'Asino e il suo Frate, Racconti Piacevolt, 1864.

" Und sie war gar sehr erstannet iiber die Adresse und List dieses Miinchleins."— Litstigc Thaten des Kloster-bruders Hannes von Lehnin, A.D. 1589.

"Monachus in claustro Non valet ova dua, Sed extra—bene valet triginta."— Rabelais.

AMONG the monks of Santa Maria Novella in ancient days was one known as Frate

Giocondo, who was truly of the kind who are of little use at home, or at any steady or reputable calling, but who was profitable enough when scouring the country on the loose, blarneying and begging from the good wives, giving counsel to the peasants, and profitable advice, while he ate their chickens and drank their wine, chucking all the pretty girls under their chins, or sub silentio, and making himself sociable, edifying, amusing, or holy—according to circumstances. Of whom it could be truly said :

"Monaco in convento Non vale niente, Ma fuori vale venti."

" Monk in monastery Is not worth a cherry ; But abroad when sent, he Often is worth twenty."

As a preaching friar of Saint Dominic, truly Brother Giocondo was not a success, but as a beggar he beat all the Zoccoloni out of Rome,[1] and that is saying a great deal. For there never was a friar with such an oiled and honeyed tongue, with which he could flatter and wheedle, tell legends of the saints, witches, or goblins by the hour, give all the gossip going ; nor was he above selling his collections, or trading donkeys, or taking a hand at a game of cards, or singing to a lute, or even fiddling to a dance — so that, being a great, burly, handsome, merry-eyed knave, he got on marvellously well in the world, his jests being reported even in Siena.

Now one evening he was returning home to Santa Maria Novella dalla cercha, " from the quest," and found himself still a few miles from Florence. And good fortune had favoured him marvellously that day, for his ass bore two panniers which were ben carichi dogni sorta di grazia di Dio — " stuffed full with all sorts of mercies of God," such as bags of wheat, maize, wheat-meal, chickens, oil, cheese, butter, wine, truffles, onions, geese, turnips, sausages, bread, ducks; in short, Signore, as I said, there was ogni sorta di grazia di Dw, and enough to support a poor family for a month.

Now, darkness coming on, and rain falling, the Friar stopped at a lonely house, where he neither knew the people nor was known to them, and begged for a night's lodging. The master of the place was a well-to-do person, but a great knave, and no sooner had he perceived that the monk had such a plentiful stock of provisions, than he saw his way to give all his neighbours a splendid feast at no expense to himself, at which he could not fail to relieve some of his guests of their money.

Now this rogue had a daughter who was scaltra e bene affilata —shrewd and sharp as a razor, one who could teach cats to see in the dark, and who had grown to villainy from her babyhood, even as a reed shoots up-

[1] Zoccoloni or Zcccolanti, sandalled friars of the lowest order, who are indeed common beggars.

wards. And she only caught a wink from her good father, which glanced off on to the load of the friar's donkey, to understand the whole game, and what was expected of her.

You must know, Signore Carlo, that the wench was very good-looking—bad wine in a silver cup, pretty to look at, but vile to sup—and had all the sweet, innocent, simple look of a saint, and she made up to Frate Giocondo like a kitten to a child, which he took in no wise amiss, being used to such conquests. And who so flattering and fawning as they all were on Brother Giocondo; how they laughed at his jests, and seemed to be in the last agonies of delight; but winked at one another withal, for there were six lusty brothers or cousins in the family, who, in case of need, did the heavy dragging out, or advanced the last argument with clubs.

By-and-by, as the night wore on, the black-eyed baggage stole away and hid herself in the room allotted to the Friar, though with no intention to break the seventh—but that against stealing—as you will see. For when the good Giocondo went to bed, which he did in full dress, he knew not that she was there. And as soon as he began to snore, she tapped gently on the wall three times, and then went and laid herself down softly by the Friar, who did not awake. At which all the band came bursting in with torches and staves, and began to beat the victim, reviling and cursing him for having deluded the poor child, so that there was a fearful fracasso — a great riot—but they left the door open, through which the pious Giocondo bolted, and none pursued, as they had already secured his provisions.

Now Giocondo shrewdly noted this, and at once understood that he had been as shrewdly robbed, and that by such a trick as left no door open to return and claim his property. So he quietly mounted his ass and rode away, and returning to the convent, thought it all over, till he came to a device to revenge himself. For he was one of those who was never bit by a wolf but what he had his skin.

So he let a long time pass by, and then went to work. First of all he got two jars, and paid a contadino to catch for him as many living vipers as would fill them both, saying it was for the apothecary of his convent to make tcriaca or Venetian treacle, which is a cure for serpents' bites. And then he disguised himself like a lord's messenger, darkening his face, and putting on long curling locks, with a bold impudent air, with cloak and feather, sword and dagger ; truly no one would ever have known him. And in this guise he went again to the Albergo de' Ladrt, or Thieves' Den, asking once more for lodging, which was cheerfully granted.

Now the part which he played, and that to perfection, was that of a foolish gasconading servant; nor had he been long in the house ere he informed his host in confidence that he served a great lord who was in love with a married lady in Florence, and to win her good graces had sent her two jars full of honey or conserves, but that there was in each a hundred crowns in gold, of which he was to privately inform the lady, lest her husband should suspect the truth ; adding artfully, " But i' faith, if I were to steal the whole myself and run away, my lord would never pursue me, so fearful is he lest the thing should be found out; and even if I were to be robbed, one could do nothing."

And as he said this he saw the knave give a wink to his daughter, and knew very well what it meant, but pretended to take no notice of it. So all went as before, and the girl stole into his room and hid herself. But he, who was prepared for everything, when he retired took from his pocket two or three large screws and a screwdriver, and closed the great strong door so that it would resist a hard assault, and left the window open so that he could easily escape, and so went to bed.

Then the girl, when she thought he was asleep, gave the signal, and the thieves tried to burst in, but could not. And Friar Giocondo, jumping up, gave the girl such a beating as she had never heard of, abusing her all the time as a song to the accompaniment of the thrashing, till at last, when he saw they were really coming in, he jumped through the window, ran to the stable, and finding there a fine horse, saddled it in haste and rode away like the wind.

The thieves were so intent on the jars that they paid no heed to anything else, not even to the girl, who was raging mad at her father for having exposed her to such danger. So they got two deep plates, and opened both jars at once to pour the honey out, when lo! there came swarming forth the vipers, hissing, and squirming, and darting out their tongues like so many devils. At which sight they all fled in fear, the girl first, nor did she stop till she got to Fiesole, where, in great terror, she (fearing for her soul) told the whole story to everybody and the monks.

The thief went to the stable, but found his horse gone, and so had to content himself with Giocondo's donkey, on which, fearing the pursuit of justice, he rode away, to be hanged somewhere else. And the Abbot of Santa Maria Novella cheerfully absolved Brother Giocondo for stealing the horse—and accepted it as a graceful gift, or in recompense for the load of provisions which had been lost.

" Thus 'twas with all of them it sped,
And the Abbot came out one horse ahead ! : '

THE LEGEND OF THE CROCE AL TREDBIO

" The bell in the Bargello called the Montanara obtained the name of the Catnpana delle Anne because it was the signal for citizens to lay aside their weapons and retire home."— Hares " Cities of Central Italy."

" Where towers are crushed, and temples fair unfold A new magnificence that vies with old, Firm in its pristine majesty hath stood A votive column."— Wordsworth, " Pillar of Trajan"

VERY near to the Church of Santa Maria Novella is the small piazza or open place of the Croce al Trebbio. This is a column with a crucifix, the whole being of beautiful proportions and of a strikingly romantic character. It is said to have been raised to commemorate a victory of "that sanguinary fanatic Saint Peter Martyr" over the Paterini. "The Croce al Trebbio/' says Leader Scott, "of the year 1244, is a work of the Pisan school, but whether it is by Niccolo or Giovanni Pisani, who were in Florence about that epoch, there is nothing to show. There was* a curious Latin inscription in Gothic letters, which began: Sanctus A mbrosius cum Sancto Zenobio propter grande mysterium hanc crucein —and went on to say that it was reconstructed by the bishops of Florence and of Aquileia in August 1308. It is evident that the connection of the cross with Saint Peter Martyr is mere conjecture, the Italian authorities say die si crede, ' believed 1 to be erected on the spot where a victory was gained over the Paterini. If this were so, where is the mystery referred to in the inscription ? "

The legend, which was after long inquiry recovered by my collector, distinctly describes the reconstruction of the

1 The partial inscription referred to is still on the column.

cross, and as certainly sets forth a mysterium magnum with an apparition of the Virgin on this very spot, which would have assuredly caused a pillar, if not a church, to be erected in the thirteenth century. The story of this mystery is as follows :

LA CROCK AL TREBBIO.

" Where the Croce al Trebbio now stands, was in very old times a great palace occupied by one of the most ancient families of Florence. And when it died out, there came into the house three families, but none could remain there, being so terrified with fearful sounds and an apparition.

"It was the custom in those days in Florence to ring a bell at ten o'clock at night, which was a signal for every citizen to go home at once ; therefore, after that hour no one was seen in the streets except police guards, military patrols, and riotous young men, whom the former aimed at arresting. It often happened that such irregular folk took refuge in the old palazzo, but if they remained there one night, they had enough of it, and never returned, so great was the horror which they were sure to feel.

"The first occurrence which gave the place a bad name was as follows : Some time after the death of the last of the old line of Signori who had occupied the palace, and the three families spoken of had come into it, on the first night at midnight they heard some one put a key in the house-door, open the same with great noise, and come storming and swearing up the stairs into the great dining-hall. Then there entered a tall and magnificently dressed gentleman, of very handsome and distinguished appearance, but his face was deadly pale, his eyes had a terrible gleam, and it seemed as if a light bluish flame flickered and crept about him, ever rising and vanishing like small serpents.

" And entering, he began to scold and blaspheme in a diabolical manner, as if at servants whom he was accustomed to have promptly at his call, saying, ' Birbanti di seruitori —you scoundrelly waiters—you have not got supper ready for me, nor laid the tables.' Saying this, he seized on plates and glasses, and dashing them down violently, broke them in mad rage. Then he entered the best bedroom in the house, where some one lay asleep, and this man he maltreated and hurled forth, saying that the bed was his own.

" And if after that any one dared to sleep in the old palazzo, he was found there dead in the morning, or else lived but a few days. So it came to pass that no one would inhabit it; nay, all the houses round about began to be deserted, and the whole neighbourhood regarded it as a pest. And from all this they were relieved by a marvellously strange occurrence and a great miracle.

" There was a gentleman who was very pious, honourable, and brave, a good man at every point, but wretchedly poor, so that he with his eight children and wife had all been turned into the street, because he could not pay his rent.

" Then in his distress he went to the city council and begged for some kind of relief or employment; and they being much concerned at the time about the haunted palazzo, knowing him to be a man who would face the devil, with little to fear on account of his integrity, proposed to him to occupy the building, adding that he and his family should every day be supplied with food and wine gratis, and that if, as was generally supposed, there was hidden treasure in the palace, and he could find it, he should be welcome to keep it.

" To which this brave man willingly assented, and at once went his way to the haunted palace. But while on the road he obtained olive sprigs, salt, and frankincense, also certain images of saints, and then with much holy water sprinkled all the rooms, stairs, and cellars, praying withal. [1]

" And the first night there was again heard the grating of the key in the lock, the crash of the door, the rapid heavy footfall, and the spirit appeared with the waving plume of flame on his splendid beretta or cap, when suddenly he was checked and could go no farther, because the hall had been blessed, yes, and thoroughly. Then the spectre began to bellow and roar, and utter whistling screams and all horrible sounds, worse than a wild beast.

" But the new master of the house did not let fear overcome him in the least, and the next day he renewed the sprinkling and blessing, and finding there was a chapel in the palace, he called in a priest, who there read a mass for the soul of the ghost, so that he might rest in peace.

"Now there was a beautiful little garden attached to the

[1] This is strikingly like the ceremony for the same purpose used by the ancient Romans, the object in both being to frighten away evil spirits. Vide " Etruscan Roman Remains," by C. G. Leland, p. 305.

C

palace, and the children of the new tenant were delighted to play in it.

" And in the middle of the garden they found a cross with a Christ on it, and the cross had been shattered. But the children took the pieces and carried them one by one into the chamber where no one dared to sleep, and there they put them piously together, and dressed a little altar before it, and began to sing hymns.

" But while they were thus singing in their simple devotion, wishing to aid their father, there was a knock at the door, and a lady entered whose face was concealed in a veil, but who seemed to be weeping as she beheld them, and she said, ' Children, keep ever as you are; always be good and love God, and He will love you !'

"Then she continued, 'The master of this house was a gambler and a blasphemer; when he lost money at gambling he would return home and beat this image of Christ, till one night, being in a mad rage, he broke it and threw it into the garden.'

" ' But soon after that he fell ill, and knowing that he was dying, he buried all his treasure in the garden. Love God, and you shall find it. So he died, blaspheming and condemned. Love God, and He will love you!' And saying this, she vanished.

" The children, all astonished, ran to their father and mother, and told them that a beautiful lady had visited them, and what she had said.

"Then they said to the children, 'You must indeed be always good, for that Lady who spoke to you was the Holy Virgin, who will always protect you.' And then the father called in a priest to say midnight mass at the time when the spirit would appear. And he came, and said, ' I am he who broke the cross, and for that I was damned!' Then the priest began to sprinkle holy water, with exorcisms, when all at once the accursed one disappeared in a tremendous, overwhelming crash of thunder, and the whole palace fell to gravel and dust—there was not left one stone standing on the other, save the cross which the children had repaired, which rose alone in the middle of the garden.

" Then the next day the good man dug away the rubbish by the cross, and when this was removed, they found a mass of charcoal, and under this the treasure.

" Then the Signore, grown rich, had, to commemorate this, a beautiful column built, on which he placed the cross, and this is known to this day as the Croce al Trebbio, or the Crucifix of the Cross-roads."

If the Croce al Trebbio really commemorates one of the most iniquitous massacres which ever disgraced even the Church, then to find this tender and graceful little tale springing up from it, reminds me of what I once heard of a violet which was found growing in the Far West, and blooming in an Indian's skull. The conception of the children playing at worshipping, and yet half-worshipping, is very Italian. I have seen little boys and girls thus rig up a small chapel in the streets of Rome, and go through the mass and other ceremonies with intense interest.

It may also be observed that in this, as in many other legends, charcoal is found over a hidden treasure. The folk-lore of coal in connection with money is so extensive and varied, that one could write on it a small book. I believe that the two are synonyms in all canting jargons or "slanguages."

"Hence probably came," remarks Flaxius, "the saying, 'To haul one over the coals,' meaning to go over money-accounts with any one who has cause to dread the ordeal. Truly 'tis but a conjecture, yet I remember that in my youth it was generally applied to such investigations.

" ' And so 'twas held in early Christian time That glowing coals were a sure test of truth And holy innocence, as was full proved By Santa Agnatesis of the Franks, And fair Lupita of the Irish isle.' "

Since writing the foregoing I have found the whole ot the ancient inscription of the cross, as it was preserved by two chroniclers. This will be found in another chapter.

THE TWO FAIRIES OF THE WELL

A LEGEND OF THE VIA CALZATOLI

" When looking clown into a well, You'll see a fairy, so they tell, Although she constantly appears With your own face instead of hers ; And if you cry aloud, you'll hear Her voice in the ringing echo clear ; Thus every one unto himself May be a fairy, or an elf."

"And truly those nymphs and fairies who inhabit wells, or are found in springs and fountains, can predict or know what is to take place, as may be read in Pausanias, and this power they derive from their hal'ifat, or, as Creuzer declares (Symlolik, part iv. 72), they are called Muses, inasmuch as they dwell in Hippocrene and Aganippe, the inspiring springs of the Muses."— On the Mysteries of Water. FRIEDRICH (Symbolik\'7d.

LONG after Christianity had come in, there were many places in the vast edifice of society whence the old heathen deities refused to go out, and there are even yet nooks and corners in the mountains where they receive a kind of sorcerer's worship ttfolletti. A trace of this lingering in a faith outworn, in nymphs, dryads, and fata, is found in the following story:

LE DUE NINFE DEL Pozzo.

" There once lived in Florence a young nobleman, who had grown up putting great faith in fate, ninfe, and similar spirits, believing that they were friendly, and brought good fortune to those who showed them respect. Now there was in his palazzo in the Via Calzaioli, at the corner of the Condotta, a very old well or fountain, on which were ancient and worn images, and in which there was a marvellous echo, and it was

said that two nymphs had their home in it. And the Signore,

believing in them, often cast into the spring wine or flowers, uttering a prayer to them, and at table he would always cast a little wine into water, or sprinkle water on the ground to do them honour.

"One day he had with him at table two friends, who ridiculed him when he did this, and still more when he sang a song praising nymphs and fairies, in answer to their remarks. Whereupon one said to him :

" ' Truly, I would like to see An example, if 't may be, How a fairy in a fountain. Or a goblin of the mountain, Or a nymph of stream or wood, Ever did one any good ; For such fays of air or river, One might wait, I ween, for ever, And if even such things be, They are devils all to me.'

" Then the young Signore, being somewhat angered, replied:

" ' In the wood and by the stream, Not in reverie or dream, Where the ancient oak-trees blow, And the murmuring torrents flow, Men whose wisdom none condemn Oft have met and talked with them. Demons for you they may be, But are angels unto me.'

" To which his friend sang in reply, laughing :

" ' Only prove that they exist, And we will no more resist; Let them come before we go, With ha I ha ! ha ! and ho! ho! ho !'

" And as they sang this, they heard a peal of silvery laughter without, or, as it seemed, actually singing in the hall and making a chorus with their voices. And at the instant a servant came and said that two very beautiful ladies were without, who begged the young Signore to come to them immediately, and that it was on a matter of life and death.

" So he rose and stepped outside, but he had hardly crossed the threshold before the stone ceiling of the hall fell in with a tremendous crash, and just where the young Signore had sat was a great stone weighing many quintale or hundredweights, so that it was plain that if he had not been called away, in

an instant more he would have been crushed like a fly under a hammer. As for his two friends, they had broken arms and cut faces, bearing marks in memory of the day to the end of their lives.

" When the young Signore was without the door and looked for the ladies, they were gone, and a little boy, who was the only person present, declared that he had seen them, that they were wonderfully beautiful, and that, merrily laughing, they had jumped or gone down into the well.

"Therefore it was generally believed by all who heard the tale that it was the Fairies of the Well, or Fonte, who thus saved the life of the young Signore, who from that day honoured them more devoutly than ever; nor did his friends any longer doubt that there are spirits of air or earth, who, when treated with pious reverence, can confer benefits on their worshippers.

" ' For there are fairies all around Everywhere, and elves abound Even in our homes unseen : They go wherever we have been, And often by the fireside sit, A-laughing gaily at our wit; And when the ringing echo falls Back from the ceiling or the walls, 'Tis not our voices to us thrown In a reflection, but their own ; For they are near at every turn, As he who watches soon may learn.'

"And the young Signore, to do honour to the fairies, because they had saved his life, put them one on either side of his coat-of-arms, as you may see by the shield which is on the house at the corner of the Via Calzaioli."

The authenticity of this legend, is more than doubtful, because it exists elsewhere, as I have read it, being unable to give my authority; but unless my memory deceives me, it goes back to classic times, and may be found in some such work as that of Philostratus de Vita Apollonii or Grosius. Neither am I well assured, to judge from the source whence I had it, that it is current among the people, though no great measure of credulity is here required, since it may be laid down as a rule, with

rarest exception, that there is no old Roman tale of the kind which may not be unearthed with pains and patience among old Tuscan peasant women. However, the shield is still on the corner of the Via Calzaioli, albeit one of the nymphs on it has been knocked or worn away. Thus even fates must yield in time to fate.

I have in a note to another legend spoken of the instinct which seems to lead children or grown people to associate wells with indwelling fairies, to hear a voice in the echo, and see a face in the reflection in the still water. Keats has beautifully expressed it in " Endymion " :

"Some mouldered steps lead into this cool cell Far as the slabbed margin of a well, Whose patient level peeps its crystal eye Right upward through the bushes to the sky. . . . Upon a day when thus I watched . . . behold ! A wonder fair as any I have told— The same bright face I tasted in my sleep Smiling in the clear well. My heart did leap Through the cool depth. . . . Or 'tis the cell of Echo, where she sits And babbles thorough silence till her wits Are gone in tender madness, and anon Faints into sleep, with many a dying tone."

" In which tale," writes the immortal Flaxius, " there is a pretty allegory. Few there are who know why truth is said to be at the bottom of a well; but this I can indeed declare to you. For as a mirror was above all things an emblem of truth, because it shows all things exactly as they are, so the water in a well was, as many traditions prove, considered as a mirror, because looking into it we see our face, which we of course most commonly see in a glass, and this disk of shining water resembles in every way a hand-mirror. And for this reason a mirror was also regarded as expressing life itself, for which reason people so greatly fear to break them. So in the Latin, Velut in specula, and in the Italian, Vero come un specchio —' True as a mirror,' we have the same idea. And a poet has written, ' Mirrored as in a well,' and many have reechoed the same pretty fancy.

" Which reminds me that in the Oberpfalz or Upper Palatinate maidens were wont to go to a well by moonlight, and if on looking therein they saw their own faces, they believed that they would soon be happily married. But if a cloud darkened the moon and they saw nothing, then they would die old maids. But luckiest of all was it if they fancied they saw a man's face, for this would be the future husband himself.

" Now it befell that a certain youth near Heidelberg fell into a well, or put himself there, when a certain maid whom he loved, came and looked in, and believing that she saw the face of her destined spouse, went away in full faith that the fairy of the well had taken his form, and so she married him. Which, if it be not true, is ben trovato.

"Truth is always represented, be it remembered, as holding a mirror.

"And note also that the hand-mirror and the well were strangely connected in ancient times, as appears by Pausanias, who states that before a certain temple of Ceres hung a speculum, which, after it had been immersed in a neighbouring well or spring, showed invalids by reflection whether they would live or die. And with all this, the holding a mirror to the mouth of an insensible person to tell whether the breath was still in the body, seemed also to make it an indicator of life."

" Thus in life all things do pass, As it were, in magic glass."

THE STORY OF THE VIA DELLE SERVE SMARRITE

"We all do know the usual way In which our handmaids go astray, But in this tale the situation Has a peculiar variation ; How an old wizard — strange occurrence ! Deluded all the girls in Florence, (It needs no magic now to do it), And how the maidens made him rue it, For having seized on him and stripped him, They tied him up and soundly whipped him."

THE author of " The Cities of Central Italy," speaking of Siena, says that " In its heart, where its different hill-promontories unite, is the Piazza, del Campo, lately — with the time-serving which disgraces every town in Italy—called Vittorio Emanuele." And with the stupidity and bad taste which seems to characterise all municipal governments in this respect all the world over, that of Florence has changed most of the old names of this kind, and in order to render the confusion more complete, has put the new names just over the old ones, with the simple addition of the word Gm or "formerly." Whence came the legend current in the Anglo-American colony, that a newly arrived young lady, not as yet beyond the second lesson in Ollendorff, being asked where she lived, answered in Gta Street. She forgot the rest of the name.

One of these gaping gias is the Via del Parlascio gia Via delle Serve Smarrite, or the street of the maidservants strayed away or gone astray. Now Florence is famous for its pretty servant-girls, and if I may believe a halfpenny work, entitled " Seven Charming Florentine Domestics," now before me, which is racy of the soil—or dirt—and appears to be written from life [as accurate portraits of all the fascinating seven are given], I opine that the damsel of this class who had never been, I do not say a wife, but a waif and a stray, must be a phenomenal rarit\'7d 7 . Therefore it was suggested to me that it was formerly in very ancient times the custom to send all such stray cattle to the pound, that is, to dwell in this street as a kind of Ghetto. But the folly of this measure soon became apparent when it was found that one might as well try to get all the cats in Tuscany into a hand-basket, or all its flies—or fleas—under one tumbler, as try to make a comprehensive menagerie of these valuable animals, who were, however, by no means curiosities. So the attempt was abandoned, and thenceforth the maidens were allowed to stray wherever they pleased, but under some slight supervision ; whence it was said of them that they were le lucertole chi comindano a sentir il sole —"fireflies which begin to see the sun"— a proverb which the learned and genial Orlando Peschetti (1618) explains as being applicable to those who, having been in prison and then set free, are still watched, but which appears to me rather to refer to the suspected who are " shadowed " before they are arrested.

But in due time I received from good authority an ancient legend of the Via delle Serve Smarrite, in which the origin of the name is explained as follows:

VIA DELLE SERVE SMARRITE.

" There was long ago, in what was afterwards called the Via delle Serve Smarrite, or Stray Maid-Servants' Street, a very ancient and immensely large house, which was generally supposed to be vacant, and in which no one cared to dwell, or even approach, since there were dreadful tales of evil deeds done in it, and reports that it was a gathering-place for witches, goblins, and diavoli. The clanking of chains and peals of horrid laughter rung from its chambers at midnight, blue and

green fires gleamed from its windows, and everybody all around had heard from somebody else that the nightmares had there their special nest, from which they sailed forth to afflict all Florence.

" Yet all this was a trick which was often played in those days, when gente non dabbene or evil folk and outlaws wanted to keep a house to themselves, and there were no newspapers to publish every mystery. For there were a great many who went in there, but few who ever came out, and these were all young and pretty servant-maids. And the way it was managed was this. When such girls were sent to the market to buy provisions, they always met there or elsewhere an old woman who pretended to be extremely pious,[1] who, by using many arts and making small gifts, and above all by subtle flatteries, persuaded them that service was only fit for gentaccia or the dregs of the people, and that, beautiful and graceful as they were, they needed only live like ladies for a little time at ease, and they would soon be fit to marry some Signore, and that she herself would thus maintain them, hoping they would pay her well for it all when once married. And I need not say that the trick generally succeeded.

" The house to which they were led was ugly and repulsive outside, but within there were beautiful rooms of all kinds, magnificently furnished, and the new-comers were promptly bathed, elegantly attired, and jewelled from head to foot, and instead of serving, had maids given them as attendants, and everything conceivable was done to make their life as pleasant and demoralising among themselves as possible. But in due time they found out that a certain Signore was lord of the house and of themselves, and that he gradually led them into the strangest and most terrible orgies, and finally into witchcraft, after which one disappeared mysteriously after the other, none knew whither, but as there were always fresh arrivals to take their places, nobody heeded it.

"However, this mournful disappearance of pretty servant-maids became at last so frequent and was so mysterious, that it began to be much talked about. Now there was a certain gentleman, a man himself of great authority and intelligence, who had heard of these vanishments and hoped to find out their cause. And one night at a very late hour, when he was passing by the mysterious house, he heard from it now and

[1] Una vecchietta, tutta Gesù e Maria.

then sounds like groans mingled with the clanking of chains, and saw red and blue and green lights at the windows, but by keeping still he also distinguished the sound of music and girls' voices laughing and singing; and stealing near in the darkness, and fearing no devils, he contrived to climb up to a window, and pulling aside a curtain, peeped in, when he beheld plainly enough a great many beautiful women in scant array, or a real dance of witches, and being marvellously attracted by the sight of so many charms so liberally displayed, he naturally desired to enter the gay party.

" And here chance favoured him beyond all hope; for on going to the door, he found an old woman about to enter, to whom he gave a gold piece, and begged her to tell him the true story of the house, and whether he could enter it. But what was his amazement to find in her his old foster-mother of the country, whom he had not seen for many years, and who loved him dearly.

" And she, being pressed, told him the whole story of the house, wherein she was a servant, but that she had grown deadly tired of such evil ways, and seeing such sin as went on there, though she was well paid, and said if he would only give her a home, she would reveal all to justice. And she added that for the present he could freely join the girls who were dancing, as the wizard, their master, was away that night.

" But when he entered, he was amazed at the splendour of the rooms and the beauty of the women. Now among these he found one who truly enchanted him, and entering into conversation with her, found that she would gladly escape with him, and that many others were inclined to leave, but dare not show it for fear of the master.

"Then the Signore, addressing all the girls, told them that in a few hours the guards or police would, by his orders, be in the house, and advised them to at once seize on all the valuables on which they could lay their hands, and pack up their bundles and depart, and that he himself would write for every one a free pass to let-her go with the property. And truly he had hardly spoken ere there began such a plundering and pillaging, sacking and spoliation, as it would have done your heart good to see, and which was like the taking of a rich town, only that the marauders were all maidens. Here was one rolling up silver spoons, cups, anything she could get, in a shawl; there another filling a bag with jewellery, and a silver ladle sticking out of her bosom or back; anon a couple of Venuses fighting

for a splendid garment, while a superb Hebe ravished a golden goblet, and an enchanting Vesta, if not a vestal, appropriated most appropriately a silver lamp. Some pulled down the curtains, others rolled up the costly Venetian rugs ; they drank wine when they were thirsty, and quarrelled and laughed and shrieked, as a parcel of wild servant-girls in a mad frolic might be expected to do. It was a fine sight—' one worthy of a great artist or De Goncourt,' notes Flaxius.

"When lo ! all at once there was an awful and simultaneous shriek as the door opened, and the Domine —I mean the headmaster, wizard, or sultan—entered, gazing like an astonished demon on the scene before his eyes. In a voice of thunder he asked the meaning of the scene, when he found himself confronted by the intruding Signore, before whom his heart run away like water when he recognised in him a man having very great authority, with the police at his back.

"Now, servant-maids, however pretty they may be, are mostly contadine with powerful muscles and mighty arms, and with one accord they rushed on their late master, and soon overpowered him. Then he was securely bound with silken curtain ropes, and the new Signore, taking his place at a great table, bade all the damsels range themselves at the sides in solemn council, for the offender was now to be tried, condemned, and punished too, should he be found guilty.

'•The trial was indeed one of peculiar interest, and the testimony adduced would have made the fortune of a French novelist, but space (if nothing else) prohibits my giving it. Suffice it to say that the wizard was found guilty of taking unto himself an undue share of pretty handmaidens, a great sin considering the number of gallant soldiers and other bachelors who were thereby defrauded of their dues. But as he had neither murdered nor stolen, it was decided to let him go and carry on his games in some less Christian town, on condition that he would divide what money he had in the house among the poor girls whom he had so cruelly cajoled.

"And as this last sentence was plaintively pronounced, there was a deep and beautiful sigh uttered by all the victims, followed by three cheers. The master's strong-box was at once hunted up, and its contents shared, and indeed they were so considerable that the maidens one and all soon married nobly and lived happily."

The written story, with a pleasing instinct of Italian
thrift, adds that the conquering Signore purchased the property, in fact, the whole street, at a very low figure, before the facts became known, and gave the place the name of the Via delle Serve Smam'te, as it is still called by the people, despite its new official christening.

" Ye may break, ye may ruin the flask if ye will, But the scent of the brandy will hang round it still."

THE BRONZE BOAR OF THE MERCATO NUOVO

"Now among the Greeks, as with the Northern races, the boar was the special type of male generation, even as the frog expressed that of the female sex. And therefore images of the boar were set in public places that fertility might be developed among women, for which reason they also wear, as among the Arabs, necklaces of silver frogs."— Notes on Symbolism.

IN front of the Mercato Nuovo, built by Cosimo I., stands a bronze copy of an ancient boar, now in the Uffizzi Gallery. It was cast by Pietro Tacca, and is now a fountain. The popular legend in relation to it is as follows:

" In the market-place of Florence, which is called // Por-cellino, because there is in it a fountain with a swine, there was anciently only a spring of water and a pool, in which were many frogs, water-lizards, shell-snails, and slugs. These were round about, but in the spring itself was a frog who was confined there because she had revealed that her lover was a boar.

"This boar was the son of a rich lord, who, being married for a very long time, had no children, and for this reason made his wife very unhappy, saying that she was a useless creature, and that if she could not bear a son she had better pack up and be off with herself, which she endured despairingly and weeping continually, praying to the saints and giving alms withal, all to bring forth an heir, and all in vain.

" One day she saw a drove of pigs go by her palace, and among them were many sows and many more very little pigs. Now among these, or at hand, was a. fata or witch-spirit. [1] And the lady seeing this said in the bitterness of her heart, ' So the very pigs have offspring and I none. I would I were as

[1] I have elsewhere explained that the fata in these traditions is a witch or sorcerer become a spirit.

they are, and could do as they do, and bring forth as they bring forth, and so escape all this suffering !'

" And the fairy heard this, and took her at her word ; and, as you will see, she cut her cloth without measuring it first, from which came a sad misfit. And soon after she was ill, and this being told to her husband, he replied, 'Good news, and may she soon be gone !' but he changed his tone when he heard that he was to have an heir. Then he flew to her and begged her pardon, and made great rejoicings.

" Truly there was horror and sorrow when in due time the lady, instead of a human child, brought forth a boar-pig. Yet the parents were so possessed with the joy of having any kind of offspring that they ended by making a great pet of the creature, who was, however, human in his ways, and could in time talk with grace and ease. [1] And when he grew older he began to run after the girls, and they to run away from him, screaming as if the devil had sent him for them.

" There lived near the palace a beautiful but very poor girl, and with her the young Boar fell desperately in love. So he asked her parents for her hand ; but they, poor as they were, laughed at him, saying that their daughter should never marry a swine. But the young lady had well perceived that this was no common or lazy pig, such as never gets a ripe pear— *porco pigro non mangia pere mature* —as he had shown by wooing her ; and, secondly, because she was poor and ambitious, and daring enough to do anything to become rich and great. 2

" Now she surmised that there were eggs under the chopped straw in this basket, or more in the youth than people supposed ; and she was quite right, for on the bridal night he not only unclothed himself of silk and purple and fine linen, but also doffed his very skin or boar's hide, and appeared as beautiful as a Saint Sebastian freshly painted.

" Then he said to her, ' Be not astonished to find me good-looking at the rate of thirty sous to a franc, nor deem thyself over-paid, for if we had not wedded, truly I should have gone on pigging it to the end of my days, having been doomed— like many men—to be a beast so long as I was a bachelor, or

1 It may be conjectured from this context that the child was partly human in form, perhaps like the Pig-faced Lady, or not more swinish than NVilliam of Ardennes in face.

2 Truly she was, to use a really ancient phrase, " ready to go the whole hog." It is said that Mahomet told his disciples that there was one part of a pig which they must not touch ; but as he did not specify what it was, they among them devoured the entire animal.

till a beautiful maid would marry me. Yet there is a condition attached to this, which is, that I can only be a man as thou seest me by night, for I must be a boar by day. And shouldst thou ever betray this secret to any one, or if it be found out, then I shall again be a boar all the time for life, and thou turn into a frog because of too much talking.

" Now as surely as that time and straw ripen medlars, as the saying is, just so surely will it come to pass that a woman will tell a secret, even to her own shame. And so it befell this lady, who told it as a great mystery to her mother, who at once imparted it under oath to all her dear friends, who swore all their friends on all their salvations not to breathe a word of it to anybody, who all confessed it to the priests. How much farther it went God knows, but by the time the whole town knew it, which was in one day of twenty-four hours, or ere the next morning, the bride had become a frog who lived in the spring, and the bridegroom a boar who every day went to drink at the water, and when there said:

"' Lady Frog ! lo, I am here !
He to whom thou once wert dear.
We are in this sad condition,
Not by avarice or ambition,
Nor by evil or by wrong,
But 'cause thou could'st not hold thy tongue ;
For be she shallow, be she deep,
No woman can a secret keep ;
Which all should think upon who see
The monument which here will be.'

" So it came to pass either that the boar turned into the great bronze *maiale* which now stands in the market-place, or else the people raised it in remembrance of the story— *chi sa* — but there it is to this day.

" As for the Signora Frog, she comforted herself by making a great noise and telling the tale at the top of her voice, having her brains in her tongue—*'/ cervello nella lingua*, as they say of those who talk well yet have but small sense. And that which you hear frogs croaking all night long is nothing but this story which I have told you of their ancestress and the bronze boar."

This is, in one form or the other, a widely spread tale. As the voice of the frog has a strange resemblance to that of man, there being legends referring to it in every language, [1] it was anciently regarded as a human being who was metamorphosed for being too impudent and loquacious, as appears by the legend of " Latona and the Lycian Boors " (Ovid, Metamorph., vi. 340). The general resemblance of the form of a frog to that of man greatly contributed to create such fables.

The classic ancient original of this boar may be seen in the Uffizzi Gallery. As the small image of a pig carried by ladies ensures that they will soon be, as the Germans say, "in blessed circumstances," or enceinte (which was all one with luck in old times), so the image of the boar is supposed to be favourable to those ladies who desire olive branches. From all which it appears that in ancient times swine were more highly honoured than at present, or, as Shelley sings :

"We pigs
Were blest as nightingales on myrtle sprigs, Or grasshoppers that live on noon-day dew."

[1] "Symbola Heroica," Antwerp, 1583.

THE FAIRY OF THE CAMPANILE, OR THE TOWER OF GIOTTO

" Bella di fronte e infino alle Calcagna, Con un corredo nobile e civile, In te risiede una cupola magna E superbo di Giotto il Campanile."— Giuseppe Moroni.

" Round as the O of Giotto, d'ye see?
Which means as well done as a thing can be."— Proverb.

MANY have wondered how it came to pass that Virgil lived in tradition not as a poet but as sorcerer. But the reason for it is clear when we find that in Florence every man who ever had a genius for anything owed it to magic, or specially to the favour of some protecting fairy or follettOj spirit or god. Is a girl musical ? Giacinto or Hyacinth, the favourite of Apollo, has given her music lessons in her dreams. For the orthodox there are Catholic saints with a specialty, from venerable Simeon, who looks after luck in lotteries, to the ever-blessed Antony, who attends to everything, and Saint Anna, ne'e Lucina, who inspires nurses. And where the saints fail, the folletti, according to the witches, take their place and do the work far better. Therefore, as I shall in another place set forth, Dante and Michel Angelo have passed into the marvellous mythology of goblins. With them is included Giotto, as appears by the following legend of " The Goblin of the Bell-Tower of Giotto."

IL FOLLETTO DEL CAMPANILE DI GIOTTO.

" Giotto was a shepherd, and every day when he went forth to pasture his herd there was one little lamb who always kept near him, and appeared to be longing to talk to him like a Christian.

" Now this lamb always laid down on a certain stone which was fast in the ground (masso); and Giotto, who loved the lamb, to please it, lay down also on the same stone.

"After a short time the lamb died, and when dying said :

" ' Giotto, cosa non far ti Se mi senti parlarti, Ti voglio tanto bene E dove andrai, Io ti seguiro sempre In forma di folletto, E col mio volere Tu verrai un bravo scultore E insegne disegnatore.'

" ' Giotto, be not astonished That I thus speak to thee ; I have such love for thee, Wherever thou shall go I will follow thee always In the form of a fairy, And through my favour Thou shall become a great sculptor And artisl."

" And so it came to pass that Giotto was an able sculptor by the aid of the lamb, and all that he did was due to the lamb which helped him.

" And when he died, the spirit of the lamb remained in the form of a folletto or fairy in the campanile, and it is still often seen there, always with the spirit of Giotto. Even in death their souls could not be separate.

" When any one desires to ascend the tower, and his or her heart fails in mounting the steps (e che ha paura di satire), the fairy below says:

" ' Vade, vade, Signora ! La vade su salgha, Non abbia paura, Ci sono io sotto.'

" ' Go on, go on, Signora, Go up the stairs—oh go ! Be not afraid, my lady ! For I am here below.'

"Then the visitor hearing this believes it is one of the guides employed (inpiegati\ or one of the gentlemen or ladies

who are ascending after. And often when half-way up there comes a great puff of wind which blows up their skirts (fa gonfiare le sottane) which causes great laughter, and they think that this is only a common thing, and do not perceive that it does not happen to others.

"And it is said that this fairy appears by night in the Piazza del Duomo, or Cathedral Square, in different forms."

The reason why Giotto is so popularly known as having been a shepherd is that on the central tablet of the tower or campanile, facing the street, there is a bas-relief of a man seated in a tent with sheep before him, and this is naturally supposed to represent the builder or Giotto himself, since it fills the most prominent place. In a very popular halfpenny chapbook, entitled "The Statues under the Uffizi in Florence, Octaves improvised by Giuseppe Moroni, called // Niccheri or the Illiterate," I find the

following :
GIOTTO.

" Voi di Mugello, nato dell' interno, Giotto felice, la da' Vespignano Procligiose pitture in ogni esterno A Brescia, a Roma, Firenze e Milano, Nelle pietre, ne' marmi nel quaderno, L'archittetura al popolo italiano. Da non trovare paragone simile, Vi basti, per esempio, il campanile."

" Thou of Mugello, born in Italy, Happy Giotto, gav'st to Vespignan Great pictures which on every front we see At Brescia, Rome, in Florence and Milan, In stone, in marble, and in poetry, And architecture, all Italian. Nothing surpassed thy wondrous art and power, Take for example, then, our great bell-tower."

The fact that this is taken from a very popular halfpenny work indicates the remarkable familiarity with such a name as that of Giotto among the people.

THE GOBLIN OF THE TOWER DELL A TRINITA, OR THE PORT A SAN NICCOLO

" They do not speak as mortals speak, Nor sing as others sing ; Their words are gleams of starry light, Their songs the glow of sunset light, Or meteors on the wing."

I ONCE begun a book—the ending and publishing of it are in the dim and remote future, and perhaps in the limbo of all things unfinished. It was or is " The Experiences of Flaxius the Immortal," a sage who dwells for ever in the world, chiefly to observe the evolution of all things absurd, grotesque, quaint, illogical — in short, of all that is strictly human. And on him I bestowed a Florentine legend which is perhaps of great antiquity, since there is a hint in it of an ancient Hebrew work by Rabbi ben Mozeltoff or the learned Gedauler Chamar— I forget which—besides being found in poetic form in my own great work on Confucius.

That money is the life of man, and that treasure buried in the earth is a sin to its possessor, forms the subject of one of Christ's parables. The same is true of all talent unemployed, badly directed, or not developed at all. The turning-point of evolution and of progressive civilisation will be when public opinion and state interests require that every man shall employ what talent he has, and every mere idler be treated as a defaulter or criminal. From this truly Christian point of view the many tales of ghosts who walk in agony because of buried gold are strangely instructive.

FLAXIUS AND THE ROSE.

" Midnight was ringing from the cloister of San Miniato in Florence on the hill above, and Flaxius sat by the Arno down below, on the bank by the square grey tower of other days, known as the Niccolb, or Torre del/a Trinita, because there are in it three arches. . . .

" It was midnight in mid-winter, and a full moon poured forth all its light over Florence as if it would fain preserve it in amber, and over the olive groves as if they had become moss agates. . . .

['"Or I,' quoth Flaxius, 'a fly in hock.']

"Yes, it was a clear, cold, Tuscan night, and as the last peal of bells went out into eternity and faded in the irrevocable, thousands of spirits of the departed began to appear, thronging like fireflies through the streets, visiting their ancient haunts and homes, greeting, gossiping, arranging their affairs just as the peasants do on Friday in the great place of the Signoria, as they have done for centuries.

" Flaxius looked at the rolling river which went rushing by at his feet, and said:

" ' Arno mio, you are in a tremendous hurry to get to the sea, and all the more so because you have just had an accessit —a remittance of rain from the mountain-banks. JBuon pro vi faccia —much good may it do you ! So every shopman hurries to become a great merchant when he gets some money, and every farmer a signore, and every signore a great lord, and every great lord a ruler at court and over all the land— prorsum et sursum. And when they get there—or when you get to the sea—then ye are all swallowed up in greater lives, interests, and actions, and so the rivers run for ever on, larger yet ever seeming less unto yourselves. And so— ad altiora tendunt omnes —the flower-edged torrent and the Florentine.' . . .

" When he suddenly heard above his head a spirit voice, clear, sweet and strange, ringing, not in words, but tones of unearthly music—of which languages there are many among the Unearthlies, all being wordless songs or airs suggesting speech, and yet conveying ideas far more rapidly. It was the Goblin of the Tower calling to him of the tower next beyond on the farther hill, and he said :

" ' How many ghosts there are out to-night!'

"'Yes; it is a fine night for ghosting. Moonlight is mid-

summer for them, poor souls! But I say, brother, who is yonder frate^ the dark monk-spectre who always haunts your tower, lingering here and there about it? What is the spell upon that spirito ?'

"' He is one to be pitied,' replied the Goblin of the Trinita. ' He was a good fellow while he lived, but a little too fond of money. He was afflicted with what doctors called, when I was young in Rome, the amor scekratus habendi. So it came to pass that he died leaving a treasure— milk aureos —a thousand gold crowns buried in my tower unknown to any one, and for that he must walk the earth until some one living wins the money.'

" Flaxius pricked up his ears. He understood all that the spirits said, but they had no idea that the man in a scholar's robe who sat below knew Goblinese.

"' What must a mortal do to get the gold ?' inquired the second goblin.

"'Truly he must do what is well-nigh impossible,'replied the Elf of the Tower; ' for he must, without magic aid—note that—bring to me here in this month of January a fresh fullblown rose.'

The voices were silent; a cloud passed over the face of the moon; the river rushed and roared on; Flaxius sat in a Vandyke-brown study, thinking how he could obtain peace and repose for the ghostly monk, and also get the pecuniam.

"' Here is,' he thought, ' aliquid laborare — something to be worked out. Now is the time, and here is a chance— ingirlan-darsi di lauro —to win the laurel wreath. A rose in January ! What a pity that it is not four hundred years later, when people will have green-houses, and blue-nosed vagabonds will be selling red roses all the winter long in the Tornabuoni! Truly it is sometimes inconvenient to be in advance of or behind the age.

"'Eureka! I have it,'he at last exclaimed, 'by the neck and tail. I will spogliar la tesoria — rob the treasury and spoil the Egyptian— si non in errore versatus sum —unless I am stupendously mistaken. Monk ! thy weird will soon be dreed —thy penance prophesied will soon be o'er.'

" Saying this he went into the city. And there the next day, going to a fair dame of his acquaintance, who excelled all the ladies of all Italy in ingenious needlework, he had made of silk a rose; and so deftly was it done, that had it been put on a bush, you would have sworn that a nightingale would have sung to it, or bee have sought to ravish it.

"Then going to a Venetian perfumer's, the wise Flaxius had his flower well scented with best attar of roses from Constantinople, and when midnight struck he was at the tower once more calling to the goblin.

"' Che vuoi? What dost thou seek?' cried the Elf.

" ' The treasure of the monk !'

" ' Bene ! Give me a rose.'

" ' Ecco ! There it is,' replied Flaxius, extending it.

" ' Non facit —it won't do,' answered the goblin (thinking Flaxius to be a monk). ' It is a sham rose artificially coloured, murice tine fa esf.'

" ' Smell it,' replied Flaxius calmly.

"' The smell is all right, I admit,' answered the guardian of the gold. ' The perfume is delicious;' here he sniffed at it deeply, being, like all his kind, enraptured with perfume, ' and that much of it is, I grant, the real thing.'

"'Now tell me,' inquired Flaxius, 'truly— religiose testimo-nium dicere —by thy great ancestress Diana and her sister-double Herodias and her Nine Cats, by the Moon and the eternal Shadow, Endamone, and the word which Bergoia whispered into the ear of the Ox, and the Lamia whom thou lovest—what is it makes a man ? Is it his soul or his body ?'

"' Man of mystery and master of the hidden lore,' replied the awe-struck goblin, ' it is his soul.'

" ' And is not the perfume of the rose its soul —that which breathes its life, in which it speaks to fairies or to men ? Is not the voice in song or sweetened words the perfume of the spirit, ever true? Is not '

" ' I give it up,' replied the goblin. ' The priest may turn in now for a long, long nap. Here, take his gold, and ne gioire tutto d 1 allegrezza —may you have a merry time with it. There is a great deal of good drinking in a thousand crowns; and if you ever try to ludere latrunculis vel afeis, or shake the bones or dice, I promise you three sixes. By the way, I'll just keep this rose to remember you by. Addio — a rivederlei / '

" So the bedesman slept amid his ashes cold, and the good Flaxius, who was a stout carl for the nonce, with a broad back and a great beard, returned, bearing a mighty sack of ancient gold, which stood him in good stead for many a day. And the goblin is still there in the tower."

" HCRC fabula docet" wrote Flaxius as he revised the proof with a red-lead pencil, for which he had paid a penny in the Calzolaio. " This tale teaches that in this life there is naught which hath not its ideal side or inner soul, which may raise us to higher reflection or greater profit, if we will but seek it. The lower the man the lower he looks, but it is all to his loss in the end. Now every chapter in this book, O my son—or daughter—may seem to thee only a rose of silk, yet do not stop at that, but try to find therein a perfume. For thou art thyself, I doubt not, such a rose, even if thy threads (as in most of us) be somewhat worn, torn, or faded, yet with a soul far better than many deem who see thee only afar off. And this my book is written for the perfume, not the silk of my reader. And there is no person who is better than what the world deems him or her to be who will not find in it marvellous comfort, solace, and satisfaction." Thus wrote Flaxius.

Since I penned the foregoing from memory, I have found the Italian text or original, which had been mislaid for years. In it the tale is succinctly told within the compass of forty lines, and ends with these words :

" ' Take the treasure, and give me the rose !' "And so the spirit gave him the treasure and took the rose, and the poor man went home enriched, and the priest to sleep in peace— fra gli eterni —among the eternals."

I ought, of course, to have given scientifically only the text word for word, but litera scripta manet —what is written remains, and Flaxius is an old friend of mine, and I greatly desired to introduce him to my readers. And I doubt not that the reviewers will tell me if I have sinned!

" Do a good deed, or aught that's fit, You never again may hear of it; But make a slip, all will detect it, And every friend at once correct it! "

THE GHOST OF MICHEL ANGELO

" If I believed that spirits ne'er Return to earth once more, And that there's naught unto them dear In the life they loved before ; Then truly it would seem to me, However fate has sped, For souls there's no eternity, And they and all are dead."

IT must have struck every one who has read the life of Michel Angelo, that he was, like King James the First of England, "nae great gillravager after the girls," or was far from being susceptible to love—in which he formed a great contrast to Raphael, and indeed to most of the Men of his Time—or any other. This appears to have impressed the people of Italy as something even more singular than his works, for which reason he appears in popular tradition as a good enough goblin, not without cheerfulness and song, but as one given to tormenting enamoured couples and teasing lady artists, whom he subsequently compliments with a gift. The legend is as follows:

Lo SPIRITO DI MICHELE ANGIOLO BUONAROTTI.

" The spirit of Michel Angelo is seen mostly by night, in woods or groves. The good man appears as he did in life, come era prima, ever walking among trees singing poetry. He amuses himself very much by teasing lovers— a dare noia agli amoretti —and when he finds a pair who have hidden themselves under leaves and boughs to make love, he waits till they think they are well concealed, and then begins to sing. And the two feel a spell upon them when they hear his voice, and can neither advance nor retreat.

"Then all at once opening the leafy covert, he bursts into a peal of laughter; and the charm being broken, they fly in fear, because they think they are discovered, and it is all nothing but the spirit of Michel Angelo Buonarotti.

"When some lady-artist goes to sketch or paint, be it al piazzale, in open places, or among the woods, it is his delight to get behind, and cause her to blunder, scrawl, and daub (fare degli scarabocchi). And when the artist is angered, she will hear a loud peal of laughter; and if this irritates her still more, she will hear a song, and yet not perceive the singer. And when at last in alarm she catches up her sketch, all scrawled and spoiled, and takes to flight, she will hear the song following her, and yet if she turns her head she will see no one pursuing. The voice and melody are always beautiful. But it is marvellously lucky to have this happen to an artist, for when she gets home and looks at her sketch, she finds that it is neither scrawled nor daubed, but most exquisitely executed in the style of Michel Angelo."

It is marvellous how the teasing faun or Silvanus of the Romans has survived in Tuscany. I have found him in many forms, under many names, and this is the last. But why it should be Michel Angelo, I cannot imagine, unless it be that his face and stump nose, so familiar to the people, are indeed like that of the faun. The dii sylvestres, with all their endless mischief, riotry, and revelry, were good fellows, and the concluding and rather startling touch that the great artist in the end always bestows a valuable picture on his victim is really godlike —in a small way.

It is remarkable as a coincidence, that Michel Angelo was himself during life terribly annoyed and disturbed by people prying and speering about him while painting — especially by Pope Leo—for whom he nevertheless painted very good pictures. It would almost seem as if there were an echo of the event in the legend. Legend is the echo of history.

"This legend," remarks Flaxius, "may give a valuable hint to collectors. Many people are aware that there are in exist-

ence great numbers of sketchings and etchings attributed to Michel Angelo, Diirer, Raphael, Marc Antonio, and many more, which were certainly executed long since those brothers of the paint or pencil passed away. May it not be that the departed still carry on their ancient callings by the aid of new and marvellous processes to us as yet unknown, or by what may be called 'pneumato-gravure'? Who knows?—'tis a great idea, my masters;—let us pass on or legit unto another legend!

" ' Well I ween it may be true That afar in fairyland
Great artists still pursue
That which in life they knew,
And practise still, with ever bettering hand,
Sculpture and painting, all that charm can bring,
While by them all departed poets sing.' "

THE APPARITION OF DANTE

" Musa profonda dei Toscani, il Dante,
II nobil cittadin, nostro Alighieri,
Alia filosofia ricco e brillante
Purgo il linguaggio e corredo i pensieri ;
E nell' opera sua fatto gigante
A Campaldino nei primi guerrieri;
Lui il Purgatorio, Paradise e Inferno
Fenomeno terren, poeta eterno ! "

— /.e Statue disotto gli Ufizi in Firemzc. Otiave improvisate da Giuseppe Moroni detto II

Nicchieri (llliterafo), Florence, 1892.

IT has been boldly asserted by writers who should know better, that there are no ghosts in Italy, possibly because the two only words in the language for such beings are the equivocal ones of spirito or spirit, and spettro or spectre—or specter, as the Websterians write it— which is of itself appalling as a terrific spell. But the truth is that there is no kind of spuk, goblin, elf, fairy, gnome, or ouphe known to all the North of Europe which was not at home in Italy since old Etruscan days, and ghosts, though they do not make themselves common, are by no means as rare as eclipses. For, as may be read in my "Etruscan Roman Legends," people who will look through a stone with a hole in it can behold no end of revenants, or returners, in any churchyard, and on fine nights the seer can see them swarming in the streets of Florence. Giotto is in the campanile as a gentle ghost with the fairy lamb, and Dante, ever benevolent, is all about town, as appears from the following, which was unexpectedly bestowed on me :

Lo SPIRITO DI DANTE ALIGHIERI.

" When any one is passionately fond of poetry, he should sit by night on the panchina 1 in the piazza or square of Santa Croce or in other places (i.e., those haunted by Dante), and having read his poetry, pronounce the following:

" ' Dante, che eri La gran poeta, Siei morto, ma vero, II tuo spirito E sempre rimasto, Sempre per nostro Nostro aiuto.

" ' Ti chiamo, ti prego ! E ti scongiuro ! A voler aiutarmi. Questa poesia Voglio imparare ; Di piu ancora, Non voglio soltanto Imparar la a cantare, Ma voglio imparare Di mia testa Foter le scrivere, E cosi venire Un bravo poeta !'

" 'Thou Dante, who wert Such a great poet, Art dead, but thy spirit Is truly yet with us, Here and to aid us.

" ' I call thee, I pray thee, And I conjure thee ! Give me assistance ! I would learn perfectly All of this poetry. And yet, moreover, I would not only Learn it to sing it, But I would learn too How I may truly From my head write it, And become really An excellent poet !'

"And then a form of a man will approach from around the statue (da canto), advancing gently— piano-piano —to the

1 Raised footway, high curbstone, causeway, bench.

causeway, and will sit on it like any ordinary person, and begin to read the book, and the young man who has invoked the poet will not fail to obtain his wish. And the one who has come from the statue is no other indeed than Dante himself.

"And it is said that if in any public place of resort or inn (bettola) any poet sings the poems of Dante, he is always present among those who listen, appearing as a gentleman or poor man — secondo il locale —according to the place.

" Thus the spirit of Dante enters everywhere without being seen.

" If his poems be in the house of any person who takes no pleasure in them, the spirit of the poet torments him in his bed (in dreams) until the works are taken away."

There is a simplicity and directness in this tradition, as here told, which proves the faith of the narrator. Washington Irving found that the good people of East Cheap had become so familiar with Shakespearian comedy as to verily believe that Falstaff and Prince Hal and Dame Quickly had all lived, and still haunted the scenes of their former revels; and in like manner the Florentine has followed the traditions of olden time so closely and lovingly, that all the magnates of the olden time live for him literally at the present day. This is in a great measure due to the fact that statues of all the celebrities of the past are in the most public places, and that there are many common traditions to the effect that all statues at certain times walk about or are animated.

One of the commonest halfpenny or soldo pamphlets to be found on the stand of all open-air dealers in ballads —as, for instance, in the Uffizzi—is a collection of poems on the statues around that building, which of itself indicates the interest in the past, and the knowledge of poets and artists possessed by the common people. For the poorest of them are not only familiar with the names, and more or less with the works, of Orcagna, Buonarotti, Dante, Giotto, Da Vinci, Raffaelle, Galileo, Machiavelli,

and man\'7d' more, but these by their counterfeit presentments have entered into their lives and live. Men who are so impressed make but one bold step over the border into the fairyland of faith while the more cultured are discussing it.

I do not, with some writers, believe that a familiarity with a few names of men whose statues are always before them, and from whose works the town half lives, indicates an indescribably high culture or more refined nature in a man, but I think it is very natural for him to make legends on them. There are three other incantations given in another chapter, the object of which, like this to Dante, is to become a poet.

" From which we learn that in the fairy faith," writes Flaxius, with ever-ready pen, " that poets risen to spirits still inspire, even in person, neophytes to song.

" ' Life is a state of action, and the store Of all events is aggregated there That variegate the eternal universe ; Death is a gate of dreariness and gloom, That leads to azure isles and beaming skies . . . Therefore, O spirit, fearlessly bear on.' "

E

LEGENDS OF LA CERTOSA

" ' Now when ye moone like a golden flowrc,

In ye sky above doth bloome, lie lett doune a basket in that houre,

And pull ye upp to my roome, And give mee a kisse if 'tis yes,' he cryed ;

Ye mayden would nothing refuse ; But held upp hir lippes—

Oh I would I had beene Just thenn in that friar's shoos."

IF we pass the Porta Roman a, and keep on for three miles, we shall arrive at the old Carthusian convent of La Certosa in Val d'Ema. Soon after passing " the village of Galluzzo, where the stream is crossed, we come to an ancient gateway surmounted by a statue of Saint Laurence, through which no female could enter except by permission of the archbishop, and out which no monk could pass." At least, it is so stated in a justly famous English guide-book, though it does not explain how any " female " could enter the saint, nor whether the female in question belonged to the human species, or was fish, flesh, or red-herring. I should, however, incline to believe the latter is meant, as "herring" is a popular synonym for a loose fish.

The Certosa was designed and built in the old Italian Gothic style by Andrea Orcagna, it having been founded in the middle of the fourteenth century by Niccolo Accia-juoli, who was of a great Florentine family, from whom a portion of the Lung Arno is named. The building is on a picturesque hill, 400 feet above the union of the brooks called the Ema and the Greve, the whole forming

a charming view of a castled monastery of the Middle Ages.

There is always, among the few monks who have been allowed to remain, an English or Irish brother, to act as cicerone to British or American visitors, and show them the interesting tombs in the crypt or subterranean church, and the beautiful chapels and celebrated frescoes in the church. These were painted by Poccetti, and I am told that among them there is one which commemorates or was suggested by the following legend, which I leave the reader to verify, not having done so myself, though I have visited the convent, which institution is, however, popularly more distinguished—like many other monasteries—as a distillery of holy cordial than for aught else :

AL CONVENTO DELLA CERTOSA.

" There was in this convent a friar called Il Beato Dyonisio, who was so holy and such a marvellous doctor of medicine, that he was known as the Frate Miraculoso or Miraculous Brother.

" And when any of the fraternity fell ill, this good medico would go to them and say, ' Truly thou hast great need of a powerful remedy, O my brother, and may it heal and purify thy soul as well as thy body !' 1 And it always befell that when he had uttered this conjuration that the patient recovered ; and this was specially the case if after it they confessed their sins with great devoutness.

" Brother Dyonisio tasted no food save bread and water; he slept on the bare floor of his cell, in which there was no object to be seen save a scourge with great knots; he never took off his garments, and was always ready to attend any one taken ill.

"The other brothers of the convent were, however, all jolly monks, being of the kind who wear the tunic as a tonic to give them a better—or bitter—relish for secular delights, holding that it is far preferable to have a great deal of pleasure for a little penitence than per poco piacer gran penitenza — much

1 " D'una gran purga bisogna avete, E questa purga davero dovete Farla all' anima, cosi guariretc ! "

penitence for very little pleasure. In short, they were just at the other end of the rope away from Brother Dyonisio, inasmuch as they ate chickens, bisteahe or beef-steaks, and drank the best wine, even on fast-days— giorni di vigiglia —and slept in the best of beds; yes, living like lords, and never bothering themselves with any kind of penance, as all friars should do.

" Now there was among these monks one who was a great bestemmiatore, a man of evil words and wicked ways, who had led a criminal life in the world, and only taken refuge in the disguise of a monk in the convent to escape the hand of justice. Brother Dyonisio knew all this, but said nothing ; nay, he even exorcised away a devil whom he saw was always invisibly at the sinner's elbow, awaiting a chance to catch him by the hair; but the Beato Dyonisio was too much for him, and kept the devil ever far away.

" And this was the way he did it:

" It happened one evening that this finto frate, or mock monk or feigned friar, took it into his head, out of pure mischief, and because it was specially forbidden, to introduce a donna di mala vita, or a girl of no holy life, into the convent to grace a festival, and so arranged with divers other scapegraces that the damsel should be drawn up in a basket.

" And sure enough there came next morning to the outer gate a fresh and jolly black-eyed tontadina, who asked the mock monk whether he would give her anything in charity. And the finto frate answering sang :

" 'You shall have the best of meat, Anything you like to eat, Cutlets, macaroni, chickens, Every kind of dainty pickings. Pasticcie and fegatelli, Salame and mortadelle, With good wine, if you are clever, For a very trifling favour !'

" To which the girl replied:

" ' Here I am, as here you see !
What would'st thou, holy man, with me ?'

" The friar answered :

" ' When thou hear'st the hoots and howlc, At midnight of the dogs and owls, And when all men are sunk in sleep, And only witches watch do keep,

Come 'neath the window unto me, And there thou wilt a basket see Hung by a rope as from a shelf, And in that basket stow thyself, And I alone will draw thee up, Then with us thou shalt gaily sup.'

" But the girl replied, as if in fear:

" ' But if the rope should break away, Oh, then there'd be the devil to pay, Oh, holy father, first for thee— But most especially for me ! For if by evil luck I'd cracked your Connecting cord, my limbs I'd fracture !'

" The friar sang :

"' The rope is good, as it is long,

The basket's tough, my arms are strong, Have thou no fear upon that score, T'as hoisted many a maid before ; For often such a basket-full Did I into a convent pull, And many more I trust will I Draw safely up before I die.'

" And at midnight the girl was there walking beneath the windows awaiting the hour to rise— Ascensionem expectans — truly not to heaven, nor from any great liking for the monks, but for a great fondness for roast-chickens and good wine, having in her mind's eye such a supper as she had never before enjoyed, and something to carry home with her.

" So at last there was a rustling sound above, as a window softly opened, and a great basket came vibrating down below; and the damsel, well assured, got into it like a hen into her nest, while the lusty friar above began to draw like an artist.

" Now the Beato frate Dyonisio, knowing all that passed round about by virtue of his holy omniscience, determined to make manifest to the monks that things not adapted to piety led them into the path of eternal punishment.

" Therefore, just as the basket-full of girl touched the window of the convent, it happened by the virtue of the holy Dyonisio that the rope broke and the damsel came with a capi tombola somerset or first-class tumble into the street; but as she, poor soul, had only sinned for a supper, which she greatly needed and seldom got, she was quit for a good fright, since no other harm happened to her.

" But it was far otherwise with the wicked monk, who had only come into that holy monastery to stir up sin ; for he, leaning too far over at the instant, fell with an awful howl to the ground, where he roared so with pain that all the other monks came running to see what was the matter. And they found him indeed, more dead than alive, terribly bruised, yet in greater agony of mind than of body, saying that Satan had tempted him, and that he would fain confess to the Beato Dyonisio, who alone could save him.

"Then the good monk tended him, and so exhorted him that he left his evil ways and became a worthy servant of God, and the devil ceased to tempt him. And in due time Brother Dyonisio died, and as a saint they interred him in the crypt under the convent, and the morning after his burial a beautiful flower was found growing from his tomb, and so they sainted him.

" The fall of the girl was a scandal and cause of laughter for all Florence, so that from that day the monks never ventured more to draw up damsels in baskets."

This story is so widely spread in many forms, that the reader can hardly have failed to have heard it; in fact, there are few colleges where it has not happened that a basket has not been used for such smuggling. One of the most amusing instances is of a damsel in New Haven, or Cambridge, Massachusetts, who was very forgetful. One day she said to a friend, " You have no idea how wicked some girls are. The other morning early—I mean late at night— I was going by the college when I saw a girl being drawn up in a basket by some students, when all at once the rope broke— and down I came."

In Germany, as in the East, the tale is told of a wooer who is drawn up half-way in a basket and then let remain for everybody to behold. In Uhland's Old Ballads there is one to this effect of Heinrich Corrade der Schreiber im Korbe. Tales on this theme at least need not be regarded as strictly traditional.

There is another little legend attached to La Certosa which owes its small interest to being told of a man who

was one of the Joe Millers of Italy in the days of the Medici. It is a curious fact that humorists do most abound and are most popular in great epochs of culture.

Domenico Barlacchi was a banditore —herald or public crier—of Florence, commonly known as II Barlacchia, who lived in the time of Lorenzo de' Medici, and who, being molto piacevole e faceto, or pleasing and facetious, as I am assured by an ancient yellow jest-book of 1636 now before me, became, like Piovano Arlotto and Gonella, one of the famous wits of his time. It is worth noting, though it will be no news to any folk-lorist, that in these flying leaves, or fleeting collections of facetiae, there are many more indications of familiar old Florentine life than are to be gleaned from the formal histories which are most cited by writers who endeavour to illustrate it.

"One morning Barlacchia, with other boon companions, went to La Certosa, three miles distant from Florence,1 where, having heard mass, they were taken over the convent by one of the friars, who showed them the convent and cells. Of which Barlacchia said 'twas all very fine, but that he would like to see the wine-cellar— sentendosi egli hauer sete —as he felt great thirst sadly stealing over him.

" To which the friar replied that he would gladly show them that part of the convent, but that unfortunately the Decano who kept the keys was absent. \Decano, dean or deacon, may be rendered roughly in English as a dog, or literally of a dog or currish.] To which Barlacchia replied, 'Truly I am sorry for it, and I wish you were all de' cani or dogs !'

Times have changed, and whether this tale brought about the reform I cannot say, but it is certain that the good monks at present, without waiting to be asked, generally offer a glass of their famous cordial to visitors. Tastes may differ, but to mine, when it is old, the green Certosa, though far cheaper, is superior to Chartreuse.

1 It appears from this story that La Certosa was " even then as now " visited by strangers as one of the lions of Florence.

Another tale of Barlacchia, which has a certain theological affinity with this story, is as follows:

"A great illness once befell Barlacchia, so that it was rumoured all over Florence that he was dead, and great was the grieving thereover. But having recovered, by the grace of God, he went from his house to the palace of the Grand Duke, who said to him :

" ' Ha ! art thou alive, Barlacchia ? We all heard that thou wert dead.'

" ' Signore, it is true,' was his reply. ' I was indeed in the other world, but they sent me back again, and that for a mere trifle, which you forgot to give me.'

'"And what was that?' asked the Duke.

" ' I knocked,' resumed Barlacchia, ' at the gate of heaven, and they asked me who I was, what I had done in the world, and whether I had left any landed property. To which I replied no, never having begged for anything. So they sent me off, saying that they did not want any such poor devils about them— non volevano la simile dapochi. And therefore, illustrious Signore, I make so bold as to ask that you would kindly give me some small estate, so that another time I may not be turned away.'

"Which so pleased the magnificent and liberal Lorenzo that he bestowed on Barlacchia a podere or farm.

" Now for a long time after this illness, Barlacchia was very pale and haggard, so that everybody who met him (and he was well known to everybody) said, 'Barlacchia, mind the rules' —meaning the rules of health; or else, ' Barlacchia, look to yourself;' or regolati! m guardatevi !— till at last he became tired with answering them. So he got several small wooden rules or rulers, such as writers use to draw lines, and hung them by a cord to his neck, and with them a little mirror, and when any one said ' Regolati' —'mind the rules,' he made no reply, but looked at the sticks, and when they cried ' Guardatevi /' he regarded himself in the mirror, and so they were answered."

This agrees with the sketch of Lorenzo as given by Oscar Browning in his admirable "Age of the Condottieri," a short history of Mediaeval Italy from 1409 to 1530:

" Lorenzo was a bad man of business; he spent such large sums on himself that he deserved the appellation of the

Magnificent. He reduced himself to poverty by his extravagance ; he alienated his fellow-citizens by his lust . . . and was shameless in the promotion of his private favourites."

Yet with all this he was popular, and left a legendary fame in which generosity rivals a love of adventure. I have collected many traditions never as yet published relating to him, and in all he appears as a bon prince.

" But verily when I consider that what made a gallant lord four hundred years ago would be looked after now by the Lord Chancellor and the law courts with a sharp stick, I must needs," writes Flaxius, "exclaim with Spenser sweet:

" ' Me seernes the world is run quite out of square, For that which all men once did Vertue call, Is now called Vice, and that which Vice was hight Is now hight Vertue, and so used of all; Right now is wrong, and wrong that was, is right, As all things else in time are changed quight, 1 "

LEGENDS OF THE BRIDGES IN FLORENCE

" I stood upon a bridge and heard

The water rushing by, And as I thought, to every word The water made reply.

I looked into the deep river,

I looked so still and long, Until I saw the elfin shades

I'ass by in many a throng.

They came and went like starry dreams,

For ever moving on, As darkness takes the starry beams

Unnoted till they're gone."

THERE is something in a bridge, and especially in an old one, which has been time-worn and mossed into harmony with surrounding nature, which has always seemed peculiarly poetical or strange to men. Hence so many legends of devil's bridges, and it is rather amusing when we reflect how, as Pontifex, he is thus identified with the head of the Church. Thus I once, when attending law lectures in Heidelberg in 1847, heard Professor Mitter-maier say, that those who used the saying of " the divine right of kings" as an argument reminded him of the peasants who assumed that every old bridge was built by the devil. It is, however, simply the arch, which in any form is always graceful, and the stream passing through it like a living thing, which forms the artistic attraction or charm of such structures. I have mentioned in my " Memoirs" that Ralph

Waldo Emerson was once impressed by a remark, the first time I met him, to the effect that a vase in a room had the effect of a bridge in a landscape—at least, he recalled it at once when I met him twenty years later.

The most distinguished bridge, from a legendary point of view, in Europe, was that of Saint John Nepomuc in Prague—recently washed away owing to stupid neglect; the government of the city probably not supporting, like the king in the opera-bouffe of "Barbe Bleu," a commissioner of bridges. The most picturesque work of the kind which I recall is that of the Ponte Maddalena—also a devil's bridge—at the Bagni di Lucca. That Florence is not wanting in legends for its bridges appears from the following:

THE SPIRIT OF THE PONTE VECCHIO OR OLD BRIDGE.

" He who passes after midnight on the Ponte Vecchio can always see a form which acts as guard, sometimes looking like a beggar, sometimes like a guardia di sicurezza, or one of the regular watchmen, and indeed appearing in many varied forms, but generally as that of a watchman, and always leaning on the bridge.

"And if the passer-by asks him any such questions as these: 'Chi siei?'—'Cosa fai?'—'Dove abiti?'—'Ma vien' con me?' That is: ' Who are you ?'—' What dost thou do ?'—' Where is your home ?'—' Wilt with me come ?'—he seems unable to utter anything ; but if you ask him, ' Who am I ?' it seems to delight him, and he bursts into a peal of laughter which is marvellously loud and ringing, so that the people in the shops waking up cry, ' There is the goblin of the Ponte Vecchio at his jests again!' For he is a merry sprite, and then they go to sleep, feeling peaceably assured that he will watch over them as of yore.

"And this he really does for those who are faithful unto him. And those who believe in spirits should say sincerely :

" ' Spirito del Ponte Vecchio, Guardami la mia bottega ! Guardami dagli ladroni! Guardami anche dalla strega !'

" ' Spirit of the ancient bridge !

Guard my shop and all my riches, From the thieves who prowl by night, And especially from witches !'

" Then the goblin ever keeps guard for them. And should it ever come to pass that thieves break into a shop which he protects, he lets them work away till they are about to leave, when he begins to scream ' Al ladro ! al ladro /' and follows them till they are taken.

" But when the police have taken the thief, and he is brought up to be interrogated, and there is a call for the individual who was witness (quando le guardie vanno per in-terrogare Findividuo che si e trovato presente\ lo and behold he has always disappeared.

"And at times, when the weather is bad, he prowls about the bridge in the form of a cat or of a he-goat, and should any very profane, abusive rascal (l>estemmiatore) come along, the spirit as a goat will go before, running nimbly, when all at once the latter sinks into the earth, from which flames play forth, to the great terror of the sinner, while the goblin vanishes laughing."

I have very little doubt that this guardian spirit of the bridge is the same as Teramo, i.e., Hermes Mercury, who is believed in the Toscana Romana to betray thieves when they commit murder. But Mercury was also a classic guardian of bridges.

This merry goblin of the Ponte Vecchio has a colleague not far away in the Spirito del Ponte alia Carraia, the legend of which is as follows. And here I would note, once for all, that in almost every case these tales were written out for me in order to secure the greater accuracy, which did not however always ensure it, since even Miss Roma Lister, who is to the manor or manner born, often had with me great trouble in deciphering the script. For verily it seems to be a decree of destiny that everything traditional shall be involved, when not in Egyptian or Himaritic, or Carthaginian or Norse-Runic, at least in some diabolical dialect, so anxious is the Spirit of the past to hide from man the things long passed away.

AL PONTE ALLA CARRAIA.

" By the Arno, or under the Bridge alia Carraia, there lived once a certain Marocchio, 1 a bestetnmiatore, or blasphemer, for he cursed bitterly when he gained but little, being truly a marocchio, much attached to money. Even in dying he still swore. And Marocchio had sold himself to the devil, and hidden his money under a stone in the arch of the bridge. Yet though he had very poor relations and friends, he confided nothing to them, and left niente a nessuno, 'nothing to nobody.' Whence it came that after his death he had no rest or peace, because his treasure remained undiscovered.

" Yet where the money lay concealed there was seen every night the form of a goat which cast forth flames, and running along before those who passed by, suddenly sunk into the ground, disappearing in a great flash of fire.

"And when the renaioli or sand-diggers, 2 thinking it was a real goat, would catch it by the hair, it cast forth fire, so that many of them died of fright. And it often overthrew their boats and made all the mischief possible.

"Then certain people thinking that all this indicated a hidden treasure, sought to find it, but in vain; till at last one who was pifi fitrbo, or shrewder than the rest, observed that one day, when the wind was worse than usual, raising skirts and carrying away caps and hats, there was a goat in all the hurly-burly, and that this animal vanished at a certain spot. ' There I ween,' he said, ' lies money hid !' And knowing that midnight is the proper time or occasion (cagione di nascosto tesoro) for buried hoards, he came at the hour, and finding the habitual goat (// ' soliio chaprone), he addressed him thus :

"' If thou art a blessed soul, then go thy way in peace, and God be with thee. But if thou sufferest from buried treasure, then teach me how I, without any fear, may take thy store, then thou mayst go in peace ! And if thou art in torment for a treasure, show me the spot, and I will take it home, and then thou'lt be at peace and grieve no more.'

1 This word is apparently allied to Marra.no, an infidel Moor, miscreant, traitor, or to ainaro, bitter or painful.

2 A peculiarly Florentine word. Renajo, sand-pii;, a place so called near the Arno in Florence (Barretti's Dictionary). I can see several of these renaioli with their boats from the window at work before me as I write. Vide " The Spirit of the Arno."

"Then the goat jumped on the spot where the money was hidden and sank as usual out of sight in fire.

"So the next day the young man went there and dug till he discovered the gold, and the spirit of Marocchio was relieved. But to this hour the goat is seen now and then walking in his old haunt, where he sinks into the ground at the same place."

The legend of a goat haunting a bridge is probably derived from the custom of sacrificing an animal to new buildings or erections. These were originally human sacrifices, for which, in later times, the animals were substituted. Hence the legends of the devil having been defrauded out of a promised soul by driving a goat or cat over the bridge as a first crosser. The spirits of the Ponte Vecchio and Ponte alia Carraia clearly indicate this origin.

The next legend on this subject is that of the Ponte alle Grazie, which was built by Capo, the fellow-pupil of Arnolfo, under the direction of Rubaconte, who filled the office of Podesta in 1235. Five hundred years are quite time enough to attract traditions in a country where they spring up in five ; and when I inquired whether there was any special story attached to the Ponte alle Grazie, I was soon supplied with the following:

LE PONTE ALLE GRAZIE.

"When one passes under a bridge, or in halls of great palaces, or the vault of a church, or among high rocks, if he calls aloud, he will hear what is called the echo of his voice.

" Yet it is really not his own voice which he hears, but the mocking voices of spirits, the reason being that they are confined to these places, and therefore we do not hear them in the open air, where they are free. But we can hear them clearly in great places enclosed, as, for instance, under vaults, and far oftener in the country, because in limited spaces their voices are confined and not lost. And these are the voices of people who were merry and jovial while on earth, and who now take delight a rifare il verso, to re-echo a strain.

" But under the Ponte alle Grazie we hear the cry of the spirit of a girl. She was very beautiful, and had grown up from infancy in constant companionship with a youth of the neighbourhood, and so from liking as children they went on to loving at a more advanced age, with greater fondness and with deeper passion.

" And it went so far that at last the girl found herself with child, and then she was in great trouble, not knowing how to hide this from her parents. Sfa beccata da una serfe, as the proverb is; 'she had been stung by a serpent,' and now began to feel the poison. But the youth was faithful and true, and promised to marry her as soon as he could possibly arrange matters. So she was quieted for a time.

" But she had a vilely false friend, and a most intimate one, in a girl who, being a witch, or of that kind, hated her bitterly at heart, albeit she knew well fortare bene la maschera, how to wear the mask.

"Now the poor girl told this false friend that she was enceinte, and that her lover would marry her; and the dear friend took her, as the saying is, a trip to Volterra, during which a man was treated like a prince and robbed or murdered at the end. For she insinuated that the marriage might fail, and meantime she, the friend, would consult witches and fate, who would get her out of her troubles and make all right as sure as the Angelus. And the false friend went to the witches, but she took them a lock of hair from the head of the lover to conjure away his love and work harm. And knowing what the bridal dress would be, she made herself one like it in every detail. And she so directed that the bride on the wedding morning shut herself up in a room and see no one till she should be sent for.

"The bride-to-be passed the morning in great anxiety, and while waiting there received a large bouquet of orange-flowers as a gift from her friend. And these she had perfumed with a witch-powder. And the bride having inhaled the scent, fell into a deep sleep, or rather trance, during which she was delivered of a babe, and knew nothing of it. Now the people in the house hearing the child cry, ran into the room, and some one ran to the bridegroom, who was just going to be married to the false friend, who had by aid of the witches put on a face and a false seeming, the very counterpart of her he loved.

" Then the unfortunate girl hearing that her betrothed was being married, and maddened by shame and grief, rushed in her bride's dress through the streets, and coming to the Bridge delle Grazie, the river being high, threw herself into it and was drowned; still holding the bouquet of orange-blossoms in her hand, she was carried on the torrent into death.

" Then the young man. who had discovered the cheat, and whose heart was broken, said, ' As we were one in life, so we will be in death,' and threw himself into the Arno from the same place whence she had plunged, and like her was drowned. And the echo from the bridge is the sound of their voices, or of hers. Perhaps she answers to the girls and he to the men ; anyhow they are always there, like the hymns in a church."

There is a special interest in the first two paragraphs of this story, as indicating how a person who believes in spirits, and is quite ignorant of natural philosophy, explains phenomena. It is precisely in this manner that most early science was confused with superstition; and there is more of it still existing than even the learned are aware of.

I know not whether echoes are more remarkable in and about Florence than elsewhere, but they are certainly specially noticed in the local folk-lore, and there are among the witches invocations to echoes, voices of the wind, and similar sounds. One of the most remarkable echoes which I ever heard is in the well of the Villa Guicciardini, now belonging to Sir John Edgar. It is very accurate in repeating every sound in a manner so suggestive of a mocking goblin, that one can easily believe that a peasant would never doubt that it was caused by another being. It renders laughter again with a singularly strange and original effect. Even when standing by or talking near this mystic fount, the echo from time to time cast back scraps of phrases and murmurs, as if joining in the conversation. It is worth observing (vide the story of the Three Horns) that this villa once belonged to—and is, as a matter of course, haunted by the ghost of—Messer Guicciardini, the great writer, who was himself a faithful echo of the history of his country, and of the wisdom of the ancients. Thus into things do things repeat themselves, and souls still live in what surrounded them. I have not seen this mystic well noticed in any of the Florentine guide-books of any kind, but its goblin is as well worthy an interview as many better known characters. Yea, it may be that he is the soul of Guicciardini himself, but when I was there I forgot to ask him if it were so ?

I can, however, inform the reader as to the incantation which is needed to call to the spirit of the well to settle this question. Take a copy of his "Maxims" and read them through; then drink off one glass of wine to the health of the author, and, bending over the well, distinctly cry— " Sei Messer Guicciardini, di cosi ? "— strongly accentuating the last syllable. And if the reply be in the affirmative, you may draw your own conclusions. For those who are not Italianate, it will do quite as well if they cry, "Guicciardini? No or yes?" For even this echo is not equal to the Irish one, which to " Hoiv do you do ? " replied, " Pretty well, I thank you ! "

There is a very good story of the Ponte alle Grazie, anciently known as the Rubaconte, from the Podesta in whose year of office it was built, told originally by Sachetti in his Novelle and Manni, Veglie Piaceuoli, who drew it indeed from Venetian or Neapolitan-Oriental sources, and which is best told by Leader Scott in "The Echoes of Old Florence." It still lives among the people, and is briefly as follows, in another form:

THE ORIGIN OF THE PONTE ALLE GRAZIE.

" There was once in Florence a Podestk or chief magistrate named Rubaconte, and he had been chosen in the year 1236, nor had he been long in office when a man called Bagnai, because he kept a public bath, was brought before him on the charge of murder.

F

" And Bagnai, telling his tale, said: ' This is the very truth— ne favola ne canzone di tavola —for I was crossing the river on the little bridge with a hand-rail by the Palazzo Mozzi, when there came riding over it a company of gentlemen. And it befell that I was knocked over the bridge, and fell on a man below who was washing his feet in the Arno, find lo ! the man was killed by my dropping on him.'

" Now to the Podesta this was neither eggs nor milk, as the saying is, and he could at first no more conclude on it than if one had asked him, ' Chi nacque prima — Puovo o la gallina ?' 1 Which was born first—the hen or the egg ?' For on one side the bagnajolo was innocent, and on the other the dead man's relations cried for vengeance. But after going from one side of his brain to the other for five minutes, he saw ' from here to the mountain,' and said:

" 'Now I have listened to ye both, and this is a case where one must—

" ' Non giudicar per legge ni per carte, Se non ascolti 1'un e Faltra parte.'

" 'Judge not by law-books nor by chart, But look with care 10 either part."

" ' And as it is said, " Berta must drink from her own bottle," so I decree that the bagnaio shall go and wash his feet in the Arno, sitting in the same place, and that he who is the first of his accusers shall fall from the bridge on his neck, and so kill him.'

" And truly this settled the question, and it was agreed that the Podesta was//w savio de gli statnti —wiser even than the law itself.

"But then Rubaconte did an even wiser thing, for he determined to have a new bridge built in place of the old one, and hence came the Ponte alle Grazie, ' of which he himself laid the first foundation-stone, and carried the first basket of mortar, with all due civic ceremony, in 1236.' 1

" But as it is said, ' he who has drunk once will drink again,' it came to pass that Bagnai had to appear once more as accused before the Podesta. One day he met a man whose donkey had fallen and could not rise. 'Twas on the Ponte Vecchio.

"The owner seized the donkey by the head, Bagnai caught him by the tail, and pulled so hard that the tail came off!

1 " Echoes of Old Florence," by Temple Leader.

" Then the contadino or asinaio had Bagnai brought before the Podesta, and claimed damages for his injured animal. And Rubaconte decided that Bagnai should keep the ass in his stable, and feed him well — until the tail had grown

again.

"As may be supposed, the asinaio preferred to keep his ass himself, and go no farther in the case."

This ancient tale recalls that of Zito, the German magician conjuror, whose leg was pulled off. It is pretty evident that the donkey's tail had been glued on for the occasion.

I may here add something relative to the folk-lore of bridges, which is not without interest. I once asked a witch in Florence if such a being as a spirit of the water or one of bridges and streams existed ; and she replied :

" Yes, there is a spirit of the water as there is of fire, and everything else. They are rarely seen, but you can make them appear. How ? Oh, easily enough, but you must remember that they are capricious, and appear in many delusive forms. 1

" And this is the way to see them. You must go at twilight and look over a bridge, or it will do if it be in the daytime in the woods at a smooth stream or a dark pool— *che sia un poco oscuro* —and pronounce the incantation, and throw a handful or a few drops of its water into the water itself. And then you must look long and patiently, always thinking of it for several days, when, *poco a poco*, you will see dim shapes passing by in the water, at first one or two, then more and more, and if you remain quiet they will come in great numbers, and show you what you want to know. But if you tell any one what you have seen, they will never appear again, and it will be well for you should nothing worse happen.

"There was a young man at Civitella in the Romagna Toscana, and he was in great need of money. He had lost an uncle who was believed to have left a treasure buried somewhere, but no one knew where it was. Now this nephew was a reserved, solitary youth, always by himself in lone places,

1 Like Proteus, the evasive slippery nature of water and the light which plays on it accounts for this.

among ruins or in the woods— *un poco streghon* —a bit of a wizard, and he learned this secret of looking into streams or lakes, till at last, whenever he pleased, he could see swarms of all kinds of figures sweeping along in the water.

" And one evening he thus saw, as in a glass, the form of his uncle who had died, and in surprise he called out ' Zio mio !'—' My uncle !' Then the uncle stopped, and the youth said, ' Didst thou but know how I am suffering from poverty !' When he at once beheld in the water his home and the wood near it, and a path, and the form of his uncle passed along the path to a lonely place where there was a great stone. Then the uncle pointed to the stone and vanished. The next day the young man went there, and under the stone he found a great bag of gold—and I hope that the same may happen to all of us !

" ' He who has sheep has wool in store; He who has mills hath plenty of flour ; He who hath land hath these at call ; He who has money has got them all."

THE BASHFUL LOVER

A LEGEND OF THE CHIESA SANTA LUCIA IN THE

VIA DE' BARDI

" She never told her love—oh no ! For she was mild and meek, And his for her he dared not show, Because he hadn't the cheek. 'Tis pity this should e'er be past, For, to judge by what all men say, 'Twere best such difference should last Unto our dying day."

ALL who have visited Florence have noticed the Church of Santa Lucia in the Via de' Bardi, from the figure of the patron with two angels over the door in Lucca della Robbia ware. Of this place of worship there is in a jest-book a droll story, which the reader may recall when he enters the building.

" A young Florentine once fell desperately in love with a beautiful lady of unsullied character and ready wit, and so followed her about wherever she went ; but he being sadly lacking in wit and sense, at all four corners, never got the nearer to her acquaintance, though he told all his friends how irresistible he would be, and what a conquest he would make, if he could only once get a chance to speak to her. Yet as this lady prized ready wit and graceful address in a man above all things, it will be seen that his chance was thin as a strip of paper.

" But one fesfa the lady went to the Church of Santa Lucia in the Via dei Bardi, and one of the friends of the slow-witted one said to him, ' Now is the lucky hour and blooming chance for you. Go up and speak to her when she approaches the font to take holy water.'

"Now the lover had prepared a fine speech for the lady, which he had indeed already rehearsed many times to his friends with great applause; but when it came to utter it to the lady a great and awful fear fell on him, the words vanished —vanished from his memory, and he was dumb as a dead ass. Then his friend poking him in the ribs, whispered in his ear, ' But say something, man, no matter what!'

"So with a gasp he brought out at last, ' Signora, I would fain be your humble servant.'

"To which the lady, smiling, replied, ' Well, I have already in my house plenty of humble servants, and indeed only too many to sweep the rooms and wash the dishes, and there is really no place for another. . . .'

"And the young man turned aside with sickness in his heart. His wooing for that holiday was o'er."

This may be matched with the story of a bashful New England lover of the olden time, for there are none such now-a-days:—

"I don't know how I ever got courage to do it; but one evening I went courting Miss Almira Chapin.

"And when she came in, I sat for half-an-hour, and dared not say a word. At last I made a desperate dash and got out, ' Things are looking very green out of doors, Miss Almira.'

"And she answered, ' Seems to me they're looking a great deal greener in doors this evening.'

"That extinguished me, and I retreated. And when I was outside I burst into tears."

LA FORTUNA

A LEGEND OF THE VIA DE' CERCHI

"One day Good Luck came to my home,

I begged of her to stay. ' There's no one loves you more than I,

Oh, rest with me for aye,' ' It may not be ; it may not be, I rest with no one long,' said she."

—" Witch Ballads? by C. G. LELAND.

THE manner in which many of the gods in exile still live in Italy is very fully illustrated by the following story:

"It is a hard thing sometimes now-a-days for a family to pass for noble if they are poor, or only poor relations. But it was easy in the old time, Signore Carlo, easy as drinking good Chianti. A signore had only to put his shield with something carved on it over his window, and he was all right. He was noble senza dubbio.

"Now the nobles had their own noble stories as to what these noble pictures in stone meant, but the ignoble people often had another story just as good. Coarse woollen cloth wears as well as silk. Now you may see on an old palazzo in the Via de' Cerchi, and indeed in several other places, a shield with three rings. But people call them three wheels. And this is the story about the three wheels."

LA FORTUNA.

"There was a man, tanto buono, as good as could be, who lived in squalid misery. He had a wife and two children, one blind and another storpia or crippled, and so ugly, both— non si dice — beyond telling !

"This poor man in despair often wept, and then he would repeat:

"' The wheel of Fortune turns, they say, But for me it turns the other way ; I work with good-will, but do what I may, I have only bad luck from day to day.'

"' Yes, little to eat and less to wear, and two poor girls, one blind and one lame. People say that Fortune is blind herself, and cannot walk, but she does not bless those who are like her, that is sure!' And so he wailed and wept, till it was time to go forth to seek work to gain their daily bread. And a hard time he had of it.

"Now it happened that very late one night, or very early one morning, as one may say, between dark and dawn, he went to the forest to cut wood. When having called to Fortune as was his wont— Ai! what was his surprise to see— tutta ad un tratto — a\\ at once, before his eyes, a gleam of light, and raising his head, he beheld a lady of enchanting beauty passing along rapidly, and yet not walking—on a rolling ball— e don-dolava le gambe —moving her limbs—I cannot say feet, for she had none. In place of them were two wheels, and these wheels, as they turned, threw off flowers from which there came delicious perfume.

"The poor man uttered a sigh of relief seeing this, and said :

"' Beautiful lady, believe me when I say that I have invoked thee every day. Thou art the Lady of the Wheels of Fortune, and had I known how beautiful thou art, I would have worshipped thee for thy beauty alone. Even thy very name is beautiful to utter, though I have never been able to couple it with mine, for one may see that I am not one of the fortunate. Yet, though thou art mine enemy, give me, I pray, just a little of the luck which flies from thy wheel!

"' Yet do not believe, I pray, that I am envious of those who are thy favourites, nor that because thou art my enemy that I am thine, for if thou dost not deem that I am worthy, assuredly I do not deserve thy grace, nor will I, like many, say that Fortune is not beautiful, for having seen thee, I can now praise thee more than ever.'

"' I do not cast my favours always on those who deserve them,'replied Fortune, 'yet this time my wheel shall assist thee. But tell me, thou man of honesty and without envy, which wouldst thou prefer—to be fortunate in all things thyself alone, or to give instead as much good luck to two men as miserable as thou art? If thou wilt gain the prize for

thyself alone, turn and pluck one of these flowers ! If for others, then take two.'

"The poor man replied : ' It is far better, lady, to raise two families to prosperity than one. As for me, I can work, and I thank God and thee that I can do so much good to so many, although I do not profit by it myself;' and saying this, he advanced and plucked two flowers.

"Fortune smiled. ' Thou must have heard,' she said, ' that where I spend, I am lavish and extravagant, and assuredly thou knowest the saying that " Three is the lucky number," or nine. Now I make it a rule that when I relieve families, I always do it by threes— la spando a tre famiglie —so do thou go and pluck a flower for thyself!'

"Then the poor man, hearing this, went to the wheels, and let them turn till a very large fine flower came forth, and seized it, whereat Fortune smiled, and said:

"' I always favour the bold. Now go and sit on yonder bench till some one comes.' And saying this, she vanished.

"There came two very poor woodcutters whom he knew well. One had two sons, another a son and a daughter, and one and all were as poor and miserable as could be.

"' What has come over thee, that thou art looking so handsome and young,' said one amazed, as he came up.

"' And what fine clothes !' remarked the second.

"' It shall be so anon for ye both,' replied the favourite of Fortune; ' only take these flowers and guard them well.'

"Si, Signore, they sat down on the bench three beggars, and they rose three fine cavaliers, in velvet and satin, with gold-mounted swords, and found their horses and attendants waiting. And when they got home, they did not know their wives or children, nor were they known unto them, and it was an hour before all was got right. Then all went with them as if it were oiled. The first man found a great treasure the very first day in his cellar—in fine, they all grew rich, and the three sons married the three girls, and they all put the three wheels on their scudi. One of the wheels is the ball on which Fortune rolled along, and the other two are her feet; or else the three men each took a wheel to himself. Anyhow, there they are, pick and choose, Signore— chi ha piii cervello, Fusi! • —let him who has brains, brain !

"Now, it is a saying that ogni fior non fa friitto —every blossom doth not bear a fruit— but the flowers of Fortune bear fruit enough to make up for the short crop elsewhere.

'•' But there is some sense and use in such stories as these, Signore, after all; for a poor devil who half believes—and very often quite believes in them—gets a great deal of hope and comfort out of them. They make him trust that luck or fairies or something will give him a good turn yet some day— chi sa ? —and so he hopes, and truly, as they say that no pretty girl is ever quite poor, so no man who hopes is ever really broken— grazie, Signore! I hope to tell you another story before long."

There is something in the making Fortune with two wheels for feet which suggests a memory of skate-rollers.

I once published an article in the Ethnologische Monats-heft of Budapest, which set forth more fully the idea expressed in this tale, that the popular or fairy tale is a source of comfort, or a Bible to the poor, for it always teaches the frequently delusive, but always cheering lesson that good-luck or fortune may turn up some day, even for the most unfortunate. The Scripture promises happiness for the poorest, or indeed specially for the poorest in the next life; the fairy tale teaches that Cinderella, the despised, and the youngest, humblest of the three, will win fortune while here on earth. It inspires hope, which is a great secret of happiness and success.

To which the learned Flaxius annotates :

" It hath escaped the author—as it hath indeed all mankind—that as the first syllable of Fortuna \sfort (La.\\\i fortis), so the true beginning of luck is strength; and if we are to understand by una, 'one' or 'only,' we may even believe that the name means strength alone or vigorous will, in accordance with which the ancients declared that ' Fortune favours the bold,' and also Fortuna conientionis studiosa est — ' Fortune delights in strife.' Therefore she is ever fleeting in this world. Fortuna sitnul cum moribus iinmutatur, as Boethius hath it."

THE STORY OF THE UNFINISHED PALACE
A LEGEND OF THE VIA DEL PROCONSOLO

" ' Yes, you have cheated me,' howled the devil to the architect. ' But I lay a curse upon your work. It shall never be finished.'"— Snow and Planches " Legends of the Rhine."

ALL great and ancient buildings which were never finished have a legend referring to their incompleteness. There was one relative to the Cathedral of Cologne, which may be found in Planche's " Legends of the Rhine," and as there is a palazzo non finito in Florence, I at once scented an old story; nor was I disappointed, it being unearthed in due time, and written out for me as follows:

IL PALAZZO NON FINITO.

" On the corner of the Via del Proconsole and the Borgo degli Albizzi there is an unfinished palace.

" The great Signore Alessandro Strozzi had a friend who, when dying, confided to him the care of his only son. And it was a troublesome task, for the youth was of a strange temper. And a vast property was left to the young man, his father imploring him not to waste it, and to live in friendship with his guardian.

"But his father had hardly closed his eyes in death before this youth began to act wildly, and above all things to gamble terribly. And as the saying is, *Il diavolo ha parte in ogni giuoco*—'The devil has a hand in every game,' so he soon brought himself into company with the gamester. Now, as you have heard, 'tis *la lingua o la bocca e quella che fa il giuoco*.

"'Every game, as it is sung,
Is won by mouth, or else by tongue.'

"So this devil or imp by smooth talk succeeded in deceiving the young heir, and leading him into a compact by which he was to achieve for the Signore all the work which might be required of him for a hundred years, no matter what it was, and then the heir must forfeit his soul.

"For some time the young man was satisfied with always winning at gambling. Yes, he ruined scores, hundreds, and piled up gold till he got sick of the sight of cards. You know the saying, 'When the belly is full the eyes are tired,' and 'A crammed dove hates to fly.'

"So for a while he kept the devil busy, bringing him a girl here, and building him a tower there, sending him to India for diamonds, or setting him at work to keep off storm and hail from his vineyards, which the devil found hard work enough, I promise you, Signore, for then he had to fight other devils and witches. Then he put him at a harder job. There was a ghost of a stregone or wizard who haunted his palazzo. Now such ghosts are the hardest to lay.

"'*È niente, Signore,*' said the devil. '*E vi passarebbe un carro di fieno.* 'Tis nothing, my lord; one could drive a cartload of hay through it.' But the devil had a devil of a time to lay that ghost! There was clanking of chains and howling, and *il diavolo scatenato* all night long ere it was done.

"'*E finito, Signore]* said the devil in the morning. But he looked so worn-out and tired, that the young man began to think.

"And he thought, 'This devil of mine is not quite so clever as I supposed.' And it is a fact that it was only a diavolino — a small devil who had thought the young man was a fool-in which he was mistaken. A man may have *un ramo di pazzo come Tolmo di Fiesole* —'be a bit of a fool,' but 'a fool and a sage together can beat a clever man,' as the saying is, and both were in this boy's brain, for he came of wizard blood. So he reflected, 'Perhaps I can cheat this devil after all.' And he did it.

"Moreover, this devil being foolish, had begun to be too officious and consequential. He was continually annoying the Signore by asking for more work, even when he did not want it, as if to make a show of his immense ability and insatiable activity. Finally, beginning to believe in his own power, he

1 "Well, yes, I think you might;
A cart of hay went through this afternoon."
I believe this is by Peter Pindar. The Italian proverb probably suggested it.

began to appear far too frequently, uncalled, rising up from behind chairs abruptly in his own diabolical form, in order to inspire fear; but the young lad had not been born in Carnival to be afraid of a mask, as the saying is, and all this only made him resolve to send his attendant packing.

"'*Chi ha pazienza, cugino,
Ha i tordi grassi a un quattvino.*

"'He who hath patience, mind me, cousin, May buy fat larks a farthing a dozen.'

"Now, amid all these dealings, the young signore had contrived to fall in love with the daughter of his guardian, Alessandro Strozzi, and also to win her affections; but he observed one day when he went to see her, having the diavo-lino invisible by his side, the attendant spirit suddenly jibbed or balked, like a horse which stops before the door, and refused to go farther. For there was a Madonna painted on the outside, and the devil said:

" ' I see a virgin form divine,
And virgins are not in my line ;
I'm not especially devout :
Go thou within—I'll wait without !'

"And the young man observing that his devil was devilishly afraid of holy water, made a note of it for future use. And having asked the Signore Alessandro Strozzi for the hand of his daughter, the great lord consented, but made it a condition that the youth should build for his bride a palace on the corner of the Via del Proconsolo and the Borgo degli Albizzi, and it must be ready within a year. This he said because in his heart he did not like the match, yet for his daughter's love he put this form upon it, and he hoped that ere the time would be out something might happen to prevent the marriage. In fin che v'e fiato v't speranza— while there is breath, Signore, there is hope.

"Now the young man having resolved to finish with his devil for good and all, began to give him great hope in divers ways. And one day he said to the imp :

" ' Truly thou hast great power, but I have a mind to make a great final game with thee. Ogni bel giuoco vnol durar poco —no good game should last long, and let us play this compact of ours out. If thou canst build for me a palace at the corner of the Via del Proconsolo and the Borgo degli Albizzi, and

finish it in every detail exactly as I shall order it, then will I be thine, and thou need'st do no more work for me. And if thou canst not complete it to my taste, then our compact will be all smoke, and we two past acquaintances.'

" Now it is said that to cook an egg to a turn, make a dog's bed to suit him exactly, or teach a Florentine a trick, sono trtcose difficile— are three very difficult things to do, and this contract for building the palace on time with indefinite ornaments made the devil shake in his shoes. However, he knew that ' Pippo found out how to stand an egg on its end,' 1 and where there's a will there's a way, especially when you have ' all hell to back you up'— httto f inferno a spalleggiarvi.

" So he built and built away, with one gang of devils disguised as workmen by day, and another, invisible, by night, and everybody was amazed to see^how the palace rose like weeds after a rain ; for, as the saying is, mala herba presto cresce —' ill weeds grow apace,' and this had the devil to water it.

" Till at last one day, when the six months were nearly up, the imp said to the master:

"' Ebbenc, Signore, it is getting to the time for you to tell me how you would like to have the palace decorated. Thus far everything has been done exactly as you directed.'

" ' Ah yes, I see—all done but the finishing. Well, it may be a little hard, but I promise you, on the word of a gentleman (tra galanf uomini unaparola e un instrumento\ that I will not ask you to do anything which cannot be executed even by the artists of this city.'

"Now the devil was delighted to hear this (for he was afraid he might be called on to work miracles unheard of), and so replied :

" ' Top ! what man has done the devil can do. I'll risk the trick if you swear that men can work it.'

" «I swear!'

" ' And what is the finish ?'

"' Oh, very easy. My wife who is to be is of a very pious turn, and I want to please her. Firstly, all the work must be equal in execution to the best by the greatest masters—painting, sculpture, and gilding.'

1 Rizzar tuovo di Pippo sh un piano. "To do a difficult thing, or achieve it by tact and skill." This hints at the egg of Columbus. But Columbus set the egg upright by breaking its end, which was not a fair game. Any egg can be set on end on a marble table (I have done it), by patient balancing, without breaking.

"'Agreed.'

" ' Secondly, the subjects. Over the front door— bisogna mettermi Gesu Cristo onnipotente unitamente a Maria e il suo divin figlio, Padre, Figlio e Spirito Santo — that is, the Holy Family and Trinity, the Virgin and Child.'

"'Wha—wha—what's that?' stammered the devil, aghast. ' It isn't fair play—not according to the game.'

' On every door,' continued the young man, raising his voice, and looking severely at the devil, ' the same subject is to be repeated on a thick gold ground, all the ultramarine to be of the very best quality, washed in holy water.'

" ' Ugh ! ugh ! ugh !' wailed the devil.

' The roof is to be covered with the images of saints as pinnacles, and, by the way, wherever you have a blank space, outside on the walls or inside, including ceilings—just cover it with the same subjects—the Temptation of Saint Antony or

Saint '

' Oh, go to the devil with your saints and gold grounds !' roared the imp. ' Truly I have lost this game; fishing with a golden hook is a fool's business. There is the compact!'

"It was night—deep, dark night—there came a blinding flash of light—an awful crash of indescribable unearthly sound, like a thunder-voice. The imp, taking the form of a dvetta or small owl, vanished through the window in the storm-wind and rain, wailing, 'Mai finite /'

"And it is said that to this day the small owl still perches by night on the roof of the palace, wailing wearily—' Unfinished ! unfinished !'"

In no country in the world has unscrupulous vigorous intellect been so admired as in Italy, the land of the Borgias and Machiavellis. In the rest of Europe man finds a master in the devil; in Italy he aims at becoming the devil's master. This is developed boldly in the legend of " Intialo," to which I have devoted another chapter, and it appears as markedly in this. The idea of having an attendant demon, whom the master, in the consciousness of superior intellect, despises, knowing that he will crush him when he will, is not to be found, I believe, in a single German, French, or any other legend not Italian.

If this be so, it is a conception well deserving study, as illustrating the subtle and powerful Italian intellect as it was first analysed by Macaulay, and is now popularly understood by such writers as Scaife. 1 It is indeed a most unholy and unchristian conception, since it is quite at war with the orthodox theology of the Church, as of Calvin and Luther, which makes the devil the grand master of mankind, and irresistible except where man is saved by a special miracle or grace.

And it may also be noted from such traditions that folk-lore, when it shall have risen to a sense of its true dignity and power, will not limit itself to collecting variants of fairy tales to prove the routes of races over the earth, but rise to illustrating the characteristic, and even the aesthetic, developments of different stocks. That we are now laying the basis for this is evident.

Though the devil dared not depict lives and legends of the saints upon the palace, he did not neglect to put his own ugly likeness there, repeated above the four front windows in a perfectly appalling Gothic style, which contrasts oddly with the later and severe character of the stately building. These faces are fiendish enough to have suggested the story.

It may here be mentioned that it was in the middle of the Borgo degli Albizzi, near this palace, that that indefatigable corpse-reviver and worker of miracles, San Zenobio, raised from the dead the child of a noble and rich French lady. "Then in that place there was put a pillar of white marble in the middle of the street, as a token of a great miracle."

" H (EC falula docet —this fable teaches," adds Flaxius the immortal, " that there was never yet anything left incomplete by neglect or incapacity or poverty, be it in buildings or in that higher structure, man himself, but what it was attributed

1 "Florentine Life during the Renaissance," by Walter B. Scaife. Baltimore, 1893.

to the devil. If it had not been for the devil, what fine fellows, what charming creatures, we would all have been to be sure ! The devil alone inspires us to sin; we would never have dreamed of it. Whence I conclude that the devil is dearer to man, and a greater benefactor, than all the saints and several deities thrown in, because he serves as a scudaway scapegoat, and excellent excuse for the sins of all the orthodox of all time. How horrible it would be were we all made unto ourselves distinctly responsible for our sins—our unfinished palaces, our good resolutions broken; and how very pleasant it is that it is all the devil's fault, and not our own ! Oh my friends, did I believe as ye do—which I don't— I would long ago have raised altars and churches to the devil, wherein I would praise him daily as the one who in spirit and in truth takes upon himself the sins of all the world, bearing the burden of our iniquities. For saying which thing, but in other words, the best Christian of his age, Bishop Agobard, was hunted down well-nigh to death. Thus endeth a great lesson !"

THE DEVIL OF THE MERCATO VECCHIO

" Have I not the magic wand, by means of which, having first invoked the spirit (Xleken, one can enter the elfin castle ? Is not this a fine trot on the devil's crupper? Here it is—one of the palaces erected by rivals of the Romans. Let us enter, for I hold a hand of glory to which all doors open. Let us enter, hie et nunc, the palace fair. . . . Here it was once on a Sabato of the Carnival that there entered four graceful youths of noble air."— Arltcchino alle Nozze di Cana.

I VERY naturally made inquiry as to whether there was not a legend of the celebrated bronze devil made by Giovanni di Bologna, which remained until lately in the Mercato Vecchio, and I obtained the following, which is, from intrinsic evidence, extremely curious and ancient.

IL DIAVOLO ALLA CAVOLAIA.

" On the corner of the Palace Cavolaia there were anciently four devils of iron. 1 These were once four gentlemen who, being wonderfully intimate, had made a strange compact, swearing fidelity and love among themselves to death, agreeing also that if they married, their wives and children and property should be all in common.

"When such vows and oaths are uttered, the saints may pass them by, but the devils hear them ; they hear them in hell, and they laugh and cry, ' These are men who will some day be like us, and here for ever !' Such sin as that is like a root which, once planted, may be let alone—the longer it is in the ground, the more it grows. Terra non avvilisce oro — earth does not spoil gold, but even virtue, like friendship, may grow into a great vice when it grows too much.

"As it happened in this case. Well, the four friends were invited to a great festa in that fatal palace of the Cavolaia, and they all went. And they danced and diverted themselves

1 The diavolino of Gian di Bologna is of bronze, but popular tradition makes light of accuracy.

with great and beautiful ladies in splendour and luxury. As the four were all singularly handsome and greatly admired, the ladies came con grandi tueletti —in their best array, sfarzose per essere corteggiate —making themselves magnificent to be courted by these gentlemen, and so they looked at one another with jealous eyes, and indeed many a girl there would have gladly been wife to them all, or wished that the four were one, while the married dames wished that they could fare i sposamenti —be loved by one or all. People were wicked in those days !

" But what was their surprise—and a fearful surprise it was—• when, after all their gaiety, they heard at three o'clock in the morning the sound of a bell which they had never heard before, and then divine music and singing, and there entered a lady of such superhuman beauty as held them enchanted and speechless. Now it was known that, by the strict rules of that palace, the festa must soon close, and there was only time for one more dance, and it was sworn among these friends that every lady who danced with one of them, must dance with all in succession. Truly they now repented of their oath, for she was so beautiful.

" But the lady advancing, pointed out one of the four, and said, ' I will dance with him alone.'

" The young signore would have refused, but he felt himself obliged, despite himself, to obey her, and when they had danced, she suddenly disappeared, leaving all amazed.

" And when they had recovered from the spell which had been upon them, they said that as she had come in with the dawn and vanished with the day, it must have been the Beautiful Alba, the enchanting queen of the fairies.

" The festa lasted for three days, and every night at the same hour the beautiful Alba reappeared, enchanting all so wonderfully, that even the ladies forgot their jealousy, and were as much fascinated by her as were the men.

"Now of the four friends, three sternly reproached the other for breaking his oath, they being themselves madly in love; but he replied, and truly, that he had been compelled by some power which he could not resist to obey her. But that, as a man of honour, so far as he could, he would comply with the common oath which bound them.

"Then they declared that he should ask her if she loved him, and if she assented, that he should inform her of their oath, and that she must share her love with all or none— altrimenti non avrebbe maipotuta sposarla.

11 Which he did in good faith, and she answered, ' Hadst thou loved me sincerely and fully, thou wouldst have broken that vile oath; and yet it is creditable to thee that, as a man of honour, thou wilt not break thy word. Therefore thou shalt be mine, but not till after a long and bitter punishment. Now I ask thy friends and thee, if to be mine they are willing to take the form of demons and bear it openly before all men.'

" And when he proposed it to his friends, he found them so madly in love with the lady that they, thinking she meant some disguise, declared that to be hers they would willingly wear any form, however terrible.

"And the fair Alba, having heard them, said, 'Yes, ye shall indeed be mine; more than that I do not promise. Now meet me to-morrow at the Canto dei Diavoli—at the Devil's Corner!'

" And they gazed at her astonished, never having heard of such a place. But she replied, ' Go into the street and your feet shall guide you, and truly it will be a great surprise.'

" And they laughed among themselves, saying, ' The surprise will be that she will consent to become a wife to us all.'

" But when they came to the corner, in the night, what was their amazement to see on it four figures of devils indeed, and Alba, who said, ' Now ye are indeed mine, but as for my being yours, that is another matter.'

"Then touching each one, she also touched a devil, and said, ' This is thy form; enter into it. Three of ye shall ever remain as such. As for this fourth youth, he shall be with ye for a year, and then, set free, shall live with me in human form. And from midnight till three in the morning ye also may be as ye were, and go to the Palazzo Cavolaia, and dance and be merry with the rest, but through the day become devils again.'

"And so it came to pass. After a year the image of the chosen lover disappeared; and then one of the three was stolen, and then another, till only one remained."

There is some confusion in the conclusion of this story, which I have sought to correct. The exact words are, " For many years all four remained, till one was stolen away, and that was the image of the young man who pleased the beautiful Alba, who thus relieved him of the spell." But as there has been always only one devil on the corner, I cannot otherwise reconcile the story with the fact.

I have said that this tale is ancient from intrinsic evidence. Such extravagant alliances of friendship as is here described were actually common in the Middle Ages ; they existed in England even till the time of Queen Elizabeth. In " Shakespeare and his Friends," or in the " Youth of Shakespeare"— I forget which— two young men are represented as fighting a duel because each declared that he loved the other most. There was no insane folly of sentiment which was not developed in those days. But this is so foreign to modern ideas, that I think it could only have existed in tradition to these our times.

There were also during the Middle Ages strange heretical sects, among whom such communism existed, like the polyandria of the ancient Hindoos. There may be a trace of it in this story.

Alba, Albina, or Bellaria, appear in several Tuscan traditions. They are forms of the Etruscan Alpan, the fairy of the Dawn, a sub-form of Venus, the spirit of Light and Flowers, described in my work on " Etruscan Roman Traditions." It may be remarked as an ingenious touch in the tale, that she always appears at the first dawn, or at three o'clock, and vanishes with broad day. This distinguishes her from the witches and evil spirits, who always come at midnight and vanish at three o'clock.

The readiness with which the young men consented to assume the forms of demons is easily explained. They understood that it meant only a disguise, and it was very common in the Middle Ages for lovers to wear something strange in honour of their mistresses. The dress of a devil would only seem a joke to the habitues of the Cavolaia. It may be also borne in mind that in other tales of Florence it is distinctly stated that spirits confined in statues, columns, et cetera, only inhabit them "as bees live in hives.'.' They appear to sleep in them by day, and come out at night. So in India the saint or demon only comes into the relic or image from time to time, or when invoked.

After I had written the foregoing, I was so fortunate as to receive from Maddalena yet another legend of the bronze imp of Giovanni di Bologna, which tale she had unearthed in the purlieus of the Mercato Vecchio. I have often met her when thus employed, always in the old part of the town, amid towering old buildings bearing shields of the Middle Ages, or in dusky vicoli and ckiassi, and when asked what she was doing, 'twas ever the same reply, "Ma, Signore Carlo, there's an old woman —or somebody—lives here who knows a story." And then I knew that there was going to be a long colloquy in dialect which would appal any one who only knew choice Italian, the end of which would be the recovery, perhaps from half-a-dozen vecchic, of a legend like the following, of which I would premise that it was not translated by me, but by Miss Roma Lister, who knew Maddalena, having taken lessons from her in the sublime art of battezare le carte, or telling fortunes by cards, and other branches of the black art. And having received the manuscript, which was unusually illegible and troublesome, I asked Miss Lister to kindly transcribe it, but with great kindness she translated the whole, only begging me to mention that it is given with the most scrupulous accuracy, word for word, from the original, so far as the difference of language permitted.

IL DIAVOLINO DEL CANTO DE* DIAVOLI.

The Imp of the Devils Corner and the Pious Fairy.

"There was once a pious fairy who employed all her time in going about the streets of Florence in the shape of a woman, preaching moral sermons for the good of her hearers, and singing so sweetly that all who heard her voice fell in love with her. Even the women forgot to be jealous, so charming was her

voice, and dames and damsels followed her about, trying to learn her manner of singing.

" Now the fairy had converted so many folk from their evil ways, that a certain devil or imp—who also had much business in Florence about that time—became jealous of the intruder, and swore to avenge himself; but it appears that there was as much love as hate in the fiend's mind, for the fairy's beautiful voice had worked its charm even when the hearer was a devil. Now, besides being an imp of superior intelligence, he was also an accomplished ventriloquist (or one who could imitate strange voices as if sounding afar or in any place); so one day while the pious fairy in the form of a beautiful maiden held forth to an admiring audience, two voices were heard in the street, one here, another there, and the first sang:

"' Senti o bella una parola,
Te la dico a te sola,
Qui nessun ci puo'l sentire
Una cosa ti vuo dire ;
Se la senti la stemperona,
L'a un voce da huffona
Tiene in mano la corona. 1
Per fare credere a questo o quella,
Che 1'e sempre una verginella.'

" ' Hear, O lovely maid, a word, Only to thyself I'd bear it, For it must not be o'erheard, Least of all should the preacher hear it. 'Tis that, while seeming pious, she, Holding in hand a rosary, Her talk is all hypocrisy, To make believe to simple ears, That still the maiden wreath she wears.'

" Then another voice answered:

"' La risposta ti vuo dare, Senza farti aspettare; Ora di un bell affare, Te la voglio raccontare, Quella donna che sta a cantare, E una strega di queste contrade, Che va da questo e quello, A cantarle indovinello, A chi racconta : Voi siete Buona donna affezionata. Al vostro marito, ma non sapete, Cie' di voi un 'altra appasionata.'

1 This is supposed to be addressed to another, not to the fairy.

"' Friends, you'll not have long to wait For what I'm going to relate ; And it is a pretty story Which I am going to lay before ye. That dame who singing there you see Is a witch of this our Tuscany, Who up and down the city flies, Deceiving people with her lies, Saying to one : The truth to tell, I know you love your husband well; But you will find, on close inspection, Another has his fond affection.'

" In short, the imp, by changing his voice artfully, and singing his ribald songs everywhere, managed in the end to persuade people that the fairy was no better than she should be, and a common mischief-maker and disturber of domestic peace. So the husbands, becoming jealous, began to quarrel with their wives, and then to swear at the witch who led them astray or put false suspicion into their minds.

" But it happened that the fairy was in high favour with a great saint, and going to him, she told all her troubles and the wicked things which were said of her, and besought him to free her good name from the slanders which the imp of darkness had spread abroad (l'aveva chalugnato).

" Then the saint, very angry, changed the devil into a bronze figure (mascherone, an architectural ornament), but first compelled him to go about to all who had been influenced by his slanders, and undo the mischief which he had made, and finally to make a full confession in public of everything, including his designs on the beautiful fairy, and how he hoped by compromising her to lead her to share his fate.

" Truly the imp cut but a sorry figure when compelled to thus stand up in the Old Market place at the corner of the Palazzo Cavolaia before a vast multitude and avow all his dirty little tricks ; but he contrived withal to so artfully represent his passionate love for the fairy, and to turn all his sins to that account, that many had compassion on him, so that indeed among the people, in time, no one ever spoke ill of the doppio povero diavolo, or doubly poor devil, for they said he was to be pitied since he had no love on earth and was shut out of heaven.

" Nor did he quite lose his power, for it was said that after he had been confined in the bronze image, if any one spoke ill of him or said, ' This is a devil, and as a devil he can never enter Paradise,' then the imp would persecute that man with

strange voices and sounds until such time as the offender should betake himself to the Palazzo della Cavolaia, and there, standing before the bronze image, should ask his pardon.

"And if it pleased the Diavolino, he forgave them, and they had peace; but if it did not, they were pursued by the double mocking voice which made dialogue or sang duets over all their sins and follies and disgraces. And whether they stayed at home or went abroad, the voices were ever about them, crying aloud or tittering and whispering or hissing, so that they had no rest by day or night ; and this is what befell all who spoke ill of the Diavolino del Canto dei Diavoli."

The saint mentioned in this story was certainly Pietro Martire or Peter the Martyrer, better deserving the name of murderer, who, preaching at the very corner where the bronze imp was afterwards placed, declared that he beheld the devil, and promptly exorcised him. There can be little doubt that the image was placed there to commemorate this probably " pious fraud."

It is only since I wrote all this that I learned that there were formerly two of these devils, one having been stolen not many years ago. This verifies to some extent the consistency of the author of the legend, " The Devil of the Mercato Vecchio," who says there were four.

There is a very amusing and curious trait of character manifested in the conclusion of this story which might escape the reader's attention were it not indicated. It is the vindication of the " puir deil," and the very evident desire to prove that he was led astray by love, and that even the higher spirit could not take away all his power. Here I recognise beyond all question the witch, the fortune-teller and sorceress, who prefers Cain to Abel, and sings invocations to the former, and to Diana as the dark queen of the Strege, and always takes sides with the heretic and sinner and magian and goblin. It is the last working of the true spirit of ancient heathenism, for the fortune-tellers, and especially those of the mountains, all come of families who have been regarded as enemies by the Church during all the Middle Ages, and who are probably real and direct descendants of Canidia and her contemporaries, for where this thing is in a family it never dies out. I have a great many traditions in which the hand of the heathen witch and the worship of " him who has been wronged " and banished to darkness, is as evident as it is here.

" Which indeed seems to show," comments the learned Flaxius, "that if the devil is never quite so black as he is painted, yet, on the other hand, he is so far from being of a pure white—as the jolly George Sand boys, such as Heine and Co., thought—that it is hard to make him out of any lighter hue than mud and verdigris mixed. In medio tutissimus ibis, 'Tis also to be especially noted, that in this legend—as in Shelley's poem—the Devil appears as a meddling wretch who is interested in small things, and above all, as given to gossip:

" The Devil sat down in London town Before earth's morning ray, With a favourite imp he began to chat, On religion, and scandal, and this and that, Until the dawn of day."

SEEING THAT ALL WAS RIGHT
A LEGEND OF THE PORTA A SAN NICOLA

" God keep us from the devil's lackics, Who are the aggravating jackies, Who to the letter execute An order and exactly do't, Or else, with fancy free and bold, Do twice as much as they are told, And when reproved, cry bravely. ' Oh ! I thought you'd like it so and so.' From all such, wheresoe'er they be, Libera nos, Dominc ! "

THE Porta a San Nicolo in Florence is, among other legends, associated with a jest played by the famous Bar-lacchia on a friend, the story of which runs as follows:

" It is an old saying that la porta di dietro e quella che ruba hi casa (it is the back gate which robs a house), and it was going back to the gate of San Nicolo which robbed a man of all his patience. This man had gone with Barlacchia the jester from Florence to Val d'Arno, and on returning they had stopped in the plain of Ripolo, where the friend was obliged to delay for a time, while Barlacchia went on. Now it was so late that although Barlacchia was certain to reach the Porto a San Nicolo in time to enter, it was doubtful whether the one who came later could do so unless a word should be spoken in advance to the guard, who for friendship or a fee would sit up and let the late-comer in. Therefore the friend said to the jester, ^ Di gratia facesse sostenere la porta 1 — ' See that the gate is all right,' or that all is right at the bridge — meaning, of course, that he should make it right with the guardian to let him in.

" And when Barlacchia came to the gate, he indeed asked the officer in charge se questi si so^tengo —whether it was all right, and if it stood firmly, and was in no danger of falling, affirming that he was making special inquiry at request of a

friend who was commissioner of the city gates and bridges, and obtained a paper certifying that the gate was in excellent condition, after which he went home.

"Trotting along on his mule came the friend, who, believing that Barlacchia had made it all right with the guard, had not hurried. But he found it was all wrong, and that 'a great mistake had been made somewhere,' as the eel said when he was thrown into boiling hot oil instead of cold water. For he found the gate locked and nobody to let him in, so that in a great rage he was obliged to go back to an inn which was distinguished for nothing but its badness, dove stette con gran disagio quella notte (where he passed the night in great discomfort).

"And when morning came, he passed the gate, but stopped and asked whether Barlacchia had been there the night before. To which the guard answered, 'Yes,' and that he had been very particular in his inquiries as to whether the doors were firm on their hinges, and if the foundations were secure ; on hearing which, the man saw that he had been sold, 1 and going to the Piazza Signoria, and meeting Barlacchia, *gli disse rilevata vi/lania*, let him have abuse in bold relief and large proportion, saying that it was infamous to snipe his equal in all things and better in most, in such a low-flung manner, unbecoming a half-grown chimney-sweep, and that if he did not respect himself too much to use improper or strong language, he would say that Barlacchia was a dastardly blackguard and a son of a priest. To which Barlacchia remonstrated that he had performed to perfection exactly what he had promised to do, yea, *a punto*, to the very letter.

" Now by this time half Florence had assembled, and being delighted beyond all measure at this racy dispute, insisted on forming a street-court and settling the question *alia fresca*. And when the evidence was taken, and all the facts, which long in darkness lay, were brought full clearly to the light of day, there was such a roaring of laughter and clapping of hands that you would have sworn the Guelfs and Ghibellines had got at it again full swing. But the verdict was that Barlacchia was acquitted without a stain on his character.

" *Hcecfabula docet*" comments Flaxius, " that there be others besides Tyll Eulenspiegel who make mischief by fulfilling laws too literally. And there are no people in this world who contrive to break the Spirit of Christianity so much as those who follow it simply to the Letter."

1 Ucellato, caught like a bird, or, as they say on the Mississippi, "sniped."

THE ENCHANTED COW OF LA VIA VACCHERECCIA

" On Dun more Heath I also slewe
A monstrous wild and cruell beaste Called the Dun Cow of Dunmore plaine, Who many people had opprest."

— Cuj r , Earl of Warwick.

THE Via Vaccereccia is a very short street leading from the Signoria to the Via For San Maria. Vaccherricia, also Vacchereccia, means a cow, and is also applied scornfully to a bad woman. The following legend was given to me as accounting for the name of the place. A well-known Vienna beerhouse-restaurant, Gilli and Letta's, has contributed much of late years to make this street known, and it was on its site that, at some time in " the fabled past," the building stood in which dwelt the witch who figures in the story.

LA VIA VACCHERECCIA.

" There lived long ago in the Via Vacchereccia a poor girl, who was, however, so beautiful and graceful, and sweet in her manner, that it seemed to be a marvel that she belonged to the people, and still more that she was the daughter of the woman who was believed to be her mother, for the latter was as ugly as she was wicked, brutal, and cruel before all the world, and a witch in secret, a creature without heart or humanity.

" Nor was the beautiful Artemisia —such being the name of the girl—in reality her daughter, for the old woman had stolen her from her parents, who were noble and wealthy, when she was a babe, and had brought her up, hoping that when grown she could make money out of her in some evil way, and live

no LEGENDS OF FLORENCE

upon her. But, as sometimes happens, it seemed as if some benevolent power watched over the poor child, for all the evil words and worse example of the witch had no effect on her whatever.

"Now it happened that Artemisia in time attracted the attention and love of a young gentleman, who, while of moderate estate, was by no means rich; and he had learned to know her through his mother, an admirable lady, who had often employed Artemisia, and been impressed by her beauty and goodness. So it happened that the mother favoured the son's suit, and as

Artemisia loved the young man, it seemed as if her sufferings would soon be at an end, for be it observed that the witch treated the maid at all times with extraordinary cruelty.

"But it did not suit the views of the old woman at all that the girl on whom she reckoned to bring in much money from great protectors, and whom she was wont to call the cow from whom she would yet draw support, should settle down into the wife of a small noble of moderate means. So she not only scornfully rejected the suit, but scolded and beat Artemisia with even greater wickedness than ever.

" But there are times when the gentlest natures (especially when supported by good principles and truly good blood) will not give way to any oppression, however cruel, and Artemisia, feeling keenly that the marriage was most advantageous for her, and a great honour, and that her whole heart had been wisely given, for once turned on the old woman and defied her, threatening to appeal to the law, and showing that she knew so much that was wicked in her life that the witch became as much frightened as she was enraged, well knowing that an investigation by justice would bring her to the bonfire. So, inspired by the devil, she turned the girl into a cow, and shut her up in a stable in the courtyard of the house, where she went every day two or three times to beat and torture her victim in the most fiendish manner.

"Meanwhile the disappearance of Artemisia had excited much talk and suspicion, as it followed immediately after the refusal of the old woman to give her daughter to the young gentleman. And he indeed was in sad case and great suffering, but after a while, recovering himself, he began to wonder whether the maid was not after all confined in the Via Vacchereccia. And as love doubles all our senses and makes the deaf hear, and, according to the proverb, ' he who finds it in his heart will feel spurs in his flanks,' so this young man, hearing the old woman spoken of as a witch, began to wonder whether she might not be one in truth, and whether Artemisia might not have been confinata or enchanted into some form of an animal, and so imprisoned.

" And, full of this thought, he went by night to the house, where there was an opening like a window or portal in the courtyard, and began to sing :

" ' Batte le dodici a una campana, Si sente appena dalla lontana.

" 'Se almeno la voce potessi sentire,
Delia mia bella che tanto deve soffrire.'

" ' Midnight is striking, I hear it afar, High in the heaven shines many a star.

" ' And oh that the voice of the one I could hear, Who suffers so sadly—the love I hold dear.

" ' Oh stars, if you're looking with pity on me, I pray you the maid from affliction to free !'

" As he sang this, he heard a cow lowing in the courtyard, and as his mind was full of the idea of enchantment, his attention was attracted to it. Then he sang:

"' If enchanted here you be,
Low, but gently, one, tivo t three I Low in answer unto me, And a rescue soon you'll see.'

"Then the cow lowed three times, very softly, and the young man, delighted, put to her other questions, and being very shrewd, he so managed it as to extract with only yea and nay all the story. Having learned all this, he reflected that to beat a terrier 'tis well to take a bulldog, and after much inquiry, he found that there dwelt in Arezzo a great sorcerer, but a man of noble character, and was, moreover, astonished to learn from his mother that this gran mago had been a friend of his father.

" And being well received by the wise man, and having told his story, the sage replied :

"' Evil indeed is the woman of whom you speak—a black witch of low degree, who has been allowed, as all of her kind are, to complete her measure of sin, in order that she may receive her full measure of punishment. For all things may be forgiven, but not cruelty, and she has lived on the sufferings of others. Yet her power is of a petty kind, and such as any priest can crush.

"' Go to the stable when she shall be absent, and I will provide that she shall be away all to-morrow. Then bind verbena on the cow's horns, and hang a crucifix over the door, and sprinkle all the floor with holy water and incense, and sing to the cow :

" 'The witch is not thy mother in truth, She stole thee in thy early youth, She has deserved thy bitterest hate, Then fear not to retaliate ; And when she comes to thee again, Then rush at her with might and main ; She has heaped on thee many a scorn, Repay it with thy pointed horn.'

"'And note that there is a halter on the cow's neck, and this is the charm which gives her the form of a cow, but it cannot be removed except in a church by the priest.'

"And to this he added other advice, which was duly followed.

" Then th'e next day the young man went to the stable, and did all that the wise man had bid, and hiding near, awaited the return of the witch. Nor had he indeed long to wait, for the witch, who was evidently in a great rage at something, and bore a cruel-looking stick with an iron goad on the end, rushed to the courtyard and into the stable, but fell flat on the floor, being overcome by the holy water. And the cow, whose halter had been untied from the post, turned on her with fury, and tossed and gored her, and trampled on her till she was senseless, and then ran full speed, guided by the young man, to the Baptistery, into which she entered, and where there was a priest awaiting her. And the priest sprinkled her with holy water, and took the halter from her neck, and she was disenchanted, and became once more the beautiful Artemisia.

" And this done, the young man took the halter, and hurrying back to the stable, put it about the neck of the witch, who at once became a cow without horns, or such as are called ' the devil's own.' And as she, maddened with rage, rushed forth, attacking everybody, all the town was soon after her with staves, pikes, and all their dogs, and so they hunted her down through the Ufifizzi and along Lung' Arno, all roaring and screaming and barking, out into the country, for she gave them a long run and a good chase, till they came to a gate of a fodere, over which was a Saint Antony, who, indignant that she dared pass under him, descended from his niche, and gave her a tremendous blow with his staff between the horns, or where they would have been if she had possessed them. Whereupon the earth opened and swallowed her up, amid a fearful flashing of fire, and a smell which was even worse than that of the streets of Siena in summer-time—which is often so fearful that the poorer natives commonly carry fennel (as people do perfumed vinaigrettes in other places) to sniff at, as a relief from the horrible odour.

" And when all this was done, the mago revealed to the maiden that her parents, who were still living, were very great and wealthy people, so that there was soon a grand reunion, a general recognition, and a happy marriage.

" ' Maidens, beware lest witches catch you ; Think of the Via Vacchereccia ; And tourists dining in the same, Note how the street once got its name.'"

II

THE WITCH OF THE PORT A ALL A CROCE

" If any secret should sacred he,
Though it guarded the life of a family, And any woman be there about, She will die but what she will find it out; And though it hurried her soul to—well— That secret she must

immediately tell."

— Sage Stuffing for Young Ducks.

THERE are in Italy, as elsewhere, families to whom a fatality or tradition is attached. The following is a curious legend of the kind :

LA FATTUCHIERA BELLA PORTA ALLA CROCK.

"There was a very old Florentine family which lived in a castle in the country. The elder or head of this family had always one room in which no one was ever allowed to enter. There he passed hours alone every day, and woe to any one who dared disturb him while there. And this had been the case for generations, and no one had ever found out what the secret was. This was, of course, a great vexation to the ladies of the family — perche la donna e sempre churiosa — women being always inquisitive.

"And most inquisitive of all was a niece of the old man, who had got it into her head that the secret was simply a great treasure which she might obtain. Therefore she resolved to consult with a certain witch, who would tell her what it was, and how she could enter the mysterious room. This sorceress lived hard by the Porta alia Croce, for there are always many witches in that quarter.

"The witch, who was a very large tall woman, made the niece go with her to an isolated small house, and thence along a path, the lady in advance. While so doing, the latter turned her head to look behind her, and at that instant heard the cry

of a civetta or small owl. The witch exclaimed, ' My dear

lady, what you wish for will hardly be granted; I fear there is a great disaster awaiting you.'

"Then they went into a field, and the fortune-teller produced a goblet of coloured glass, and called to the swallow, which is a bird of good omen, and to the small owl, which forebodes evil, and said, ' Whichever shall alight first on the edge of this cup will be a sign to you of success or failure.'

" But the first which came and sat upon the cup was the owl.

" Then the witch said, ' What there is in that room I cannot reveal, for it disturbs my soul far too much. But I know that the number of that room is thirteen, and you can infer for yourself what that portends; and more I cannot tell you, save that you should be extremely careful and keep a cheerful heart — otherwise there is great trouble awaiting you.'

" But the lady returned home in a great rage at her disappointment, and all the more resolved to enter the room. Then all the family finding this out, reproached her, and urged her not to be so distracted ; and she, being obstinate, only became the more determined ; for she was furious that she could not force an old man to reveal a secret which had been handed down for many generations, and which could only be confided to one, or to the eldest, when the old man should die.

"And at last her evil will or mania attained such command over her, that she resolved to kill all the family one by one, till the succession of the secret should come to her. And so, after boiling deadly herbs with care, she made a strong subtle poison. And by this means she put to death her parents, brothers and sisters, aunts and all the family, without remorse, so resolved was she to master the secret.

" The last to perish was her grandfather, and calling her to his bedside he said, ' We have all died by thy hand ; we who never did thee any harm ; and thou hast felt no remorse. This thou didst to gain a treasure, and bitterly wilt thou be disappointed. Thy punishment will begin when thou shalt learn what the thing was so long hidden : truly there was sorrow enough therein, without the misery which thou hast added to it. That which thou wilt find in the chamber is a skull— the skull of our earliest ancestor, which must always be given to the care of the eldest descendant, and I now give it to thee. And this thou must do. Go every morning at seven o'clock into the room and close the windows. Then light four candles before the skull. In front of it there lies a great book in which is written the history of all our family, my life and thine; and see that thou do this with care, or woe be unto thee!'

" Therewith the old man died, and scarcely had he departed ere she called an old woman who was allied and devoted to the family, and in a rage told her all the secret. The old woman reproved her, saying that she would bring punishment on herself. But, without heeding this, the lady ran to the chamber, entered, and seeing the skull, gave it a kick and hurled it from the window, far below.

" But a minute after she heard a rattling sound, and looking at the window, there the skull was grinning at her. Again she threw it down, and again it returned, and was with her wherever she went; day after day, waking or sleeping, the skull was always before her eyes.

" At last fear came over her, and then horror, and she said to the old woman, ' Let us go to some place far, far away, and bury the skull. Perhaps it will rest in its grave.' The old woman tried to dissuade her, and they went to a lonely spot at a great distance, and there they dug long and deep.

" Dug till a great hole was made, and the lady standing on the edge dropped the skull into it. Then the hole spread into a great pit, flame rose from it—the edge crumbled away—the guilty woman fell into the fire, and the earth closed over it all, and there was no trace left of her.

" The skull returned to the castle and to its room; people say it is there to this day. The old woman returned too, and being the last remote relation, entered into possession of the property."

There is perhaps not one well-educated person in society in England who has not had the opportunity to remark how very much any old family can succeed in being notorious if it can only once make it known that it has an hereditary secret. Novels will be written on it, every member of it will be pointed out everywhere, and people who do not know the name of a sovereign in Europe can tell you all about it and them. And the number is not small of those who consider themselves immensely greater because they have in some way mastered something which they are expected to keep concealed. I could almost believe that this " 'orrible tale " was composed as a satire on family secrets. But I believe that she who told it firmly believed it. Credo quia absurdum would not be well understood among humble folk in Italy.

" To this I may add," writes Flaxius, " that there is an English legend of a certain skull which always returned to a certain window in a tower. Apropos of which there is a poem called The Student and the Head in ' Hans Breitmann in Germany' (London: T. Fisher Unwin, 1895), prefaced by a remark to the effect that the subject is so extensive as to deserve a book— instancing the head of the physician Douban in the ' Arabian Nights,' with that of Orpheus, which spoke to Cyrus, and that of the priest of Jupiter, and another described by Trallianus, and the marvellously preserved head of a saint in Olaf Tryggvason's Saga, and the Witch's Head of Rider Haggard, with many more, not to speak of the talking Tera-phim heads, and Friar Bacon's bust. With which a thoroughly exhaustive list should include the caput mortuum of the alchemists

" ' And the dead-heads of the Press.' "

THE COLUMN OF COSIMO, OR DELL A SANTA TRINITA

"Columna Florentina. —Prope Sanctae Trinitatis oedem ingens et sublimis columna erecta, cujus in fastigio extat justitia. Earn erexit Cosmus Magnus Dux, cui per urbem deambulanti, illic de victoria renunciatum fuit quam Malignani Marchio in Senarum finibus anno 1555 contra Petrum Strozium obtinuit."— Teniflum Natures Historiciim, Darmstadt, 1611.

"Vesti una Colonna, Le par una donna."— Italian Proverb.

THE central spot of Florence is the grand column of granite which stands in the middle of the Piazza di Santa Trinita, in the Via Tornabuoni, opposite the Palazzo Feroni. It was brought from the Baths of Caracalla in Rome, and erected in 1564 by Cosimo I., "in commemoration of the surrender of Siena in 1554, and of the destruction of the last liberties of Florence by the victory at Monte Murlo, 1537, over those whom his tyranny had driven into exile, headed by Filippo and Piero Strozzi. It is surmounted by a statue of 'Justice' in porphyry, by Ferruci" says Murray's Guide-Book—the Italian declares it to be by Taddi t adding that the column was from the Baths of Antoninus, and was a gift to Cosimo I. from Pius IV.

There is a popular legend that once on a time a poor girl was arrested in Florence for having stolen a chain, a bracelet, or some such article of jewellery of immense value. She was thrown into prison, but though there was collateral or indirect evidence to prove her guilt, the stolen article could not be found. Gossip and rumour constituted ample grounds for indictment and trial, and torture did the rest in the pious times when it was generally taught and believed that Providence would always rescue the innocent, and that everybody who came to grief on the gallows had deserved it for something or other at some time, and that it was all right.

So the girl was executed, and almost forgotten. When a long time after, some workman or other was sent up to the

top of the column of the Piazza Trinita, and there found that a jackdaw or magpie had built a nest in the balance or scales held by Justice, and in it was the missing jewel.

This is an Italian form of "The Maid and the Magpie," known the world over from ancient times. The scales suggest a droll German story. There was in front of a certain palace or town-hall, where all criminals were tried, a statue of Justice holding a pair of scales, and these were not cast solid, but were a bona fide pair of balances. And certain low thieves having been arrested with booty—whatever it was—it was discovered that they had divided it among themselves very accurately, even to the ounce. At which the magistrate greatly marvelling, asked them how they could have done it so well, since it had appeared that they had not been in any house between the period of the theft and their arrest. Whereupon one replied : " Very easily, your Honour, for, to be honourable, honest, and just as possible, we weighed the goods in the scales of Justice itself, here on the front of the Raih-haus"

It is for every reason more probable that the bird which stole the jewel of the column was a jackdaw than a magpie, and it is certainly fitter that it should have been thus in Florence. " It is well known," says Oken in his " Natural History" (7 B. Part I. 347), "that the jackdaw steals glittering objects, and carries them to its nest." Hence the ancient legend of Arne, who so greatly loved gold, that she sold her native isle Siphnos to Minos, and was for that turned by the gods into a daw (Ovid's "Metamorphoses," vii. 466). As a mischief-making, thieving, and chattering bird of black colour, the jackdaw was naturally considered evil, and witches, or their imps, often assumed its form. In fact, the only really good or pious bird of the kind on record known to me, is the jackdaw of Rheims sung by Ingoldsby Barham.

According to Kornmannus, the column was placed where it now stands, because Cosimo was in the Piazza Trinita when he heard the news of the surrender of Siena.

After I had written the foregoing legend, I found the following:

LA COLONNA DI SANTA TRINITA.

"The pillar di Santa Trinita was in old times a meeting-place for fairies \'7bFaie\ whither they went afoot or in their carriages. At the base of the column there was a great stone, and there they exchanged greetings or consulted about their affairs. They were all great ladies, of kindly disposition. And when it came that any one was cast into the city prison, they inquired into the affair, and then a fate would go as a magistrate in disguise and question the accused. Now they always knew whether any one spoke the truth, and if the prisoner did so, and was deserving mercy, they delivered him; but if he lied, they left him to be hanged, with a buon pro vi faccia! —Much good may it do you!

"Of evenings they assembled round the rock at the foot of the column in a great company, and had great merriment and love-making. Then in the crowd a couple would descend, or one after another into their vaults below, and then come again, often taking with them mortals who were their friends or favourites.

"Their chief was a matron who always held a pair of scales. Now when they were to judge the fate of any one, they took with great care the earth from one of his footprints, and weighed it most scrupulously, for thereby they could tell whether in his life he had done more good or evil, and it was thus that they settled the fate of all the accused in the prisons.

"And it often came to pass that when prisoners were young and handsome, these fate or fairy-witches took them from their cells in the prison through subterranean ways to their vaults under the Trinita, and passed the time merrily enough, for all was magnificent there.

"But woe unto those, no matter how handsome they might be, who betrayed the secrets and the love of the fate. Verily they had their reward, and a fine long repentance with it, for they were all turned into cats or mice, and condemned to live in the cellars and subterranean passages of the old Ghetto, which is now destroyed—and a nasty place it was. In its time people often wondered that there were so many cats there, but the truth is that they were all people who had been enchanted by those who were called in olden time le Gran Dame di Firenze —the Great Ladies of Florence.

"And the image holding the scales is called la Giustizia, but it really represents the Matrona, or Queen of the Fate, who of old exercised such strict justice with her scales in Florence."

This is, I am confident, a tradition of great antiquity, for all its elements are of a very ancient or singularly witch-like nature. In it the fate are found in their most natural form, as fates, weighing justice and dealing out rewards and punishments. Justice herself appears naïvely and amusingly to the witches as Queen of the Fate, who are indeed all spirits who have been good witches in a previous life.

What is most mystical and peculiarly classic Italian is the belief that the earth on which a human being has trod can be used wherewith to conjure him. This subject is treated elsewhere in my "Etruscan Roman Traditions."

The great stone at the base of the column was a kind of palladium of the city of Florence. There are brief notices of it in many works. It would be curious if it still exists somewhere and can be identified.

"A great palladium, whose virtues lie In undefined remote antiquity; A god unformed, who sleeps within a stone, Which sculptor's hand as yet has never known; Brought in past ages from some unknown shore; Our fathers worshipped it—we know no more."

LEGENDS OF OR' SAN MICHELE

" The spirit of Antiquity, enshrined
In sumptuous buildings, vocal in sweet song, In pictures speaking with heroic tongue, And with devout solemnities entwined."

— WORDSWORTH, "Bruges"

OR' SAN MICHELE is a very beautiful church in the Italian Gothic style in the Via Calzaioli. It was originally a market or stable below and a barn or granary above, whence some derive its name from Horreum Sancti Michaelis, and others from the Italian Orto, a garden, a term also applied to a church-congregation. " The statues and decorations on the exterior are among the best productions of the Florentine school of sculpture." As that of Saint Eloy or San Eligio, the blacksmith, with great pincers at an anvil, in a sculpture representing a horse being shod, is the most conspicuous on the facade, the people have naturally concluded that the church was originally a stable or smithy. The legend of the place is as follows:

LA CHIESA OR' SAN MICHELE.

" This was originally a stable and coach-house (rtmessd), and there was a hayloft above. Every night the horses were heard to neigh, and in the morning they were found all curried and well managed, and no one knew who did it; but none of the grooms ever shed any tears over it that ever] heard of.

" Now, the master of the place had a son, a priest named Michele, who was so holy that he worked many miracles, so that all began to call him a saint. And after he died he appeared to his parents in a dream, and told them that the stable and barn should be transformed into a church, and that he would read mass therein thrice a day.

" But his parents wished to have him buried under the altar of a church which was on their estate in the country, but the saint did not wish to be buried there.

" One day one of the grooms of the stable found that a horse could not move a foot, so he ran to call the manescalco, or blacksmith, who led the horse to his forge. And when he took the hoof to examine it, lo ! it came off at the joint and remained in his hand. Then the smith said that the horse should be killed, because he was now worthless. But the horse struck his stump on the hoof, and the latter joined itself to his leg as firmly as ever it had been. But in doing this the old shoe fell off, whence it comes to this day that whoever finds an old horse-shoe gets luck with it.

" When the smith had shod the horse anew, he tried to lead it back into the stable, but it refused to enter. Then it was plain that this was a miracle worked by San Michele. So they removed all the horses and hay from the building, and made of it the fine church which is now called La Chiesa di Or 1 San Michele."

There is a vast mass of tradition extant relative to the Horse, enough to make a large volume, and in it there is a great deal which is so nearly allied to this story as to establish its antiquity. Karl Blind has found an old Norse spell, in which, by the aid of Balder and Odin, the lameness of a horse's ankle or pastern joint can be cured. There is another version of this story, which runs as follows :

THE SMITH AND SAINT PETER.

" It is a good thing in this world to be bold and have a good opinion of one's self; yes, and to hold your head high — but not so high as to bend over backwards — else that may happen to you which befell the celebrated cock of Aspromonte."

" And what happened to him ? "

" Only this, Signore — he was so cocky, and bent his head so far backwards, that his spurs ran into his eyes and blinded him. Now, the cock reminds me of Saint Peter, and too much cheek of the ferrajo spacciato, or the saucy smith, who wanted to equal him.

"It happened once that the Lord and Saint Peter came to a forge, and the smith was about to lead a horse from the stable to the anvil to shoe him. Saint Peter said:

"'Thou hast boasted that thou art the best smith in the world, and canst work such wonders in shoeing as man never beheld. Canst thou not shoe this horse without taking him to the forge?'

"'Neither thou, nor I, nor any man can do it,' replied the smith.

"Saint Peter took the hoof in his left hand, gave it a rap with the side of his right across the joint, and the hoof fell off. Then Saint Peter carried it to the anvil, fastened a new shoe on it, returned and put it on the horse again, who stamped with it as if nothing had happened.

"Now the smith, like all boasters, was a great fool, and he only thought that this was something which he had not learned before, and so cried boldly, 'Oh, that is only the Bolognese manner of taking hoofs off and putting them on—we do it much better here in Florence!' So he seized the horse's hoof, and with one blow of a hatchet cut it off.

"'And now put it on again,' said Saint Peter. The smith tried, but it would not stick.

"'The horse is bleeding to death rapidly,' remarked the Saint.

"'I believe,' said the smith ruefully, 'that I am a fool in folio.'

"'Piit matto che un granchio —as crazy as a crawfish,' solemnly added one of his assistants.

"'Pazzo a bandiera —as wild and witless as a flapping flag,' quoth another.

"'Matto di sette cotte —an idiot seven times baked,' chimed in Saint Peter.

"'A campanile —a church bell-tower of a fool,' contributed his wife, who had just come in.

"The poor horse continued to bleed.

"'You are like the mouse,' added a neighbour, 'who thought because he had dipped the end of his tail in the meal, that he owned and could run the mill.'

"'The Florentine method of shoeing horses,' remarked Saint Peter gravely, 'does not appear to be invariably successful. I think that we had better recur to mine.' And with this he put the hoof to the ankle, m& presto! the miracle was wrought again. That is the story. In most cases, Signore, un pazzo gitta una pietra nel pozzo —a fool rolls a rock into a well which it requires a hundred wise men to get out again. This time a single sage sufficed. But for that you must have the Lord at your back, as Saint Peter had."

"Why do they say, as foolish as a crawfish or lobster?" I inquired.

"Because, Signore, the granchio, be he lobster or crawfish, carries his head in the scarsella, which is a hole in his belly. Men who have their brains in their bellies—or gluttons—are generally foolish. But what is the use of boasting of our wisdom? He who has neither poor men nor fools among his relations was born of the lightning or of thunder."

There is another story current among the people, though it is in print, but as it is a merry one, belonging truly enough to the folk-lore of Florence, I give it as it runs:

"You have heard of Piovano Arlotto, who made this our town so lively long ago. It was rich then, indeed. There are more flowers than florins in Florence now: ogni fior non fa frutto — all flowers do not bear fruit.

"Well, it happened one day that Piovano, having heard a good story from Piero di Cosimo de' Medicis, answered with another. Now the tale which Messer Piero di Cosimo told was this:

"Once there lived in Florence a poor shoemaker, who went every morning to the Church of San Michele Berteldi —some say it was at San Bartolommeo, and maybe at both, for a good story or a big lie is at home anywhere.

"Well, he used to pray before a John the Baptist in wood, or it may have been cast in plaster, or moulded in wax, which was on the altar. One morning he prayed scalding hot, and the chierico —a boy who waits on the priest, who was a young rascal, like all of his kind— overheard him say: ' Oh, Saint John, I pray thee make known to me two things. One is whether my wife is good and true to me, and the other what will become of my only son.'

"Then the mass-boy, who had hidden himself behind the altar, replied in a soft, slow, strange voice: ' Know, my son, that because thou hast long been so devout to me, thou shalt be listened unto. Return hither to-morrow, and thou wilt be answered ; and now go in peace.'

" And the shoemaker, having heard this, verily believed that Saint John had spoken to him, and went his way with great

rejoicing. So, bright and early the next morning, he was in the church, and said: 'Saint John, I await thy reply.'

" Then the mass-boy, who was hidden as before, replied: ' Oh, my son, I am sorry to say that thy wife is no better than she should be— ha fatto fallo con piu d'uno — and everybody in Florence except thee knows it.'

" 'And my son ? ' gasped the shoemaker.

" ' He will be hung,' replied the voice.

" The shoemaker rose and departed abruptly. In the middle of the church he paused, and, without a sign of the cross, and putting on his cap, he cried: ' What sort of a Saint John are you, anyhow?'

" ' Saint John the Baptist,' replied the voice.

" ' Sia col malanno e con la mala Pasque die Iddio ti dia ! —• Then may the Lord give you a bad year and a miserable Easter-tide! You never utter aught save evil, and it was for thy evil tongue that Herod cut thy head off—and served thee right! I do not believe a word of all which thou hast told me. I have been coming here every day for twenty-five years, and never asked thee for anything before; but I will make one more vow to thee, and that is—never to see thy face again.'

"And when Messer Cosimo had ended, Piovano Arlotto replied:

" ' One good turn deserves another. It is not many years ago since a poor farsettajo, or doublet-maker, lived in Florence, his shop being close to the Oratorio di Orto San Michele,[1] and every morning he went to worship in the church, and lit a candle before a picture representing Christ as a child disputing with the Doctors, while his mother enters seeking him.

"' And after he had done this daily for more than twenty-five years, it happened that his little son, while looking on at a game of ball, had a tile fall on his head, which wounded him terribly. The doctors being called in, despaired.

" ' The next morning the poor tailor went to his devotions in Or' San Michele, bearing this time, instead of a farthing taper, a great wax-candle; and kneeling, he spoke thus: "Dolce Signor mio Gesii Cristo^ I beg thee to restore my son to health. Thou knowest that I have worshipped thee here for twenty-five years, and never asked for anything before, and thou thyself can best bear witness to it. This my son is all my happiness on earth, and he was also most devoted to thee.

[1] The reader may observe that these popular names of Oratorio and Orto are most likely to have given the prefix Or'.

Should he be taken away, I would die in despair, and so I commend myself to thee!"

"'Then he departed, and coming home, learned that his son had died.

"'The next morning, in grief and anger, he entered Orto San Michele, and, without any candle, he went directly to the picture, and, without kneeling, broke forth in these words: "Jo ti disgrazio — I dislike, disown, and despise thee, and will return here no more. Five-and-twenty years have I worshipped thee, and never asked for anything before, and now thou dost refuse me my request. If I had only gone to the great crucifix there, I daresay I should have got all I wanted; but this is what comes of trusting to a mere child, for, as the proverb says, Chi Jimpaccia con fanciulli, con fanciulli si ritrova —he who troubles himself with children will himself be treated as a child.'"

It is worth remarking, as regards the tone and character of this tale, that such freedom was commonest when people were most devout. The most sceptical critics generally agree that these stories of Piovano Arlotto are authentic, having been dictated by him, and that he had a very exceptional character in his age for morality, honesty, and truth. He himself declared, without being contradicted, that he was the only priest of whom he knew who did not keep a mistress; and yet this story is simply an average specimen of the two hundred connected with his name, and that they in turn are identical in character with all the popular wit and humour of the time.

Regarding the image of the Holy Blacksmith, Saint Eiigius or Eloi, the authors of "Walks in Florence" say that it is attributed to Nanni di Banco, and is meagre and stiff, but has dignity, which accords admirably with the character of most saints, or their ideals. It is evident that the bon roi Dagobert was considered as the type of all that was free and easy—

"Le bon roi Dagobert Mcttait son culotte a l'envers."

Therefore he is contrasted with the very dignified Saint Eloy, who was (like the breeches) quite the reverse, declining to lend the monarch two sous, which Dagobert had ascertained were in the holy man's possession. "The bas-relief below," continue the critics cited, "is more certainly by the hand of Nanni. It records a miracle of Saint Eloy, who one day, when shoeing a restive horse which was possessed by a demon, and was kicking and plunging, cut off the animal's leg to fasten the shoe, and having completed his task, made the sign of the cross and restored the severed limb." I regret to say that this was written without careful reference to the original. It was not the leg of the horse which was severed, nor a limb, but only the hoof at the pastern joint.

There is yet another explanation of this bas-relief, which I have somewhere read, but cannot now recall— more's the pity, because it is the true one, as I remember, and one accounting for the presence of the female saint who is standing by, evidently invisibly. Perhaps some reader who knows Number Four will send it to me for a next edition.

It is worth noting that there is in Innsbruck, on the left bank of the Inn, a blacksmith's shop, on the front of which is a very interesting bas-relief of the fourteenth or fifteenth century, representing Saint Peter or Eligius with the horse in a smithy.

There is another statue on the exterior of this church, that of Saint Philip, by the sculptor Nanni de Banco, concerning which and whom I find an anecdote in the Facetie Diverse, A.D. 1636:

"Now, it befell in adorning the church of Or' San Michele in Florence, that *I Consoli d'Arte* (Art Directors of Florence) wanting a certain statue, wished to have it executed by Donatello, a most excellent sculptor; but as he asked fifty scudi, which was indeed a very moderate price for such statues as he made, they, thinking it too dear, refused him, and gave it to a sculptor *mediocre e mulo* —indifferent and mongrel—who had been a pupil of Donatello; nor did they ask him the price, supposing it would be, of course, less. Who, having done his best, asked for the work eighty scudi. Then the Directors in anger explained to him that Donatello, a first-class sculptor, had only asked fifty; but as he refused to abate a single quattrino, saying that he would rather keep the statue, the question was referred to Donatello himself, who at once said they should pay the man seventy scudi. But when they reminded him that he himself had only asked fifty, he very courteously replied, ' Certainly, and being a master of the art, I should have executed it in less than a month, but that poor fellow, who was hardly fit to be my pupil, has been more than half a year making it.'

" By which shrewd argument he not only reproached them for their meanness and his rival for incapacity, but also vindicated himself as an artist."

This is the story as popularly known. In it Nanni is called Giovanni, and it is not true that he was an unworthy, inferior sculptor, for he was truly great. There is another legend of Or' San Michele, which is thus given by Pascarel, who, however, like most writers on Florence, is so extravagantly splendid or "gushing " in his description of everything, that untravelled readers who peruse his pages in good faith must needs believe that in every church and palazzo there is a degree of picturesque magnificence, compared to which the Pandemonium of Milton, or even the Celestial City itself as seen by Saint John, is a mere cheap Dissenting chapel. According to him, Or' San Michele is by right " a world's wonder, and a gift so perfect to the whole world, that, passing it, one should need say (or be compelled to pronounce) a prayer for Taddeo's soul." Which is like the dentist in Paris, who proclaimed in 1847 that it was—

" Presque une crime De ne pas crier, ' Vive Fattet!"

The legend, as told by this writer, and cited by Hare,

is as follows:

i

"Surely nowhere in the world is the rugged, changeless, mountain force of hewn stone piled against the sky, and the luxuriant, dream-like poetic delicacy of stone carven and shaped into leafage and loveliness, more perfectly blended and made one than where San Michele rises out of the dim, many-coloured, twisting streets, in its mass of ebon darkness and of silvery light.

" The other day, under the walls of it, I stood and looked at its Saint George, where he leans upon his shield, so calm, so young, with his bared head and his quiet eyes.

" ' That is our Donatello's,' said a Florentine beside me— a man of the people, who drove a horse for hire in the public ways, and who paused, cracking his whip, to tell this tale to me. ' Donatello did that, and it killed him. Do you not know ? When he had done that Saint George he showed it to his master. And the master said, " It wants one thing only." Now this saying our Donatello took gravely to heart, chiefly because his master would never explain where the fault lay; and so much did it hurt him, that he fell ill of it, and came nigh to death. Then he called his master to him. " Dear and great one, do tell me before I die," he said, "what is the one thing my statue lacks ? " The master smiled and said : " Only speech." " Then I die happy," said our Donatello. And he— died—indeed, that hour.'

" Now I cannot say that the pretty story is true—it is not in the least true; Donatello died when he was eighty-three, in the Street of the Melon, and it was he himself who cried, ' Speak then—speak !' to his statue, as it was carried through the city. But whether true or false, this fact is surely true, that it is well—nobly and purely well—with a people when the men amongst it who ply for hire on its public ways think caressingly of a sculptor dead five hundred years ago, and tell such a tale, standing idly in the noonday sun, feeling the beauty and the pathos of it all."

Truly, in a town half of whose income is derived from art-hunting tourists, and where every vagabond offers himself, in consequence, as a cicerone, it is no sign that "all is well —

nobly and purely well—with a people," because a coachman who had been asked which was Donatello's Saint George by about five hundred English " fares," and nearly as many American young ladies—of
whom many of the latter told him all they knew about it —should have picked up such a tale. In fact, while I have been amazed at the incredible amount of legend, superstitious traditions, and incantations existing among the people, I have been struck by their great ignorance of art, and all pertaining to it; of which, were it worth while, I could cite convincing and amusing instances.

" But as regards a vast proportion of the ' sweet and light' writing on the Renaissance and on Italy which is at present fashionable," writes Flaxius, " I am reminded of the ' esthetic axe'ems' of an American writer, the first of which were :

"' Art is a big thing. Always bust into teers wen you see a pictur.'

" ' Bildins and churches arn't of no account unless they drive you clean out of your census.' "

THE WITCH OF THE ARNO

" Il spirito usci dal fiume a un iratto, E venne come Dio l'aveva fatto, E presentando come un cortegiano Alia donna gentil la destra mano, ' Scusate,' disse si io vengo avanti E se vi do la mano sensa guanti."— Paranti.

THE following, as a French book of fables says, is "a poem, or rather prose rhymed : "

" Two pretty maids one morning sat by the rushing stream. It murmured glittering in the sun; it seemed to sing as on it run, enchanting while a wantoning, as in a merry dream.

" Said one unto the other : ' I wish, and all in truth, that the glorious dancing river were as fine and brave a youth. Its voice is like an angel's, its drops of light like eyes so bright are beautiful I wis. Oh, ne'er before, on sea or shore, did I love aught like this.'

" A voice came from the river: ' For a love thou hast chosen me; henceforward, sweet, for ever thine own love I will be. Wherever there is water, of Florence the fairest daughter, by night or day or far away, thou'lt find me close by thee.'

"She saw bright eyes a shining in dewdrops on her path —she returned unto the palace, she entered in a bath. ' How the water doth caress me; 'tis embracing me, I vow! M'abbraria, mi baccia —my lover has me now. Since fate has really willed it, then to my fate I bow.'

"Seven years have come and vanished, seven years of perfect bliss. Whenever she washed in water, she felt her lover's kiss. She washed full oft, I ween; 'twas plain to be seen there was no maid in Florence who kept herself so clean.

" Little by little, as summer makes frogs croak in a ditch, there spread about a rumour that the damsel was a witch. They showed her scanty mercies; with cruelty extreme, with
blows and bitter curses, they cast her in the stream. ' If she
be innocent, she'll sink, so hurl her from the Arno's brink; if guilty, she will swim !'

" Up rose from the sparkling river a youth who was fair to see. ' I have loved thee, and for ever thine own I'll truly be.' He took her in his arms; she felt no more alarms. ' Farewell to you all!' sang she; ' a fish cannot drown in the water ; now I am a fish, you know—the Arno's loving daughter. Per sempre addio !' :

The foregoing is not literal, nor do I know that it is strictly " traditional;" it is a mere short tale or anecdote which I met with, and put into irregular metre to suit the sound of a rushing stream. I take the liberty of adding to it another water-poem of my own, which has become, if not " popular," at least a halfpenny broadside sold at divers street-stands by old women, the history whereof is as follows:—I had written several ballads in Italian in imitation of the simplest old-fashioned lyrics, and was anxious to know if I had really succeeded in coming down to the level of the people, for this is a very difficult thing to do in any language. When I showed them to Marietta Pery, she expressed it as her candid opinion that they were really very nice indeed, and that I ought for once in my life to come before the public as a poet. And as I, fired by literary ambition, at last consented to appear in this role, Marietta took a ballad, and going to E. Ducci, 32 Via Pilastri, who is the Cat-nach of Florence (I advise collectors of the really curious to buy his soldo publications), made an arrangement whereby my song should appear as a broadside, the lady strictly conditioning that from among his blocks Signore Ducci should find a ship and a flying bird to grace the head and the end of the lyric. But as he had no bird, she took great credit to herself that for five francs she not only got a hundred copies, but also had specially engraved for the work and inserted an object which appears as flying to the right hand of the ship. The song was as follows:

LA BELLA STREGA. Nuova Canzonetta di CHARLES GODFREY LELAND.
Era una bella Strega Che si bagnava alia riva; Vennero i pirati Lei presero captiva.
Il vento era in poppa Sull' onde la nave ballo La donna lacrimante Al capitan parlo.
" O Signer capitano ! O Capitano del mar ! Darb cento ducati, Se tu mi lasci andar."
" Non prendero cento ducati,
Tu costi molto piii
Io ti vendro al Sultano,"
Disse il Capitano,
" Per mille zecchini d'oro
Vi stimi troppo giu."
" Non vuoi i cento ducati Ebben tu non gli avrai, Ho un' amante amato Non mi abbandona mai."

Essa sede sul ponte Principio a cantar, " Vieni il mio amante," Da lontano il vento Si mette a mugghiar.

Forte e piu forte
La tempesta ruggio,
Gridava il capitano:
" Io credo che il tuo amante
E il vento che corre innante,
Ovvero il diavolo."

THE WITCH OF THE ARNO
Forte e piu forte
La procella urlb,
" Sono rocce davanti,
E il vento vien di dietro
Benvenuto sei tu mio amante ! "
La bella donna canto.

" Vattene al tuo amante All' inferno a cantar! " Disse il Capitano E getto la donna Tuori, Delia nave nel mar.

Ma come un gabbiano Sull' onde essa void. " O mio Capitano, Non sarai appiccato, Ma sarai annegato : Per sempre addio !"

THE BEAUTIFUL WITCH.

A pretty witch was bathing In the sea one summer day; There came a ship with pirates, Who carried her away.

The ship due course was keeping On the waves as they rose and broke ; The lovely lady, weeping, Thus to the captain spoke :

" O Signor Capitano !

0 captain of the sea !

I'll give you a hundred ducats If you will set me free."

" I will not take a hundred,

You're worth much more, you know ;

1 will sell you to the Sultan For a hundred gold sequins ; You set yourself far too low."

" You will not take a hundred— Oh well! then let them be, But I have a faithful lover, Who, as you may discover, Will never abandon me."

Upon the windlass sitting, The lady began to sing : " Oh, come to me. my lover ! " From afar a breeze just rising In the rigging began to ring.

Louder and ever louder

The wind began to blow:

Said the captain, " I think your lover

Is the squall which is coming over,

Or the devil who has us in tow."

Stronger and ever stronger

The tempest roared and rang,

"There are rocks ahead and the wind dead aft,

Thank you, my love," the lady laughed;

And loud to the wind she sang.

" Oh, go with your cursed lover, To the devil to sing for me !" Thus cried the angry rover,

And threw the lady over Into the raging sea.
But changing to a seagull,
Over the waves she flew :
" Oh captain, captain mine," sung she,
" You will not swing on the gallows-tree,
For you shall drown in the foaming sea—
Oh captain, for ever adieu ! "

I must in honesty admit that this my debut as an Italian poet was not noticed in any of the reviews— possibly because I did not send it to them—and there were no indications that anybody considered that a new Dante had arisen in the land. It is true, as Marietta told me with much delight, that the printer, or his foreman, had declared it was a very good song indeed; but then he was an interested party. And Marietta also kindly praised it to the skies (after she had corrected it) ; but then Marietta was herself a far better poet than I can ever hope to be, and could afford to be generous.

The reader will pardon me if I avail myself of the opportunity to give another Italian ballad which I wrote on a theme which I also picked up in Florence.

IL GIARDINO D'AMORE, o LA FIGLIA DEL RE, E IL CONTINO STREGONE.

Era un giovine Contino, Di tutto il paese il fior, Aveva un bel giardino, II bel giardin d'amor.

" Chi batte alia mia porta ? " Domanda il bel Contin'. " Son la figlia del re, Vo vedere il tuo giardin' ?"

" Entra pur nel mio giardino,
0 bella figlia del re, Purche tu non tocchi niente, A cio che dentro v'e !"

Entrata nel giardino, La bella figlia del re, Non vidde cola niente, Che fiori e foglie.

Le foglie eran d'argento, Di oro ogni fior,
1 frutti eran' gemmi, Nel bel giardin d'amor.

Sedi sulla panchetta, Sotto il frascame la ; Che vissi nel sentiero ? Un bell' anello c'era.

Non seppe che il Contino, Fu stregone appostator; Non seppe che 1'anello, Era lo stesso signer.

Ella ando nel suo letto, Con 1'anello nella man', Non 'n sospetto che la trasse Sul dito un giovan.

Svegliato da un bacino, Tra la mezzanotte e tre; Si trovb il bel Contino Accanto alia figlia del re.

Credo che fu ben contenta Con la cosa come era; Come molte donne sarebbero Con tal stregoneria.

Portar dei gioielli, A de' sposi il fior; II di un di-amante, La notte un bel signor,

D'avere un bel diamante Piace ognuno, si; Ma meglio e un amante Quando non ha piu il di.

Chi scrisse questa canzone Un gran Contino e, Anch 'egli il stregone Ch' amava la figlia del re.

THE GARDEN OF LOVE, OR THE KING'S DAUGHTER AND THE WIZARD COUNT.

There was a Count of high degree, All others far above; He had a garden fair to see, 'Twas called the Garden of Love.

" Now who is knocking at my gate ? Who is it that makes so free ? " " Oh, I am the daughter of the king, And your garden I would see !"

"Oh, come into my garden, Fair daughter of the king ! Look well at all that's growing, But touch not anything ! "

She entered in the garden, The princess young and fair, She looked it all well over, Yet nothing but trees were there.

But every leaf was of silver, The flowers of gold; in the grove The fruits were gems and jewels In the beautiful Garden of Love.

She sat beneath the foliage, The daughter of the king; What shone in the path before her ? A beautiful diamond ring !

She knew not that the County Was a wizard wondrous wise ; She did not know that the diamond Was the wizard in disguise.

And when at night, fast sleeping, The diamond ring she wore, She never dreamed that her finger Was bearing a young signer.

Awakened by his kisses As she heard the midnight ring, There was the handsome wizard By the daughter of the king.

I ween she was well contented, As many dames would be, If they could be enchanted With just such sorcery.

To have not only a jewel, But a husband, which is more, All day a dazzling diamond, And by night a bright signor!

Who was it wrote this ballad About this loving pair? He was the Count and wizard Who won the princess fair.

STORIES OF SAN MINIATO

" The picturesque height of San Miniato, now the great cemetery of the city, which dominates the Arno from the south, has an especial religious and saintly interest. The grand Basilica, with its glittering ancient mosaic, shines amid the cypresses against the sky, and whether it gleams in the sunlight against the blue, or is cut in black on the primrose sky of twilight, it is equally imposing."— "Echoes of Old Florence" by LEADER SCOTT.

To the old people of Florence, who still see visions and dream dreams, and behold the wind and the stars at noonday (which latter thing I have myself beheld), the very ancient convent of San Miniato, " the only one in Tuscany which has preserved the ancient form of the Roman basilica," and the neighbourhood, are still a kind of Sleepy Hollow, where witches fly of nights more than elsewhere, where ghosts or folletti are most commonly seen, and where the orco and the nightmare and her whole ninefold disturb slumbers a bel agio at their easiest ease, as appears by the following narrative:

SAN MINIATO FRA LE TORRE.

"This is a place which not long ago was surrounded by towers, which were inhabited by many witches.

" Those who lived in the place often noticed by night in those towers, serpents, cats, small owls, and similar creatures, and they were alarmed by frequently seeing their infants die like candles blown out— struggere i bambini come candele ; nor could they understand it ; but those who believed in witchcraft, seeking in the children's beds, often found threads woven together in forms like animals or garlands, and when mothers had left their children alone with the doors open, found their infants, on returning, in the fireplace under the ashes. And at such times there was always found a strange cat in the room.

"And believing the cat to be a witch, they took it, and first tying the two hind-paws, cut off the fore-claws (zampe, claws or paws), and said:

"' Fammi guarire La mia creatura ; Altrimenti per te saranno Pene e guai!'

"'Cure my child, Or there shall be Trouble and sorrow Enough for thee !'

"This happened once, and the next day the mother was sitting out of doors with her child, when she saw a woman who was her intimate friend at her window, and asked her if she would not wash for her her child's clothes, since she herself was ill. But the other replied : ' I cannot, for I have my hands badly cut.'

"Then the mother in a rage told this to other women whose children had been bewitched or died.

"Then all together seized the witch, and by beating her, aided with knives crossed, and whatever injuries they could think of, subdued her and drenched her under a tower with holy water. And the witch began to howl, not being able to endure this, and least of all the holy water!

" When all at once there came a mighty wind, which blew down the witch-tower, and carried away the witch, and killed all the uncanny animals which dwelt in the ruins. And unbelievers say that this was done by an earthquake; but this is not true, for the witches were really the cause (chagione) of its overthrow.

"And though many old things are destroyed and rebuilt, there are many cats still there which are assuredly witches.

" And in the houses thereabout people often perceive and see spirits, and if any one will go at night in the Piazza San Miniato fra le Torri, especially where those old things (chose vecche) were cleared away, he will see sparks of fire (faville di fuocho) break out, and then flames; and this signifies that some diabolical creature or animal is still confined there which needs relief (che a bisogna di bene), or that in that spot lies a treasure which requires to be discovered."

I consider this as very interesting, because I most truthfully guarantee that this specimen of witch-lore was written in good faith and firm belief, and is not at all, like most of the tales gleaned or gathered now-a-days, taken from people who got them from others who perhaps only half believed in them. She who wrote it has no more doubt that witch-cats prowl, and that wildfire hisses forth from evil spirits in durance pent 'neath the soil of San Miniato, than that the spirit of the Arno appears as " a small white hand pointing tremulously upwards."

There is given in the Facetice of Piovano Arlotto, which is considered a truthful record of the adventures of its subject, a tale relative to San Miniato which cannot here be deemed out of place. It is as follows:

LA TESTA DI SAN MINIATO.

"There was in Florence a poor and learned gentleman— savio e da bene, who was a good friend of Piovano Arlotto, who was also good to him, since he had often aided the former with money, meal, and many other things, and indeed without such help he could hardly have fed his family ; for he had fourteen sons and daughters, and though the proverb says Figliuoli, mioli, 'lenzuoli non sono mat troppi in una casa — there are never too many children, glasses, or linen sheets in a house, this good man found indeed that he had too many of the former.

" Now to help dire need, this gentleman tried to buy on credit two bales of cloth, one wherewith to clothe his family, and the other to sell in order to make some money. To do this, he needed some one to be his security, and he had recourse to Piovano Arlotto, who willingly agreed to pay the manufacturer in case the friend who gave his note could not meet it. Now he found that the manufacturer had sadly cheated the purchaser in the measure or quantity, fully one-half, as was also evident to many others ; however, as matters stood, he was obliged to let it pass.

" As things were thus, the poor gentleman died and passed away from this misera vita or sad life, and Piovano was in deep grief for his loss, and as much for the poor orphans.

"When the note fell due, the manufacturer went to Piovano Arlotto and asked for his money, saying that he only demanded what was justly due to him.

"And after a few days' delay, he paid the man two-thirds of the sum, and ten florins for the time and trouble, and said he would not give a farthing more. Then the dealer begun to dun him, but he evaded every demand. Then the merchant employed a young man, eighteen years of age, who had not his equal in Florence to collect debts. And this youth set to work in earnest to get from the priest the sum of about twenty-eight gold florins, still due from the account.

" In a few days he had attacked Piovano a hundred times with the utmost impudence, in the market, in the public squares, on the streets at home, and in the church, without regard to persons present, at all times, and in every aggravating way, until the priest conceived a mortal hatred of the dun, and turned over in his head many ways to get rid of him.

"At last he went one day to the Abbot of San Miniato or Monte, and said to him: ' Padre reverendo, I seek your paternal kindness to relieve a very distressing case in which I am concerned. I have a nephew who is possessed by the devil, one into whom an evil spirit has entered, and who has a monomania that I owe him money, and is always crying to me everywhere, 'When are you going to pay me? I want twenty-eight florins.' J Tis a great pity, for he is a fine young man, and something really ought to be done to cure him. Now I know that the holy relic which you possess, the worthy head of the glorious and gracious San Miniato, has such a virtue, that, if it be once placed on the head of this poor youth, 'twill certainly cure him. Would you so contrive, in any way, to put it on him some time this week ?'

"The Abbot answered, 'Bring him when you will.'

" Piovano thanked him and said: ' I will bring him on Saturday, but when he shall be here, I pray you be at the gate with seven or eight strong men, that he may not escape; for you know, holy father, that these demoniacs are accustomed to rage when they see relics and hear prayers, and it will be specially so with this poor youth, who is young and vigorous—yea, it may be that 'twill be necessary to give him sundry cuffs and kicks, so terrible is the power of Satan—

lupus esuriens. Do so, I pray, without fearing to hurt my feelings—nay, it would be a great pleasure to me, so heartily do I desire to see him cured.'

" The Abbot answered, ' Bring him here, my son, and I will see that all is rightly done.'

"Piovano returned, saying to himself:

"' Chi vuol giusta vendetta, In Dio la metta.'

"' Leave vengeance to the Lord, or to his ministers— videlicet^ the monks of San Miniato. Which I will do.'

"On Friday he went to the merchant who had sold the cloth, and said : ' As for this which I owe you, it is all rubbish. You cheated the man who gave you the note out of half the cloth—you know it, and I can prove it. However, to avoid further trouble and litigation, I am willing to pay all, but you must allow time for it. Dura cosa e Paspettare —'tis hard to wait, but harder still to have nothing to wait for. The monks of San Miniato owe me for forty cords of wood, which is to be paid for at the end of two years, and then you shall have your money.'

"This sounded like 'for ever and a day' to the creditor, and in a rage he had recourse to his collector, who on Saturday morning went to San Miniato. When he arrived, he had to wait till the grand mass was over, to the great vexation of the young man, and meanwhile eight powerful monks with long staves had grouped themselves about the door, awaiting a little healthy exercise.

"And mass being over, the dun hastened up to the Abbot, who, taking him by the hand, said: 'Oh, my son, put thy trust in God and in San Miniato the blessed; pray that he may take this evil conceit from thy head,' and with this much more, till the young man grew impatient and said:

"'Messer Abbot, to-day is Saturday, and no time for sermons. I have come to know what you are going to do about this debt of Piovano of twenty-eight florins, and when it will be paid?'

"Then the Abbot, hearing, as he expected, the demand for money, began to exhort and exorcise. And the youth began to abuse the Abbot with all kind of villanies, and finally turned to depart; but the Abbot caught him by the cloak, and there was a fight. Then came the eight monks, who seizing him, chastised him lustily, and bound him with cords, and

K

bearing him into the sacristy, sprinkled him with holy water, and incensed him indeed—and then set the holy head of San Miniato on his head—he thinking they were all mad as hatters. Then they exorcised the evil spirits in him — 'Maledicti! excommunicati et rebelles — sitis in pixna czternali nulla requies sit in vo-o-o-bis si statim non eritis obedientes, præceptis me-e-e-e-is!' — until the youth had to give in, and beg the Abbot's pardon, and being released, fled as for dear life.

"But he met outside Piovano Arlotto, who said to him: 'Thou hast had a dainty drubbing, my son, but there is plenty more where that came from— non v'e nefin, nefondo —there is neither end nor bottom to it. Now go to thy master, and say that if he goes further in this business he will fare worse than thou hast done.'

"The youth, returning to Florence, told the tale to his employer, and how Piovano Arlotto had declared if they dunned him any more he would do his best to have them drubbed to death. So they dropped the matter—like a hot shot.

"Everybody in Florence roared with laughter for seven days— sparsa la piacevolezza per Firenze, vi fu che ridere per setti giorni —that is to say, everybody laughed except one clothmaker and his collector, and if they smiled, 'twas sour and bitterly—the smile which does not rise above the throat— the merriment like German mourning grim. And as for the young man, he had to leave Florence, for all of whom he would collect money told him to go to—the monks of San Miniato!"

There was a curious custom, from which came a proverb, in reference to this monastery, which is thus narrated in that singular work, La Zucca del Doni Fiorentino ("The Pumpkin of Doni the Florentine"):

"There is a saying, E non terrebbe tin cocomere afterta —He could not catch a cucumber if thrown to him. Well, ye must know, my masters and gallant signers, that our Florentine youth in the season of cucumbers go to San Miniato, where there is a steep declivity, and when there, those who are above toss or roll them down to those below, while those below throw them up to those above, just as people play at toss-and-pitching oranges with girls at windows. So they keep it up, and it is considered a great shame and sign of feeble-ness (dapocaggine) not to be able to catch; and so in declining the company of a duffer one says: 'I'll have nothing to do with him—he isn't able to catch a cucumber.'

"It is one of the popular legends of this place that a certain painter named Gallo di San Miniato was a terribly severe critic of the works of others, but was very considerate as regarded his own. And having this cast at him one day, and being asked how it was, he frankly replied: 'I have but two eyes wherewith to see my own pictures, but I look at those of others with the hundred of Argus."

And indeed, as I record this, I cannot but think of a certain famous critic who is so vain and captious that one must needs say that his head, like a butterfly's, is all full of little z's.

" And this tale of two optics reminds me of the story of Messer Gismondo della Stufa, a Florentine of Miniato, who once said to some friends: ' If I had devoted myself to letters, I should have been twice as learned as others, and yet ye cannot tell why.' Then some guessed it would have been due to a good memory, while others suggested genius, but Messer Gismondo said: ' You are not there yet, my children; it is because I am so confoundedly cross-eyed that I could have read in two books at once."

In the first legend which I narrated, the fall of the tower is attributed to witchcraft or evil spirits. In the very ancient frescoes of San Miniato there is one in which the devil causes a wall or tower to fall down and crush a young monk. What confirms the legend, or its antiquity, is that the original bell-tower of San Miniato actually fell down in 1499. The other then built was saved from a similar fate by the genius of Michael Angelo Buonarotti, who built a bank of earth to support it.

" Hcec fabula of the head of San Miniato," wrote the immortal Flaxius on the proof, " teaches that he who would get round a priest in small trickery must arise uncommonly early—nay, in most cases 'twould be as well not to go to bed at all—especially when dunning is 'on the tap.' Con-

cerning which word dun it is erroneously believed in England to have been derived from the name of a certain Joseph Dunn, who was an indefatigable collecting bailiff. But in very truth 'tis from the Italian dotiare, to give oneself up to anything with ardour—to stick to it; in accordance with which, donar guanto, or to give the glove, means to promise to pay or give security. And if any philologist differs from me in opinion as to this, why then— let him diff! Which magnanimously sounding conclusion, when translated according to the spirit of most who utter it, generally means :

" Let him be maledict, excommunicate, and damnated ad inferos — in stzcula sceculornm ! —twice over ! "

THE FRIAR'S HEAD OF SANTA MARIA MAG-GIORE—THE LADY WHO CONFESSED FOR EVERYBODY—HOLY RELICS

" He who speaks from a window or a pulpit, or the top of a good name or any high place, should speak wisely, if he speak at all, unto those who pass."

THE Church of Santa Maria Maggiore " remounts," as the Italians say, or can be traced back to 700 A.D., but it was enlarged and renewed by the architect Bueno in the twelfth century, and according to Pitre it was the germ of a new style of architecture which we find much refined (ringentilata) in Santa Maria del Fiore. "There were, regarding its bell-tower, which no longer exists, many tales and curious anecdotes, which might form a part of a fine collection of local legends." There is still to-day on the wall above the little side-door facing the Via de' Conti, a much worn head of stone, coming out of a round cornice, which is in all probability the one referred to in the following legend:

" There was once a condemned criminal being carried along to execution, and on the way passed before the Church of Santa Maria Maggiore. One of the friars put his head out of a little round window, which was just large enough for it to pass through, and this was over the entrance on the lesser side of the church, facing the Via de' Conti. As the condemned passed by the friar said :

" ' Date gli da here, 'un morira mai.'

"'Give him a drink and he never will die.'

"To which the condemned replied:

"'E la testa di costi tu 1 un la levrai'. "'And thy head shall stick where it is for aye.' 149

"And so it came to pass that they could not get the head of the friar back through the hole, so there he died. And some say that after they got the body out they carried his likeness in stone and put it there in the little round window, in remembrance of the event, while others think that it is the friar himself turned to stone— chi sa?"

The conception of a stone head having been that of a person petrified for punishment is of the kind which would spring up anywhere, quite independently of tradition or borrowing; hence it is found the world over. That ideas of the kind may be common, yet not in common, nor yet uncommon, is shown by the resemblance of the remark of the friar:

"Give him a drink and he never will die,"—

which was as much as to say that inebriation would cause him to forget his execution—to a verse of a song in "JackSheppard":

"For nothing so calms, Our dolorous qualms,

And nothing the transit to Tyburn beguiles, So well as a drink from the bowl of Saint Giles."

There is a merrier tale, however, of Santa Maria Maggiore, and one which is certainly far more likely to have occurred than this of the petrified pater. For it is told in the ancient Facetice that a certain Florentine nobleman, who was a jolly and reckless cavalier, had a wife who, for all her beauty, was bisbetica e cattiva, capricious and spiteful, malicious and mischievous, a daughter of the devil, if there ever was one, who, like all those of her kind, was very devout, and went every day to confession in Santa Maria Maggiore, where she confessed not only her own sins, but also those of all her neighbours. And as she dwelt with vast eloquence on the great wickedness of her husband—having a tongue which would serve to sweep out an oven, or even a worse place 1 —the priest

1 Ha tanta lingua che spazzarebbe un fotno, b nn cesso. Said of virulent gossips.

one day urged the husband to come to confession, thinking that it might lead to more harmony between the married couple. With which he complied; but when the priest asked him to tell what sins he had committed, the cavalier answered, "There is no need of it, Padre; you have heard them all from my wife many a time and oft, and with them a hundred times as many which I never dreamed of committing—including those of all Florence." It was in the first Church of Santa Maria Maggiore, which stood on the site of the present, that San Zenobio in the fourth century had walled into the high altar an inestimable gift which he had received from the Pope. This was "the two bodies of the glorious martyrs Abdon and Sennen, who had been thrown unto wild beasts, which would not touch them, whereupon they were put to death by swords in the hands of viler human beasts." I may remark by the way, adds the observant Flaxius, that relics have of late somewhat lost their value in Florence. I saw not long ago for sale a very large silver casket, stuffed full of the remains of the holiest saints, and the certificates of their authenticity, and I was offered the whole for the value of the silver in the casket—the relics being generously thrown in! And truly the mass of old bones, clay, splinters, nails, rags with blood, bits of wood, dried-up eyes, et cetera, was precisely like the Voodoo-box or conjuring bag of an old darkey in the United States. But then the latter was heathen! "That is a very different matter."

BI AN CONE, THE GIANT STATUE IN THE SIGNORIA

"Fons Florentinus. —In foro lympidas aquas fons effundit marmoreis figuris Neptuni et

Faunorum ab Amanate confectis."— Templum Natures Historicum. HENRICI KORNMANNI, A.D. 1614.

THE most striking object in the most remarkable part of Florence is the colossal marble Neptune in the Fountain of the Signoria, by Ammanati, dating from 1575. He stands in a kind of car or box, drawn by horses which Murray declares "are exceedingly spirited." They are indeed more so than he imagined, for according to popular belief, when the spirit seizes them and their driver, and the bronze statues round them, they all go careering off like mad beings over the congenial Arno, and even on to the Mediterranean ! That is to say, that they did so on a time, till they were all petrified with their driver in the instant when they were bounding like the billows, which are typified by white horses.

Neptune has, however, lost his name for the multitude, who simply call him the Biancone, or Great White Man ; and this is the legend (given to me in writing by a witch), by which he is popularly known:

BIANCONE, THE GOD OF THE ARNO.

"Biancone was a great and potent man, held in great respect for his grandeur and manly presence, a being of tremendous strength, and the true type of a magician, 1 he

1 Mago, which, like magus, implies more dignity than magician or sorcerer.

being a wizard indeed. In those days there was much water in the Arno, 1 and Biancone passed over it in his car.

" There was then in the Arno a witch, a beautiful girl, the vera dea or true goddess of the river, in the form of an eel. And Biancone finding this fish every day as he drove forth in his chariot, spurned it away con cattivo garbo —with an ill grace. And one day when he had done this more contemptuously than usual, the eel in a rage declared she would be revenged, and sent to him a smaller eel. But Biancone crushed its head (le stiaccio il chapo\'7d.

" Then the eel appeared with a little branch of olive with berries, and said:

" ' Entro in questa carozza, Dove si trove l'uomo, L'uomo il piii potente, Che da tutti e temuto ; Ed e un uomo grande, E grande, e ben vero ; Ma il gran dio del Arno, II potente Biancone, Non sara il solo potente ; Vi sara una piccola pesce, Una piccola anguilla ; Benche piccola la sia ; Fara vedere la sua potenza Tu Biancone, a mi, Le magie, e siei mezzo stregone

10 una piccola anguillina, Sono una vera fata,

E sono la Fata dell Arno, Tu credevi d'essere

11 solo dio d'Arno, Ma ci, no, io che sono La regina, e la vera, Vera dea qui del Arno.'

" ' Lo, I enter in this chariot!

Where I find the man of power, Who is feared by all before him, And he is a mighty being, Great he is, there's no denying ; But the great god of the Arno, The so powerful Biancone, Is not all alone in power; There's a little fish or eel, who,

1 "The Mugnone, whose course has been shifted to the west, formerly flowed into the Arno through the heart of the city."— Murray's Handbook for Travellers in Central Italy.

Though but little, has the power,
Mighty man, to make thee tremble !
Biancone, thou art only
Unto me as half a wizard ;
I, a little eel of the Arno,
Am the fairy of the river ;
Thou didst deem thyself its ruler ;
I deny it—for I only

Am the queen and the true goddess— The true goddess of the Arno.'

" Having said this, she touched with the twig of olive the little eel whom Biancone had killed, and repeated while touching it:

" 'Anguillina che dal Grande Siei stata stiacciata, Io con questo ramoscello Ti faccio in vita tornare, E al Grande, io, del Arno Tutto il mio pensiero, Tutto posso raccontare.'

" ' I, little eel, who by the mighty Man hast been to death delivered, Do call thee back unto the living ! Wake thee with this twig of olive ! Now unto this Biancone, Thou who art too of the Arno, Shalt speak out thy mind and freely.'

"Then the little eel, resuscitated and influenced by the goddess of the Arno, said :

" ' Biancone, tu che siei

Il potente dio dell' Arno, L'anguilla discacciata, Che tu ai discacciata,

E di te inamorata, E di te piu potente, E se tu la discaccerai, Ti giura la vendetta, E si vendichera. . . .'

" ' Biancone, Biancone!

Thou great spirit of the Arno, Lo, the eel by thee despised Turns again with love unto thee : She surpasses thee in power ; If she is by thee rejected, She will vow revenge upon thee, And will be avenged truly.'

" Biancone replied :

" ' Io non voglio amar donne, Sia pure d'una bellezza Da fare a cecare, Ma per me non mi fa niente, Non voglio amare donne, Sara per bellezza una Gran persona, ma non vero, Per potenza, per che piu, Piu potente di me non Vi e alcun '

" ' I seek not the love of women. Thou art of a dazzling beauty ; Unto that I am indifferent; I seek not the love of ladies. Thou may'st be full great in beauty, Not in power, for in power I shall ever be the greater.'

" Then the eel arose 1 and said :

" ' Biancone, or guardami, Guarda mi bene perche piu, Non mi vedrai vedermi, E se mi vedrai, Non mi potrai toccare, Dici che piu potente Di te non ce nessuno, Ma sa io la prima, Mia potenza e quella Di vederti inamorato, Di me vere inamorato, Ma che ora sono io, Che ti discaccio per la tua, Al te si guardami mi vedi.'

" ' Biancone, now regard me,

Look well at me now, for never, Wilt thou ever more behold me, Or if thou behold'st me, touch me, And thou say'st that thou hast power, And that none can rival with thee. Thou shall learn that I am stronger, For I've power to make thee love me, But 'tis I who now reject thee, If thou doubtest — now behold me !'

"And then, instead of an eel, appeared a maid of dazzling

1 L'anguilla si rizzo in piedi —"The eel rose upon her feet." This will remind the reader of some of the difficulties experienced by Gothic artists in depicting Eve and the Serpent.

beauty, and Biancone sought to embrace her, but could not, and said:

" ' Contentami una volta

Sola, o dea dell' Arno ;

Lascia che ti abbraci

Una volta sola, o dea.'

" ' For a single time content me, Lovely goddess of the Arno ; Let me but for once embrace thee, Yield to me I pray, O fairy !'

" But the goddess of the Arno replied :

" ' Una donna piu potente Di te, non si lascia Vincere da uno superbo ; Tuo pari mi basta di Far ti vedere, che c'e Persona ancora di te Piu potente . . . Ora io Mi voglio vendi care per che, Tu mi ai discacciata, Tante volte, ed ora invece Tu saresti bene contento Di abbraciarmi anche, Anche or per una volta, Ma no. Addio Biancone !'

"' A woman who has greater power
Than thine will surely not be conquered Merely by pride in outward seeming, But now, in brief, I will content me By proving mine the greater power ; I seek to avenge myself upon thee, Since of old thou didst despise me Many times, but now wouldst gladly, Though it were but for once, embrace me — Farewell for ever, Biancone !'

"And Biancone fled, but he always bore the beautiful goddess in his mind, and could not forget her, so he too meditated a vengeance.

"But the vengeance of a woman strikes more powerfully than that of a man.

"One day when Biancone was passing over the Arno in his chariot, with all his attendants, he thought he saw the eel engaged in forming the basin of a fountain (vasca), and bear it away in a car, she herself being in it, 1 and it was covered

1 There is much confusion here. It appears that the faiiy made the fountain now in the Signoria, and that Biancone saw this in a vision.

with glass; but in the time that he thought (or dreamed) that he saw this, the eel appeared and said :

" ' Il momento della mia vendetta E arrivato, e ti giuro Giuro che la mia vendetta E potente, or Turanna, Mia regina clelle Fate, E dea dell Arno, commanda Che questa carroza sprafondi, E che tu e la tua servitu, Non vi potrete salvare.'

" ' Now the time to wreak my vengeance Has arrived, and I swear thee That my vengeance shall be fearful, Very great, because my sovereign, Turanna, queen of all the fairies, Orders that thy chariot Shall be firmly fixed for ever, And that thou and all thy following Never more canst hope for rescue. 1

" Then she sang again :

" ' Confine i tuoi servitori, Quelli che ti aiut avanno A discacciar sui, o Diventare della forma, Mezze bestie, mezzi uomini, E tu o Biancone, Che tanto grande siei, Ti confino a stare sempre, Sempre ritto e non potrete Mai ragionare, ne camminare Solo quando sara luna, Luna piena, passero io Ti vedro, e mi vedrai, Ma parlarmi non potrai.

" ' Quando sara luna piena, E che sara una notte, Che sara mezza nuvola, E mezza serena s'enderai, Della tua carozza nei, Nei momenti che la Luna Resta sotto le nuvole, E cosi potrei favellare, Con tutte le statue, che ai Attorno, allor tua carozza, E col mio permesso potrai Andare anche dai tuoi amici!'

" ' I hereby compel thy servants, Those who aided thee, to vanish, Or take forms half brute, half human. 1 As for thee, O Biancone ! Thou who art so tall and stately, Thou shall stand erect for ever, Without power to speak or wander, Only when the full moon shining Falls upon thee, I will pass thee, I shall see thee ; thou wilt see me, Without power to address me !

" ' When the moon in full is shining, Yet when clouds begin to gather ; Half in light and half in darkness, Thou may'st only in the moment When the moon is overclouded, Leave thy chariot, and have converse With the statues who are round thee, Then thou may'st, by my permission, Go among thy friends, then only."

I may here explain to the reader that this tale with its elaborate invocations is not current as here given among the people. Such forms and formulas are confined to the witches, who, as in all countries, are the keepers of mysterious traditions. All that is generally heard as regards this subject is, that when the full moon shines on Biancone at midnight, he becomes animated, and walks about the Signoria conversing with the other statues.

The Neptune was, with horses and all, produced by Bartolommeo Ammanati between 1564 and 1565. It has a certain merit of grandeur, but in lesser degree is like its neighbour Cacus, by Baccio Bandinelli, which Benvenuto Cellini justly regarded as resembling a mere bag of fat. When Michael Angelo saw the Neptune he exclaimed : " Ammanato ! Ammanato ! che bel blocco che hai sciupato ! "—"Ammanato, what a fine block of marble thou hast spoiled ! "

The Italians say that the satyr at the corner of the Palazzo Vecchio is a copy, because the original was stolen

1 This refers to the satyrs who are among the bronze figures below Neptune.

one night in January in 1821, "and is now one of the finest bronzes in the British Museum of London." It may be so; there was a great deal of fine stealing in those days. I suspect, however, that the truth is that as these images return to life now and then, the satyr availed himself of his revivification to set forth on his travels, and coming to London and finding good company in the British Museum, settled down there. But truly, when I think of the wanton and heartless destruction of beautiful and valuable old relics which has gone on of late years in Florence, to no earthly purpose, and to no profit whatever, I feel as if all the tales of such things being stolen or sold away to foreign museums were supremely silly, and as if it were all just so much saved from ruin—in case the tales are true.

" Hacfabula docet" wrote Flaxius, " a strange lesson. For as it was anciently forbidden to make images, because it was an imitation of God's work; and secondly, because men believed that spirits would enter into them—even so doth it become all novel-writers, romancers, and poets, to take good heed how they portray satyrs, free-love nymphs, and all such deviltry, because they may be sure that into these models or types there will enter many a youthful soul, who will be led away thereby to madness and ruin. Which is, I take it, the most practical explanation for commandment, which hath been as yet set coram populo."

THE RED GOBLIN OF THE BARGELLO

" Lord Foulis in his castle sat, And beside him old Red-cap sly ; ' Now tell me, thou sprite, who art mickle of might, The death which I shall die ? "

—SCOTT'S Border Minstrelsy.

THE Bargello has been truly described as one of the most interesting historical monuments of Florence, and it is a very picturesque type of a towered mediaeval palace. It was partly burned down in 1322, and rebuilt in its present form by Neri di Fioravanti, after which it served as a prison. Restored, or modernised, it is now a museum. As I conjectured, there was some strange legend connected with it, and this was given to me as follows:

IL FOLLETTO Rosso.

" The Red Goblin is a spirit who haunts the Bargello, or was there of old in the prisons, nolle carceri, and he always foretold to every prisoner what his sentence would be before it was pronounced.

"He always appeared in the cell of the condemned, and first lighting a candle, showed himself all clad in red, and said to the prisoner :

" ' Piangi, piangi, ma piangi forte, E prepararti che e giunta L'ora della tua morte.'

« < Weep, oh weep full many a tear ;

Make ready; thy hour for death is near.'

" Then if the prisoner replied boldly :

" ' Anima chi siei!

Ti prego di volermi aiutare A liberarmi dalla morte !' 160

" 'Spirit, whoe'er thou be, I beg thee now for aid ; From death pray set me free !'

" Then the goblin would burst into a laugh and say :

" ' Non piangere, ridi, ridi! Ma ride sempre, e spera Che io ti aiutera !'

"But if the prisoner had replied badly, or cursed, or said ' Vai al diavolo !' or ' Che il diavolo ti porti !' —then there were heard dreadful sounds, such as frightened all the prisoners and assistants, and the goblin vanished crying :

" 'Woe, woe, and woe to thee ! For thou soon shalt punished be ; Away be led, to lose your head, There is no hope for thee !'

" And after that the man might well despair. Yet the Red Goblin was a jolly sprite when not crossed, and made great sport for the prisoners, who all knew him. He went into every cell, and would tell wild tales, and relate to every one all that he, the prisoner, had done since he was a boy, and how he came to be locked up, and what would be the end of it, and told all this with such peals of laughter that the most unhappy were fain to laugh with him.

"Then the assistants and the director hearing such sounds, thought it was the prisoners rioting, but could not detect them. 1 And the spirit relieved many innocent men from punishment, and especially visited those condemned to wear the iron collar or gogna, which was fastened to a post, but at the Bargello it was on the Campanile outside, in sight of all the people. 2

" Now there was a young man in the prison who was good at heart, and deeply repented that he had done wrong, and now feared that he indeed was in the power of Satan, and destined to be in prison for all this life and in inferno all the next.

" And when he was thus sunk in misery one night, he heard a voice call to him, and was in great alarm, but it said, ' Fear

1 I here omit a long, detailed, and wearisome account of the research, which, however, indicates the accuracy with which the tradition had been preserved, and the full belief in it of the narrator.

2 A kind of cruel pillory.

not, for I am the protecting spirit of the prisoners in the Bar-gello, and have come to free thee; put thy trust in me and I will save thee !'

" Then he told the youth how he was to act, and bade him say certain things when examined, and follow closely all the goblin would whisper to him; but whether it was his fault or his failure, he missed every point and went wrong in his replies, the end being that he was condemned to prison for life. Truly it went to his heart to think that while he lived he should always see the sun looking like a chess-board, 1 and bitterly reflected on the proverb :

" ' Ne a torto ne a ragione,

Non ti lasciar metter prigione.'

" ' Whether you're right or wrong, my man, Keep out of prison as long as you can.'

" But it went most bitterly to his heart to think that he had by his own stupidity and want of study lost the chance of freedom. And for some time the Red Goblin never came near him. But at last the prisoner heard him call, and then the spirit said, ' Now thou see'st to what a pass thy neglect of my advice has brought thee. Truly // diavolo non ti tenterebbe —the devil takes no pains to tempt such a fool as thou, for he knows that he will get him without the trouble of asking. And yet I will give thee one more chance, and this time be thou wide awake and remember that a buona volonth, non manca facoltd —where there's a will there's a way.'

" Now there was a great lord and mighty man of the state who had been in the Bargello, and greatly comforted by the Red Goblin, who now went unto this Signore, speaking so well of the young man that the latter ere long had a new trial. And this time, I warrant you, he studied his case like a lawyer; for asino punto, convien che trotte —when an ass is goaded he must needs trot—and the end thereof was that he trotted out of prison, and thence into the world, and having learned repentance as well as the art of watching his wits and turning them to account, prospered mightily, and to his dying day never forgot to pray for the Red Goblin of the Bargello."

There have been other spirits which haunted prisons; there was one in the Bastile, and the White Ladies of

1 In allusion to seeing it from behind the squares formed by the grates of iron before

prison windows.

Berlin and Parma are of their kind. This of the Bargello is certainly the household sprite with the red cap, in a short shirt, who was very well known to the Etruscans and Romans, and afterwards to the Germans, the Lutin of the French castles, the Robin Goodfellow of England, and the Domovoy of the Russians. His characteristics are reckless good nature mingled with mischief and revenge; but he is always, when not thwarted, at heart a bon gar$on. Of the Bargello I have also the following anecdotes or correlative incidents:

GIORGIO.

" Truly I will not swear that this is a story of the Bargello, for I am very particular as to truth, Signore, but I will swear that 'tis of a prison in Florence, and that when it happened the Bargello was the only prison there. And it runs thus : Giorgio, whoever he was, had killed a man, and as the law ran in his case, in those strange days, he could not be executed till he had confessed or owned the deed. And he would not confess.

" Now there was a lawyer, un notaio, b chi che si fosse (or whoever he was), who declared that he would bring to pass with a trick what justice had not been able to do with torture. So going to the prison, he called for wine, and when they had drunk deep he cried heartily :

" ' Orsti, Giorgio, stiamo un poco allegri t cantiam qualche cosa ' —' Come now, Giorgio, let's be merry and sing something !'

"' Come ti piace' —'As you please,' quoth Master Giorgio. ' You sing one line.'

" So the notary began, touching a lute :

" ' Giorgi ha morto l'huomo.' " ' Giorgio once killed a man.'

" To which Giorgio, who was sharp as a razor, added :

" ' Cos! non canta Giorgio.'

" ' But it was not thus that Giorgio sang.'

"So it passed into a proverb, meaning as much as Cost non dico io — I don't say that; or Cost non Nintendo to —I don't see

it in that light. And so the notary found that you cannot see Verona from the top of every hill.

"And there is another story of a prisoner, who had long curling hair in the old Florentine style. Hair, Signore, like charity, may cover much sin. Now this man, after he had been a while in the Bargello, got his sentence, which was to have his ears cropped off. But when the boia or hangman came to do the job, he found that the man had had his ears cut off smooth long before. Whence came the proverb :

" ' Quel che havea mozzi gli orecchi, E'ci sara de gli arreticati.'

" ' He whose ears had been cut away, Fooled another, or so they say.'

Which is a proverb to this day, when a man finds that somebody has been before him.

" And it may have been that Donatello, the great sculptor, was in the Bargello when he said, ' Erise a me ed io riso a lui' —' He laughs at me, and I do laugh at him.' Donatello was in quistione, or in trouble with the law, and in prison, for having killed one of his pupils. The Marquis di Ferrara asked him if he was guilty. But Donatello had already received from the Marquis a license to slay any one in self-defence, and so he made that answer."

A LEGEND OF THE BARGELLO.

" One day a young man, who had been gaming and lost, threw some dirt at an image of the Virgin in one of the numerous shrines in the city, blaming her for his bad luck. He was observed by a boy, who reported it to the authorities, and was soon arrested. Having confessed that he did it in a rage at having lost, he was hanged the same night from one of the windows of the Bargello." 1

Thereby adding another ghost or folletto to those who already haunt the place. It should be noted that according to Italian witch-lore a ghost is never simply the spirit of the departed as he was, but a spirit transformed. A witch becomes a. fata, good or bad, and all men something more than they were.

1 Landucci, 233, cited by Scaife.

Among other small legends or tales in which the Bar-gello is referred to, I find the following, of which I must first mention that debito in Italian means not only debt but duty, and that fare tin debito is not only to get into debt, but to do what is just, upright, and honourable.

" It happened once, long ago, that a certain good fellow was being escorted, truly not by a guard of honour, but by several bum-bailiffs, to the Bargello, and met a friend who asked him why he was in custody. To which he replied, ' Other men are arrested and punished for crime or villainy, but I am treated thus for having acted honourably, per aver fatto il debito mio.'

" And it happened to this same man that after he had been entertained for a time at the public expense in that gran albergo, or great hotel, the Bargello, that the Council of Eight, or the public magistracy, gave him a hearing, and told him that he must promptly pay the debt which he owed, which was one of fifty scudi or crowns. To which he replied that he could not. Then the chief of the Eight said, ' We will find out a way to make you pay it, be sure of that.' To which he answered, ' De gratia, Sigtwre, while you are about it, then, make it a hundred, for I have great need just now of another fifty crowns.'"

Prisoners in the Bargello, as elsewhere, were subject to the most appalling injustice and cruelty. Thus we are told of Cosimo di Medici, when he was doing all in his power to assassinate or poison Piero Strozzi, that he was always very circumspect as regarded the venom, " and did not use it till he had studied the effects and doses on condemned prisoners in the Bargello." But "condemned prisoners " here means doubtless those who were simply condemned to be made the subjects of such experiments, as may be supposed, when we learn that Cosimo obtained the recipe of making up a poison from Messer Apollino, secretary of Piero Luigi, by torturing him. It was thus they did in good old pious times. Poisoning, as a most familiar and frequent thing, even in England, did not pass

out of practice, even in politics, until that great beginning of a moral era, the Reformation.

" ffac fabula docet" wrote the good and wise Flaxius on the revise, " that as a Zoccolone friar is the best priest for a peasant, so even a buon diavolo, or jolly devil, or a boon blackguard who knows his men, is, perhaps, generally the best guide for certain kinds of rough sinners, often setting them aright in life where a holy saint would be inter sacrem et saxnm, or in despair. As for poisoning, I fear that cup, far from passing away, is, under another form, passed round far more frequently now than it ever was. For Francois Villon declared that lying gossip, tittle-tattle, and second-hand slander were worse than poison (which simply kills the body), and this with infinite refinement prevails far more in modern society (being aided by newspapers) than it ever did of yore anywhere. This is the poison of the present day, which has more veneficcR to spread it than the Locustan or Borgian venoms ever found. Now for a merrier tale ! "

" If all that's written, talked or sunge

Must be of the follies of menne, 'Twere better that no one moved his tongue, Or that none could use a penne.

" J°g on > j°g on the foot path-waye,

And cheerily jump the stile ; A merry heart goes all the daye, A sad one tires in a mile ! "

LEGENDS OF SAN LORENZO

THE CANON AND THE DEBTOR, AND THE CATS IN THE CLOISTER

" Pazienza, paziendum !

Disse il diavolo a Sant Antonium."

" A scratching he heard and a horrible groan,

As of hundreds of cats with mollrowing and moan : ' Oh !' said he to himself, ' sure the devil is come.' "

— Mr, Jones and the Cats.

THE celebrated Church of San Lorenzo is a grand museum of art, even among the many of its kind in Florence. It was originally a Roman Christian basilica, built by the matron Giuliana, which edifice was consecrated A.D. 373 by Saint Ambrose, and called the Basilica Ambrosiana. It was partially rebuilt by Brunel-leschi in 1435, and completed with sad alteration, and finished by Antonio Manetti. As is well known, or has been made known by many great poets, it contains the grandest statuary by Michael Angelo in its monuments of Lorenzo de' Medici and his uncle Giuliano.

This church served as a sanctuary in the olden time, and of this there is a tale told in the old collections of facetiae, which, though trifling, is worth recalling as connected with it.

IL DEBITORE.

" Messer Paolo dell' Ottonaio, a Canon of San Lorenzo in Florence, a cheerful and facetious man, found a certain citizen, one of his friends, who had taken refuge as a debtor in the church; and the latter stood in sorrowful and pensive attitude, having in no wise the appearance of one who had found a treasure, or who was going to be married, or to dine with the Duke, or anything of the kind.

"'Man, what aileth thee?' cried the Canon. 'Has thy wife beaten thee, or the cat broken thy best crockery, or thy favourite housemaid run away?'

" ' What I have,' replied the poor man, ' is ten times worse than all that put together.' And so, havendo caro di sfogarsi, being glad to relieve himself, he told Messer Paolo all his sorrows, wailing that his creditors, having taken all his property, threatened his person, swearing that they would put him in the Stinche, which was so horrible a prison that it was infamous even then all the world over as an inferno where every one confined at once became infermo, or a hell which made men ill, and that, being in despair, he would have taken his own life had he not come across a charming book on patience which had consoled him.

"Messer Paolo asked him whether the creditors had been paid in full.

"'Alas, no!' replied the debtor; 'not one half; nor will they ever get the rest, for I have naught.'

" ' In that case,' answered the Canon, ' it seems to me that it is your creditors and not you who should read that charming book, since it is evident that, as they are to have nothing till the Greek Kalends, or on Saint Never's day, that they must have patience whether they will or no.'

" Well, as the saying is, Pazienza vince scienza (Patience beats knowledge), and Chi ha pazienza vede le sue vendette (Wait long enough and you'll get your revenges), the Canon got for the poor man money enough to make a composition with his creditors, and he, having expectations which they knew not of, compounded with them for five per cent., on conditions written, that he should pay all up ' as he earned more money.'

" And so he was set free, and it befell on a day that some relation died and left him a fortune, whereupon his creditors summoned him to pay his old debts, which he refused to do. Then they cited him before the Council as a fraudulent debtor, but he replied by showing his quittance or agreement, and declared that he was only obliged to pay out of his earnings, and that he had inherited his money and not earned it. Whereupon there was great dispute, and one of the creditors who had shown himself most unfeeling and inhuman protested that to get money in any way whatever was to guadagnare (a gain by labour), since it was labour even to put it in one's

pocket. Now, this man had a handsome wife, who, it was generally known, greatly enriched her husband by dishonouring him, at which he willingly winked.

"Whereupon the debtor asked the magistrate if an ox carried off a bundle of hay on his horns, which had by chance been stuck into it, he could be said to have earned it by honest labour ? At which there was such a roar of laughter, and so many cries of ' No ! no ! no !' that the court went no further, and acquitted the culprit."

There is an odd bit of folklore attached to this church. As may be supposed, and as I have frequently verified, " the idle repetition of vain words," as the heathen do, or prayers in a language which people do not understand, generally lead to most ridiculous perversions of the unknown tongue. A popular specimen of this is the Salve Regina delle Ciane Florentine di San Lorenzo, or the " Salve Regina of the Florentine women of the lower class, as given in San Lorenzo." Ciana is given by Barretti as a specially Florentine word.

LA SALVE REGINA.

" Sarvia della Regina, dreco la Misericordia, vita d'un cieco, spezia nostra, sarvia tua, te chiamao esule, fili e vacche!

" Ate sospirao, i' gemeo fetente in barca e lacrima la valle.

" L' la eggo educata nostra, illons in tits.

" Misericordia se' cieli e in ossi e coperte, e lesine benedette, frutti, ventri, tubi, novi, posti cocche, esilio e tende !

" O crema, o pia, o dorce virgola Maria !—Ammenne ! "

This is perfectly in the spirit of the Middle Ages, of which so much is still found in the cheapest popular Italian literature. I have elsewhere mentioned that it was long before the Reformation, when the Church was at the height of her power, that blasphemies, travesties of religious services, and scathing sarcasms of monkish life reached their extreme, and were never equalled afterwards, even by Protestant satirists. The Epistolce Obscitrorum Virorum of Hiitten and Reuchlin was an

avowed caricature by an enemy. The revelations of monkish life by Boccaccio, Cintio, Arlotto, and a hundred other good Catholics, were a thousand times more damaging than the Epistolcz, because they were the unconscious betrayals of friends.

Since writing the foregoing, I have obtained the following, entitled, The Pater Noster of tJie Country People in the Old Market, or,

IL PATER NOSTER DEI BECERI DI MERCATO.

" Pate nostro quisin celi sanctifice tuore nome tumme; avvenia regno tumme; fia te volunta stua, in celo en terra.

"Pane nostro cotediano da nobis sodie, e dimitti nobis debita nostra, sicutte ette nos dimittimus debitori nostri, sette ananossie in due casse, intenzione sedie nosse e mulo.— Amenne !"

There is, however, this great difference in the two prayers here given, that the Salve Regina is intended for a jest, while the paternoster is given as actually taken down from a ciana, and is rather a specimen of dialect than a jeu d'esprit. The following Ave Maria is also serious, and simply a curiosity of language :

L'AvE MARIA.

" Avemmaria grazia piena, domino teco beneditta e frustris, e mulieri busse e benedetti fruttus ventris tui eiusse !

" Santa Maria Materdei, ora pro nobisse, pecatoribusse, tinche, tinona, mortis nostrisse.—Ammenne !"

These specimens of Italianised Latin are not so grotesque as some which were written out for me in all seriousness by a poor woman. A specimen of the latter is given in my work on " Etruscan-Roman Traditions."

Last of all, there came to me a small tale of little value, save that it professes to account for the reason why so many cats have ever flourished and been nourished in the cloister of San Lorenzo, these felines being, indeed, in a small way among the lions of Florence. It is as follows :—

I GATTI DI SAN LORENZO.

"In the cloisters of San Lorenzo there are many cats, and every evening people may be seen who go there to feed them, among whom are many old men and women. But these cats were long ago themselves human, that is to say, they were once all wizards and witches, who bear their present form for punishment of an evil deed.

" There was once a very wealthy and powerful family in Florence, at the head of which was a gentleman and lady who had an only daughter, in whom was all their love and hope. Among their servants in a higher position was an old woman, who was very vindictive and easily offended, so that she could brood over deadly revenge for years for the least affront, and she fancied she had a great many, because when she had neglected her duty at times she had been scolded by her mistress or master.

" Now this old woman knew that death or disaster to the daughter would drive the parents mad ; and so having recourse to witchcraft, she put into the drink of the young lady a decoction, the result of which was that she began to waste away, growing weaker and paler, without feeling any pain.

" Then her parents, in great fear, consulted the best physicians, who did no good, for indeed it was a case beyond their skill. And at last, beginning to believe that there was something unearthly in it all, they sent for an old woman who cured by occult art.[1] And when she came she looked steadily at the girl, then frowned and shook her head, and asked for a ribbon or cord, no matter what, so that it were one which the young lady had worn about her waist. With this she measured accurately the height of the patient from head to foot, and then the width from hand to hand, it being desirous that the arms be of equal length; but there was the disproportion of the thickness of a piece of money. Then the witch said :

" ' This is none of my affair as regards the cure. Your daughter is bewitched, and I can indeed make the witch appear, but to beat her and compel her to remove the spell depends on you alone.'

[1] Una medichessa.

" Now they, suspecting the old servant, sent for her, but she had disappeared and could not be found. Then the doctress took a caldron, and put into it hot water and the undergarments of the girl and certain herbs, and boiled them all together, singing an incantation, and, taking a knife, sharpened it on the table, whetting it on the chemise of the young lady.

" Then the old servant woman appeared at the door, against her will, forced by the power of the spell, in an agony of rage and bitterness; but she was at once seized and beaten, whereupon she consented to unbewitch the girl, who speedily recovered.

" Now Florence was at that time fearfully afflicted with evil witches, who defied all authority, and spread disease and death far and wide; but this affair of the bewitched lady being made known, both priests and laymen rose up in wrath, and the sorceress fled for sanctuary to the cloisters of San Lorenzo.

" Then to save their lives the Strege made a compromise with the priests, and it was agreed that they should no longer live as witches, or do any harm, but all live and die as cats in the cloister, where they should be regularly fed, and exist in peace. Which agreement has been duly carried out to this day, and among these cats are many who were once witches in human form hundreds of years ago."

This narrative is not so much a story as an account of the manner in which bewitchment is undone by another witch. The reader will find the incantations in the chapter entitled " The Spell of the Boiling Clothes," in my work on "Etruscan-Roman Remains." One of the most serious riots which has occurred in Milan for many years took place March 3, 1891, when the populace tortured terribly and tried to kill a witch, who had, it was believed, been detected by this spell.

" H<zc fabula docet" adds the wise Flaxius, " this story suggests a reason why a certain kind of ladies of ecclesiastical proclivities are always called tabbies. And that there is something in it I can well believe, knowing one who, when she calls her rector or bishop ' De-ar man !' does so in a manner

which marvellously suggests the purring of a cat. And the manner in which the tabby pounces on the small birds, mice, and gold-fish of others— i.e., their peccadilloes, and small pets or pleasures, which in good faith do her no harm—seems like literally copying the feline—upon line. . . .

"Oh ! ye who visit the cloister, and see the cats, think well on this legend, and especially on the deep identity of witches with tabbies !

" And for a moral, note that, with all their sins, what the witches and cats aimed at above all things was food, with which they have remained content, according to the exquisite lyric by the divine Shelley, p. 661, Dowden's edition :—

' ' ' This poor little cat Only wanted a rat, To stuff out its own little maw, And it were as good Some people had such food To make them hold their jaw? "

LEGEND OF THE PIAZZA SAN BI AGIO

" For by diabolical art he assumed varied forms, even the human, and deceived people by many occult tricks."— FROMANN, Tracfatus de Fascina-tione, 1675.

THIS is a slight tale of light value, and not new, but it has assumed local colour, and may amuse the reader.

" It was a great art of witches and sorcerers of old to give a man or woman by art the appearance of another person, and this they called ' drawing white lines with charcoal,' and there is many a fine tale about it. Now it was about the time when Berta spun and owls wore silk cloaks that a Signore Nannin-cino lived in the old Piazza San Biagio. He had many small possessions in Florence, but the roast chickens of the supper, or his great piece, was an estate in the country called the Mula a Quinto, for which all his relations longed, like wolves for a fat sheep. And Nannincini, being sharp to a keen edge, and knowing how to lend water and borrow wine, had promised this estate in secret to everybody, and got from them many a gratification, and supped and dined with them for years, yet after this died without leaving a will.

" Then six of his relations assembled and resolved to secure the property, though they invoked the devil. And to aid them they took a certain scamp named Giano di Selva, who somewhat resembled the departed Nannincino, and he, calling in a witch of his acquaintance, was made by sorcery to look as much like the defunct as two beads of the same rosary. So Nannincino was removed and Giano put in his place, where he lay still for an hour, and then began to show signs of life. And after a time he called for a notary and began to make his will. First he left a house to one, and his sword to another, and so on, till it came to the Mula a Quinto.

" ' And who shall have the Mula a Quinto, dear good uncle ?' asked a nephew.

"' That,' replied the dying man, ' I leave to my good friend, the only true friend I ever had, the noblest of men '

" ' But what is his name ?' asked the nephew.

" Giano di Selva,' gasped the dying man. And it was written down by the notary, and the will was signed, and the signer died immediately after. All their shaking could not revive him.

" The tale ends with these words : E cosi ingannati gli in-gannatori, rimase Giano herede delpodere —And thus the biters being bit, d'ye see, Giano took a handsome property."

" And does his ghost still promenade the palace ?"

" To oblige you, Signore, for this once— piace a lei il coman-dare —it does. The ghost walks—always when the rent fails to come in, and there is no money in the treasury— cammina, cammina per un fil di spada —walks as straight as an acrobat on a rope. But I cannot give you a walking ghost of a rascal to every house, Signore. If all the knaves who made fortunes by trickery were to take to haunting our houses in Florence, they would have to lie ten in a bed, or live one hundred in a room, and ghosts, as you know, love to be alone. Millegrazie, Signore Carlo! This will keep our ghost from walking for a week."

"Of which remark here made that ' the ghost doth walk,'" comments the sage Flaxius, " when money is forbidden unto man (which is so commonly heard in theatrical circles when the weekly salary is not paid), I have no doubt that it comes from the many ancient legends which assign a jealous guardian sprite to every hoard. And thus in Spenser's wondrous ' Faerie Queene ' the marvellous stores in Mammon's treasury, ' em-bost with massy gold of glorious guifte,' were watched by

" ' An ugly feend more fowle than dismall day ;

The which with monstrous stalk behind him stept, And ever as he went dew watch upon him kept.'

" The which quotation is in its turn otherwise curious since it gave, I doubt not, the original suggestion to Coleridge of the verse wherein mention is made in simile of one who walks in fear and dread, and dares not turn his head—

" ' For well he knows a griesly fiend Doth close behind him tread.'

" ' More or less accurately, my masters, more or less.' ' Tis sixty years since'—I read the original."

THE SPIRIT OF THE PORTA SAN GALLO

" And both the undying fish that swim Through Bowscale Tarn did wait on him : The pair were servants of his eye In their immortality; They moved about in open sight, To and fro, for his delight."

—WORDSWORTH, *Poems of the Imagination.*

THE reader should never at once infer that a legend is recent because it is attached to a new place. Spirits and traditions are like the goblin of Norse tale, who moved with the family. The family changed its home to get rid of him, but on the way the elf popped his head out and remarked, " Wiflatten " (" We're flitting " or moving). The ghost of Benjamin Franklin long haunted the library which he had founded in Philadelphia, and when the library or books were transferred to a new building, the ghost went with them and his statue. And in like manner the legend of the religious person, male or female, who is also a fish has travelled over many lands, till it came to the vasca or basin of the Porto San Gallo. Thus Leonard Vair, in his charming Trots Livres des Chanties, Sorcelages ou EncJiantemens, Paris, 1583, tells us that "there is a cloister in Burgundy, by which there is a pond, and in this pond are as many fish as there be monks in the cloister. And when one of the fish swims on the surface of the water and beats with its tail, then one of the monks is ever ill." But there is a mass of early Christian or un-Christian folklore which identifies "Catholic clergy-women " with fish, even as Quakers are identified in Philadelphia with shad. In Germany all maids just in their teens are called Backfisch, that is, pan-fish or fritures, from their youth and liveliness, or delicacy. We may read in Friedrich that the fish is a common Christian symbol of immortality, which fully accounts for all legends of certain of them living for ever. The story which I have to tell is as follows:—

Lo SPIRITO BELLA VASCA BELLA PORTA SAN GALLO.

" In this fountain-basin is found a pretty little fish, which is always there, and which no one can catch, because it always escapes with great lestezza or agility.

"And this is the queen of all the other fish, or else the Spirit of the Fountain.

" This spirit, while on earth, was a beautiful girl who loved an official, and he fell ill and was in the military hospital.

" The parents of the maid opposed her marriage with this official, though he was so much in love with her that it and anxiety had made him ill. Then the maid became a nun so that she might be near him in illness, and nurse him in his last moments, which indeed came to pass, for he died, nor did she long survive him.

" Then her mother, who had magic power (essendo stata una fata *), regretted having opposed her daughter's love and that of the young man, since it had caused the death of both. And to amend this she so enchanted them that by night both became folletti or spirits haunting the hospital, while by day the maid becomes a little fish living in the fountain. But when seen by night she appears as a pretty little nun (una bella monachina\ and goes to the hospital to nurse the invalids, for which she has, indeed, a passion. And if any one of them observes her, he feels better, but in that instant she vanishes, and is in the arms of her lover. But sometimes it happens that he becomes jealous of a patient, and then he vexes the poor man in every way, twitching off his covering, and playing him all kinds of spiteful tricks."

It is otherwise narrated, in a more consistent, and certainly more traditionally truthful manner, that both

1 Not a fairy here, but a witch of a certain degree.

M

the lovers are fish by day and folletti by night. This brings the legend to close resemblance with the undying fish of Bowscale Tarn, recorded in Wordsworth's beautiful song at the feast of Brougham Castle in the " Poems of the Imagination."

"'Tis worth noting," pens the observant Flaxius on this, "that in days of yore fish, feminines, and fascination were considered so inseparable that Dr. Johannes Christian Fro-mann wrote a chapter on this mystical trinity, observing that music was, as an attractor, connected with them, as shown by dolphins, syrens, Arions, and things of that sort. And he quoted—yea, in the holy Latin tongue—many instances of fishers who entice their finny prey by playing flutes :

" ' Which thing I doubted till I saw that Doubt

Pursued, its refutation oft begets, When in America I once found out
That shad were caught by means of castin" nets!"

STORY OF THE PODESTA WHO WAS LONG ON HIS JOURNEY
A LEGEND OF THE DUOMO

"Were I ten times as tedious, I would find it in my heart to bestow it all on you."—Dogberry.

THIS little tale is told by the Florentine Poggio, who was born in 1380 and died in 1459, yet lived—in his well-known Facezie. But as it ever was and is a folk-story, independently of the great jester, I think it worthy of a place in this collection.

"There was once a podesta sent from Rome to govern Florence, and truly he was of that kind who to a farthing's worth of sense have ten ducats' value in self-conceit; for if vanity could have kept a man warm, he never would have had need to buy blankets. And this was most shown in his belief that he was a great orator, though he was so intolerably stupid and slow that his speeches were like the post-rider of Giordano, who in good weather sometimes got as far as five miles a day.

" Now he was to be inducted into office in the Cathedral, in the presence of the priori, or notables of the city of Florence, and so begun a discourse in which he first of all described how great a man he had been as senator in Rome, and what he had done, and what everybody else connected with him had done, and all the details of his departure from the Eternal City; and then depicted a banquet given to him at Sutro, and so went on, telling everything about everybody, till, after several hours of terribly tiresome discourse, he had got no farther than Siena.

" Now by this time, as Poggio words it, ' This excessive length of wearisome narration had so exhausted his auditors

that they began to fear that the entire day would be spent on

the road,' and at last, as the shades of night began to fall, one who was present rose and said :

" ' Monsignore, I beg you to remember that it is growing late, and you must really get on a little faster in your journey, for if you are not in Florence to-day, the gates will be shut, and unless you get here in time you will not be allowed to enter, and thus you will miss being ordained, and cannot enter on your office.'

"Which having heard, the man of many words promptly concluded his speech by saying that he was really in Florence."

Southey, in " The Doctor," has narrated a number of instances of tedious discourse, but none, I think, quite equal to this.

There is a shadow under every lamp, a devil's chapel close by every church, and even of the venerable and holy Duomo of Florence there are such tales as the following:

LA MESSA DE' VILLANI.

" If there is any faith to be put in old stories and ancient books, even the ladies and gentleman, to say nothing of priests, used such language in their ordinary conversation, in good old Medici times, as would not be heard among any but the lowest people now-a-days. Well, as the saying is :

" ' Ne di tempo, ne di Signoria, Non ti dar malinconia.'

" ' Fret not thyself for time long past away,
For weather, nor for what the great may say.'

" Well, it happened one morning in Florence that a gentil donna, who, I take it, was more donna than truly gentil, whatever her rank may have been, meeting at the door of the Duomo a very ordinary and rough figure of her acquaintance, who had only made himself look more vulgar by new and gaudy clothes, asked him as he came out: " ' Is the Cads' Mass¹ over already ?' " To which he, in nowise put out, promptly replied : " 'Yes, Madonna, and that of the Demireps is just going to

¹ Si la Messa de Villani era finite.

begin; 1 only hurry, and you'll be there in time with the rest of 'em !'

" And that lifted him to celebrity, for in those famous days a small joke often made a great reputation. Ah ! Signore—a great many of us have been born into this world four hundred years too late—more's the pity! However, the lady learned the truth of the old proverb, ' Guardati del villan, quando ha la camicia bianca' —' Look out for a vulgar fellow when he has a clean shirt on,' for then he thinks himself fine enough to say anything saucy.

" And there is yet another story of the same sort, Signore; indeed, I think that while the world lasts there will always be a few of them left for steady customers, under the counter, like smuggled goods in Venice; and it is this : It befell once that a Florentine fell in love with a lady, who was like her mother, come il ramo al franco s'assomiglia —' as the bough to the tree, or very much worse than she ought to be ;' for the dear mamma was like the Porta San Niccolb, only not so well famed.

" However, the gentleman wedded her, never heeding the proverb:

" ' Let every wooer be afraid
To wed a maiden not a maid ;
For sooner or later, as 'tis said,
She'll turn again unto her trade.'

" However, in this case the proverb got the lie, for the lady after she was married behaved with great propriety, and yet was often reminded that she had better have repented before she sinned than after; for many would not speak to her, for all her wealth, till she was well convinced that Che profitta ravedersi dopo il fatto ?

" ' When the deed has once been done, What is the use of repenting, my son ?'

" So it befell one morning that the poor soul was praying in the Cathedral or Duomo, as many another poor sinner had done before her (doubtless on the same spot), when a noble lady, who had never been found out in any naughtiness (some people are certainly very lucky in this world, Signore Carlo !), came by, and seeing the penitent, drew in her robe, turned up her nose, and retreated as if the other had the plague. To which the Magdalen replied, in a sad but firm voice,' Madonna,

¹ E appunto hora comincia quella delle puttane, pero caminate, che farete a tempo con l'altre.

you need not be afraid to touch me, for I assure you that the malady (of which I have, I trust, been thoroughly cured) attacks none save those who wish to have it."

When standing in the Cathedral, the visitor may remember that here Santo Crescenzio, who died in 424, once wrought a miracle, thus recorded in his "Life" of the fourteenth century:

"A poor man had come into the Cathedral and saw no light (i.e., was blind), and going to where Saint Crescentius was, implored him with great piety that he would cause the light to return unto him. And being moved to pity, he made the sign of the cross in the eyes of the blind man, and incontinently the light was restored unto him. Saint Crescentius did not wish this to be made known, and pretended to know nothing about it, but he could not conceal such miracles."

Of which the immortal Flaxius remarks, that " it is singular that so many saints who wished to keep their miracles unknown had not the forethought to make silence a condition of cure. Also, that of all the wonder-working once effected by the holy men of the Church, the only gift now remaining to them is the miraculous power of changing sons and daughters into nephews and nieces; the which, as I am assured, is still as flourishing as ever, and permitted as a proof of transubstantiation." Thus it is that simple heretics deride holy men. And Flaxius is, I bid ye note, a sinner, in whose antique, unsanctified derision I most assuredly do take no part, " it being in bad form in this our age to believe or disbelieve in anything," and therefore in bad style to laugh at aught.

It may be worth recalling, when looking out on the Cathedral Square, that it was here that San Zenobio performed another great miracle, recorded in all his lives, but most briefly in the poetical one:

" Then did he raise an orphan from the dead, The only son of a poor widow, he, A cart with oxen passing o'er his head, Died in the Duomo Square in misery ;

But though all crushed, the Saint restored his life, And, well and gay and bright as stars do shine, He went to his mother, and the pious wife Gave thanks to God for mercy all divine."

Which being witnessed, says the Vita San Zenobii, all who were present began to sing, " Gloria tibi Domine qui mirabilia per servos tuos in nobis operari dignatus es t gloria sit tibi-i et laus in sczcu-la — sec-u-lo-o-o-rum, A-men.

Which, if they sung it as I heard it sung yesterday in the Cathedral of Siena, must have had an extremely soporific effect, lulling all others to sleep, and causing them to see beatific visions beyond all belief. I had in my boyhood a teacher named Professor Sears C. Walker, who was wont to tell how he had once heard in a rural New England village a church congregation sing:

" Before thy throne the angels bow-wow-wow-ow ! "

But to hear the bow-woiv in perfection, one must go to Rome. A pack in full cry or a chorus of owls is nothing to it. But let us pass on to a fresh story.

LEGENDS OF THE BOBOLI GARDENS: THE OLD GARDENER, AND THE TWO STATUES AND THE FAIRY

" He found such strange enchantment there, In that garden sweet and rare, Where night and day The nightingales still sing their roundelay, And plashing fountains 'neath the verdure play, That for his life he could not thence away ; And even yet, though he hath long been dead, 'Tis said his spirit haunts the pleasant shade."

— The Ring of Charlemagne.

A GREAT showman, as I have heard, once declared that in establishing a menagerie, one should have the indispensable lion, an obligato elephant, a requisite tiger, an essential camel, and imperative monkeys. One of the " indispensable lions " of Florence is the Boboli Gardens, joining the Pitti Palace, which, from their careful preservation in their original condition, give an admirable idea of what gardens were like in an age when far more was thought of them than now as places of habitual resort and enjoyment, and when they entered into all literature and life. Abraham a Santa Clara once wrote a discourse against gardens, as making life too happy or simple, basing his idea on the fact that sin originated in the Garden of Eden.

The Boboli Gardens were planned by II Tribolo for Cosimo di Medici. The ground which they occupy is greatly varied, rising high in some places, from which very beautiful views of Florence, with its "walls and churches, palaces and towers," may be seen. Of their many attractions the guide-book remarks poetically in very nearly the following words :—

" Its long-embowered walks, like lengthened arbours, Are well adapted to the summer's sun; While statues, terraces, and vases add Still more unto its splendour. All around We see attractive statues, and of these A number really are restored antiques, And many by good artists; best of all Are four by mighty Michel Angelo, Made for the second Julius, and meant To decorate his tomb. You see them at The angles of the grotto opposite The entrance to the gardens. Of this grot The famous Redi sang in verse grotesque:

" Ye satyrs, in a trice

Leave your low jests and verses rough and hobbly, And bring me a good fragment of the ice Kept in the grotto of the Garden Boboli.

With nicks and picks
Of hammers and sticks,
Disintegrate it
And separate it,
Break it and split it,
Splinter and slit it!

Till at the end 'tis fairly ground and rolled Into the finest powder, freezing cold."

There are also, among the things worth seeing, the Venus by Giovanni of Boulogne (called di Bologna); the Apollo and Ceres by Baccio Bandinelli; the group of Paris carrying off Helen by V. de' Rossi, and the old Roman fountain-bath and obelisk. The trees and flowers, shrubbery and boschetti, are charming; and if the reader often visits them, long sitting in the sylvan shade on sunny days, he will not fail to feel that strange enchantment which seems to haunt certain places, and people them with dreams, if not with elves.

The fascination of these dark arbours old, and of the antique gardens, has been recognised by many authors, and there are, I suppose, few visitors to Florence who have not felt it and recalled it years after in distant lands as one recalls a dream. Therefore, I read with interest or sympathy the following, which, though amounting to nothing as a legend, is still valuable as setting forth the fascination of the place, and how it dates even from him who gave the Boboli Gardens their name:

IL GIARDINO BOBOLI.

' The Boboli Garden is the most beautiful in Europe.

" Boboli was the name of the farmer who cultivated the land before it was bought by Cosimo de' Medici and his wife Eleanora.

"After he had sold the property he remained buried in grief, because he had an attachment for it such as some form for a dog or a cat. And so great was his love for it that it never left his mind, nor could he ever say amen to it; for on whatever subject he might discourse, it always came in like one who will not be kept out, and his refrain was, 'Well, you'll see that my place will become il -nido degli amori (the nest of loves), and I myself after my death will never be absent from it.' His friends tried to dissuade him from thinking so much of it, saying that he would end by being lunatic, but he persevered in it till he died.

" And it really came to pass as he said; for soon after his death, and ever since, many have on moonlight nights seen his spirit occupied in working in the gardens."

The story is a pretty one, and it is strangely paralleled by one narrated in my own Memoirs of the old Pening-ton mansion in Philadelphia, the gardens of which were haunted by a gentle ghost, a lady who had lived there in her life, and who was, after her death, often seen watering the flowers in them by moonlight. And thus do—

" printless footsteps fall By the spots they loved before."

The second legend which I recovered, relating to the Boboli Gardens, is as follows:

LE DUE STATUE E LA NINFA.

"There are in the Boboli Gardens two statues of two imprisoned kings, and it is said that every night a beautiful fairy of the grotto clad in white rises from the water, emerging perfectly dry, and converses with the captive kings for one hour, going alternately from one to the other, as if bearing mutual messages, and then returns to the grotto, gliding over the ground without touching the grass with her feet, and after this vanishes in the water."

"This tale is, as I conceive," writes the observant Flaxius, "an allegory, or, as Petrus Berchorius would have called it, a moralisation, the marrow whereof is as follows: The two captive kings are Labour and Capital, who have, indeed, been long enchained, evil tongues telling each that the other was his deadly foe, while the fairy is Wise Reform, who passes her time in consoling and reconciling them. And it shall come to pass that when the go-betweens or brokering mischief-makers are silenced, then the kings will be free and allied."

"Then indeed, as you may see, All the world will happy be!"

Vivat Sequenz! Now for the next story.

HOW LA VIA DELL A MOSCA GOT ITS NAME

" Puer—abige Muscas ! "

— Cicero tie Orat., 60.

THE following story contains no new or original elements, as it is only an ordinary tale of transformation by witchcraft, but as it accounts for the origin of the name of a street in Florence I give it place:—

LA VIA BELLA MOSCA.

"This is the way that the Via della Mosca, or the Street of the Fly, got its name. There once dwelt in it, in a very old house, a family which, while of rank, were not very wealthy, and therefore lived in a retired manner. There were father, mother, and one daughter, who was wonderfully beautiful— 2in vcro occhio di sole.

"And as the sun hath its shadow, so there was a living darkness in this family in a donna di scrvizio, a servant woman who had been many years with them, who had a daughter of her own, who was also a beauty of a kind, but as dark as the other was fair; the two were like day and night, and as they differed in face, so were they unlike in soul. For the young signora had not a fault in her; she would not have caused any one pain even to have her own way or please her vanity, and they say the devil will drop dead whenever he shall meet with such a woman as that. However, he never met with this young lady, I suppose, because he is living yet. And the young lady was so gentle of heart that she never said an ill word of any one, while the maid and her mother never opened their mouths save for gossip and slander. And she was so occupied with constant charity, and caring for poor children, and finding work for poor people, that she never thought about her own beauty at all, and when people told her that chi nasce bella, nasce maritata (Whoever is born pretty is born to be married), she would reply, ' Pretty or ugly, there are things more important in life than weddings.'

"And so far did she carry this, that she gave no heed at all to a very gallant and handsome yet good-hearted honourable wealthy young gentleman who lived in a palazzo opposite, and who, from watching and admiring her, had ended by falling desperately in love. So he made a proposal of marriage to her through her parents, but she replied (having had her mind, in truth, on other things) that she was too much taken up with other duties to properly care for a husband, and that her dowry was not sufficient to correspond to his wealth, however generous he might be in dispensing with one. And as she was as firm and determined as she was gentle and good, she resolutely kept him at arm's length. But firmness is nothing against fate, and he ' who runs away with nimble feet, in the war of love at last will beat.'[1]

"Now, if she was indifferent to the young signore, the dark maid-servant was not, for she had fallen as much in love with him as an evil, selfish nature would permit her, and she planned and plotted with her mother by night and by day to bring about what she desired. Now, the old woman, unknown to all, was a witch, as all wicked women really are—they rot away with vanity and self-will and evil feelings till their hearts are like tinder or gunpowder, and then some day comes a spark of the devil's fire, and they flash out into witches of some kind.

" The young signore had a great love for boating on the Arno, which was a deeper river in those days; he would often pass half the night in his boat. Now, the mother and daughter so contrived it that the young signorina should return very late on a certain night from visiting the poor, accompanied by the old woman. And when just in the middle of the Ponte Vecchio the mother gave a whistle, and lo ! there came a sudden and terrible blast of wind, which lifted up the young lady and whirled her over the bridge into the rushing river underneath.

" But, as fate would have it, the young man was in his boat just below, and fortune fell down to him, as it were, from heaven; for seeing a form float or flit past him in the water and the darkness, he caught at it and drew it into the boat,

[1] Nella guerra d'amor, che fugge vince.

LEGENDS OF FLORENCE

and truly Pilate's wife was not so astonished when the roast capon rose up in the dish and crowed as was this boatman at finding what he had fished up out of the stream.

" There is a saying of a very unlucky contrary sort of man that casco in Arno ed arse (He fell in the Arno and burnt himself). But in this case, by luck, the falling of the young lady into the river caused her heart to burn with love, for so bravely and courteously and kindly did the young signore behave, conveying her promptly home without a sign of love-making or hint of the past, that she began to reconsider her refusal, and the end thereof was a betrothal, by which the mother and daughter were maddened to think that they had only hastened and aided what they had tried to prevent.

"Now, it is true that bad people put ten f.mes as much strong will and hard work into their evil acts a:, good folk do into better deeds, because the latter think their cause will help itself along, while the sinners know perfectly well that they must help themselves or lose. So the witch only persevered the more, and at last she hit on this plan. With much devilish ado she enchanted a comb of thorns, so that whoever was combed with it would turn into a fly, and must remain one till the witch bade the victim assume his or her usual form.

"Then on the bridal morn the old woman offered to comb out the long golden locks of the young lady, and she did so, no other person being present, so she began her incantation :

" ' Earthly beauty fade away, Maiden's form no longer stay, For a fly thou shalt become, And as a busy insect hum, Hum — hum — bruin — brum ! Buzz-uz-uz about the room !

" ' Ope thine eyes and spread thy wings, Pass away to insect things. Now the world will hate thee more Than it ever loved before When it hears thy ceaseless hum, Buzz-uz-uz about the room !'

" And hearing this, the bride sank into a deep sleep, during which she changed into a fly, and so soared up to the ceiling and about the room, buzzing indeed.

" Now, with all her cleverness, the witch had missed a stitch in her sorcery, for she had not combed hard enough to draiv blood, being afraid to wake the maid; hence it came to pass that instead of a small common fly she became a very large and exquisitely beautiful one, with a head like gold, a silver body, and beautiful blue and silver wings like her bridal dress. And she was not confined to buzzing, for she had the power to sing one verse. However, when the change took place, the old woman rushed from the room screaming like mad, declaring that her young mistress was a witch who had turned into a fly as soon as she had touched her with a consecrated comb which had been dipped in holy water, and to this she added many lies, as that a witch to avoid the holy sacrament of marriage always changed her form, and that she had always suspected the signorina of being a witch ever since she had seen her fly in the wind over the Arno to the young signore.

" But when they went to look at the fly, and found it so large and beautiful, they were amazed, nor were they less astonished when they heard it begin to buzz with a most entrancing strangely sweet sound, and then sing :—

" ' Be ye not amazed that I Am enchanted as a fly, Evil witchcraft was around me, Evil witches' spells have bound me : Now I am a fly I know, But woe to her who made me so !'

" And when the young signore stretched out his hand, the fly came buzzing with joy and lighted like a bird on his finger, and this she did with great joy whenever any of the poor whom she had befriended came to see her, and so she behaved to all whom she had loved. And when it was observed that the fly had no fear of holy things, but seemed to love them, all believed in her song.

" Till one day the young signore, calling all the family and friends together, said : ' This is certainly true, that she who was to have been my wife is here, turned into a fly. And as for her being a witch, ye can all see that she fears neither holy water nor a crucifix. But I believe that these women here, her nurse and daughter, have filled our ears with lies, and that the nurse herself is the sorceress who hath done the evil deed. Now, I propose that we take all three, the fly, the mother, and daughter, and hang the room with verbena, which I have provided, and sprinkle the three with much holy water, all of us making the castagna and jettatiira, and see what will come of it.'

"Then the two witches began to scream and protest in a rage, but as soon as they opened their mouths, holy water was dashed into their faces, whereat they howled more horribly than ever, and at last promised, if their lives should be spared in any manner, to tell the whole truth, and to disenchant the bride. Which they forthwith did.

" Then those present seized the witches, and said: ' Your lives shall indeed be spared, but it is only just that ere ye go ye shall be as nicely combed, according to the proverb which says, "Comb me and I'll comb thee !"

" Said and done, but the combing this time drew blood, and the mother and daughter, shrinking smaller and smaller, flew away at last as two vile carrion-flies through the window.

" And as the story spread about Florence, every one came to see the house where this had happened, and so it was that the street got the name of the Via della Mosca or Fly Lane."

There is a curious point in this story well worth noting. In it the sorceress lulls the maiden to sleep before transforming her, that is, causes her death before reviving her with a comb of thorns. Now, the thorn is a deep symbol of death—naturally enough from its dagger-like form—all over the world wherever it grows. As Schwenck writes:

" In the Germanic mythology the thorn is an emblem of death, as is the nearly allied long and deep slumber—the idea being that death kills with a sharp instrument which is called in the Edda the sleep-thorn, which belongs to Odin the god of death. It also occurs as a person in the Nibelungen Lied as Hogni, Hagen, 'the thorn who kills Siegfried.' The tale of Dornroschen (the sleeping beauty), owes its origin to the sleep-thorn, which is, however, derived from the death-thorn, death being an eternal sleep."

This is all true, and sleep is like death. But the soothing influence of a comb produces sleep quite apart from any association with death.

Apropos of flies, there is a saying, which is, like all new or eccentric sayings, or old and odd ones revived, called "American." It is, "There are no flies on him," or more vulgarly, " I ain't got no flies on me" and signi-

fies that the person thus exempt is so brisk and active, and " flies round " at such a rate, that no insect has an opportunity to alight on him. The same saying occurs in the Proverbi Italiani of Orlando Pescetti, Venice, 1618, Non si lascia posar le mosche addosso (He lets no flies light on him).

When I was a small boy in America, the general teaching to us was that it was cruel to kill flies, and I have heard it illustrated with a tale of an utterly depraved little girl of three years, who, addressing a poor fly which was buzzing in the window-pane, said : " Do you love your Dod, 'ittle fy ? " " Do you want to see your Dod, 'ittle fy ? " " Well " (with a vicious jab of the finger), "you SHALL ! " And with the last word the soul of the fly had departed to settle its accounts in another world. Writing here in Siena, the most fly-accursed or Beelzebubbed town in Italy, on July 25th, being detained by illness, I love that little angel of a girl, and think with utter loathing and contempt of dear old Uncle Toby and his " Go—go, poor fly!" True, I agree with him to his second "go," but there our sentiments diverge—the reader may complete the sentence for himself—out of Ernulphus !

On which the wise Flaxius comments as follows on the proof with his red pencil:

"It hath been observed by the learned that the speed of a fly, were he to make even a slight effort to go directly onwards, would be from seventy to eighty miles an hour, during which transit he would find far more attractive food, pleasanter places wherein to buzz about, and more beautiful views than he meets with in this humble room of mine, wherein I, from hour to hour, do with a towel rise and slay his kind. Oh, reader! how many men there are who, to soaring far and wide in life amid honeyed flowers and pleasant places, prefer to buzz about in short flights in little rooms where they can tease some one, and defile all they touch as domestic gossips do—but, 'tis enough ! Mutato nomine de te fabula narratur !"

N

THE ROMAN VASE
A LEGEND OF BELLOSGUARDO

" From Tuscan Bellosguardo Where Galileo stood at nights to take The vision of the stars, we have found it hard," Gazing upon the earth and heavens, to make A choice of beauty."— ELIZABETH BARRETT BROWNING.

BELLOSGUARDO is an eminence on a height, crowned with an ancient, castle-like monastery, from which there is a magnificent view of Florence. It is a haunted legendary spot; fate and witches sweep round its walls by night, while the cry of the civetta makes music for their aerial dance, and in the depths of the hill lie buried mystic treasures, or the relics of mysterious beings of the olden time, and the gnome of the rocks there has his dwelling in subterranean caves. Of this place I have the following legend from Maddalena :

IL VASO ROMANO.

" There was, long ago, in the time of Duke Lorenzo di Medici, a young gardener, who was handsome, clever, and learned beyond the other men of his kind, a man given somewhat to witchcraft and mysteries of ancient days, for he had learned Latin of the monks and read books of history.

" And one day when he was working with his companions in the garden of Bellosguardo, taking out stones, they came to an old Roman vase, which the rest would fain have broken to pieces as a heathenish and foul thing, because there was carved on it the figure of a beautiful Pagan goddess, and it was full of the ashes of some dead person. But the young man suddenly felt a great passion, a desire to possess it, and it seemed as if something said to him, ' Con questo vaso tie un mistero.'

" ' Mine own in truth that vase shall ever be, For there is in it some strange mystery.'

" So he begged for it, and it was readily granted to him. And looking at it, he perceived that it was carved of fine marble, and that the figure on it was that of a beautiful nymph, or a Bellaria flying in the air, and there came from the ashes which it held a sweet odour of some perfume which was unknown to him. Now as he had, sentito ragionare tanto difate, heard much talk of supernatural beings, so he reflected : ' Some fa fa must have dwelt here in days of old, and she was here buried, and this vase is now as a body from which the spirit freely passes, therefore I will show it respect.'

" And so he hung round the neck of the vase a wreath of the most beautiful and fragrant roses, and draped a veil over it to shield it from dust, and set it up under cover in his own garden, and sang to it as follows :

" ' Vaso ! o mio bel vaso ! Di rose ti ho contornato. La rosa e un bel fior, Piii bello e il suo odor."

" ' Vase, oh lovely vase of mine ! With roses I thy neck entwine ; The rose is beautiful in bloom, More beautiful its sweet perfume, The finest rose above I place, To give the whole a crowning grace, As thou dost crown my dwelling-place Another rose I hide within, As thou so long hast hidden been, Since Roman life in thee I see, Rosa Romana thou shalt be ! And ever thus be called by me ! And as the rose in early spring Rises to re-awakening, Be it in garden, fair, or plain, From death to blooming life again, So rise, oh fairy of the flowers, And seek again these shady bowers ! Come every morning to command My flowers, and with thy tiny hand Curve the green leaf and bend the bough, And teach the blossoms how to blow ; But while you give them living care, Do not neglect the gardener ;

And as he saved your lovely urn, I pray protect him too in turn, Even as I this veil have twined, To guard thee from the sun and wind : Oh, Fairy of the Vase—to you, As Queen of all the Fairies too, And Goddess of the fairest flowers In earthly fields or elfin bowers, To thee with earnest heart I pray, Grant me such favour as you may.' l

" Then he saw slowly rising from the vase, little by little, a beautiful woman, who sang :

" ' Tell me what is thy desire,

Oh youth, and what dost thou require ?

From realms afar I come to thee,

For thou indeed hast summoned me,

With such sweet love and gentleness,

That I in turn thy life would bless,

And aye thy fond protectress be.

What would'st thou, youth, I ask, of me ?'

" And the young man replied :

" ' Fair lady, at a glance I knew,

Thy urn and felt thy spirit too, .

And straight the yearning through me sped, To raise thee from the living dead ; I felt thy spell upon my brow, And loved thee as I love thee now. Even as I loved unknown before, And so shall love thee evermore, And happiness enough 'twould be If thou would'st ever live with me !'

"Then the spirit replied :

"'A debt indeed to thee I owe, And full reward will I bestow ; The roses which thou'st given me With laurel well repaid shall be ; Without thy rose I had not risen Again from this my earthly prison, And as it raised me to the skies, So by the laurel thou shall rise !'

1 Viene tutte le mattine Colle sue belle manine.

Though very rude, even to illiteracy inform, the train of thought is here very gracefully managed in the original.

"The youth answered :

"'Every evening at thy shrine Fresh roses, lady, I will twine ; But tell me next what 'tis for fate That I must do, or what await ?'

"The fairy sang :

"'A mighty mission, youth, indeed

Hast thou to fill, and that with speed, Since it depends on thee to save All Florence from a yawning grave, From the worst form of blood and fire, And sword and conflagration dire. Thou dost the Duke Lorenzo know ; Straight to that mighty leader go ! The Chieftain of the Medici, And tell him what I tell to thee, That he is compassed all about With armed enemies without, Who soon will bold attack begin, Linked to conspiracy within ; And bid him ere the two have crossed, To rise in strength or all is lost, Ring loud the storm-bell in alarms, Summon all Florence straight to arms : Lorenzo knows well what to do. Take thou thy sword and battle too ! And in the fray I'll look to thee: Go forth, my friend, to victory.'

"Then the young man went to the Duke Lorenzo, and told him, with words of fire which bore conviction, of the great peril which threatened him. Then there was indeed alarming and arming, and a terrible battle all night long, in which the young man fought bravely, having been made captain of a company which turned the fight. And the Grand Duke, impressed by his genius and his valour, gave him an immense reward.

"So he rose in life, and became a gran signore, and one of the Council in Florence, and lord of Bellosguardo, and never neglected to twine every day a fresh wreath of roses round the Roman vase, and every evening he was visited by the fairy. And so it went on well with him till he died, and after that the spirit was seen no more. The witches say that the vase is, however, somewhere still in Florence, and that while it exists the city will prosper ; but to call the fairy again it must be crowned with roses, and he who does so must pronounce with such faith as the gardener had, the same incantation."

What is remarkable in the original text of this tale is the rudeness and crudeness of the language in which it is written, which is indeed so great that its real spirit or meaning might easily escape any one not familiar with such composition. But I believe that I have rendered it very faithfully.

There seems to be that, however, in Bellosguardo which inspires every poet. Two of the most beautiful passages in English literature, one by Elizabeth Barrett Browning, and another by Hawthorne, describe the views seen from it. The castle itself is deeply impressed on my memory, for during the past nine months I have never once raised my eyes from the table where I write without beholding it in full view before me across the Arno, even as I behold it now.

I cannot help observing that the mysterious sentiment which seized on the hero of this tale when he found his virgin relic, was marvellously like that which inspired Keats when he addressed his Ode to a Grecian Urn:

"Thou still unravished bride of quietness ! Thou foster-child of Silence and slow Time, Sylvan historian who canst thus express A flowery tale more sweetly than our rhyme : What leaf-fringed legend haunts about thy shape ? "

That which I have here given is truly a leaf-fringed legend, for it is bordered with the petals of roses and embalmed with their perfume, and one which in the hands of a great master might have been made into a really beautiful poem. It came near a very gay rhymer at least in the Duke Lorenzo de' Medici, whose songs, which were a little more than free, and rather more loose than easy, were the delight and disgrace of his time. And yet I cannot help rejoicing to meet this magnificent patron of art and letters at so late a day in a purely popular tale. There are men of beauty who are also a joy for ever, as well as things, and Lorenzo was one of them.

It is worth noting that just as the fairy in this tale reveals to Lorenzo that Florence is threatened by enemies, just so it happened that unto Saint Zenobio, standing rapt in divine contemplation in his cavern, it was announced that the same city was about to be assailed by cruel barbarians, who, as Sigbert relates in his Chronicle of 407 A.D., were the two hundred thousand Goths led by Radagasio into Italy. But they were soon driven away by the Saint's prayers and penitence. It would be curious if one legend had here passed into another:

" So visions in a vision live again, And dreams in dreams are wondrously transfused ; Gold turning into grey as clouds do change, And shifting hues as they assume new forms."

Apropos of Saint Zenobio of Florence, I will here give something which should have been included with the legend of the Croce al Trebbio, but which I obtained too late for that purpose. It would appear from the Iscrizioni e Memorie di Firenze, by F. Bigazzi (1887), that the pillar of the cross was really erected to commemorate a victory over heretics, but that the cross itself was added by the Saints Ambrosio and Zenobio, " on account of a great mystery"—which mystery is, I believe, fully explained by the legend which I have given. The inscription when complete was as follows :

SANCTUS AMBROSIUS CUM SANCTO ZENOBIO PROPTER GRANDE MISTERIUM
HUNC CRUCEM HIC LOCAVERUNT. ET IN MCCCXXXVIII NOVITER DIE
10 AUGUSTI RECONSECRATA EST P. D. M. FRANCISC. FLOR. EPISCOPUM UNA CUM ALIIS EPISCOPIS M.

A slightly different reading is given by Brocchi (Vite de 1 Santi fiorentini, 1742).

" Of which saint, be it observed," writes Flaxius, "that there is in England a very large and widely extended family, or stirps, named Snobs, who may claim that by affinity of name to Zenobio they are lineally or collaterally his descendants, even as the Potts profess connection with Pozzo del Borgo. But as it is said of this family or gens that they are famed for laying claim to every shadow of a shade of gentility, it may be that there is truly no Zenobility about them. Truly there are a great many more people in this world who are proud of their ancestors, than there ever were ancestors who would have been proud of them. The number of whom is as the sands of the sea, or as Heine says, ' more correctly speaking, as the mud on the shore.'

" ' The which, more eath it were for mortall wight, To sell the sands or count the starres on hye ; Or ought more hard, then thinke to reckon right . . . Which—for my Muse herselfe now tyred has, Unto another tale I'll overpas.'"

THE UNFORTUNATE PRIEST
A LEGEND OF LA VIA DELLO SCHELETRO

" Fear and trembling Hope, Silence and Foresight— Death the Skeleton, And Time the Shadow."— WORDSWORTH.

" If God were half so cruel as His priests, It would go hard, I ween, with all of us."

I HAVE elsewhere remarked that there is—chiefly about the Duomo—a group of small streets bearing the dismal names of Death, Hell, Purgatory, Limbo, Crucifixion, Our Lady of Coughing (delle Tosse), The (last) Rest of Old Age, Gallows Lane (Via della Forca), The Tombs, The Way of the Discontented, 1 Dire Need, Small Rags, Fag-End or Stump, Bad Payers, and finally, the Via dello Scheletro, or Skeleton Street. To which there belongs, as is appropriate, a melancholy legend.

LA VIA DELLO SCHELETRO.

" There once dwelt in what is now called the Street of the Skeleton a priest attached to the Cathedral, who was in every respect all that a good man of his calling and a true Christian should be, as he was pious, kind-hearted, and charitable, passing his life in seeking out the poor and teaching their children, often bringing cases of need and suffering to the knowledge of wealthier friends—which thing, were it more frequently done by all, would do more to put an end to poverty than anything else.

1 So called because criminals passed through it on their way to execution.

" ' But he who is in everything most human May highest rise and yet the lowest fall ; And when a brave kind heart meets with the woman, Our greatest duties seem extremely small, And those which were the first became the least : Even so it happened to this gentle priest.

" ' In the old dwelling where he had his home, Which otherwise had been most drear and dull At morn or eve did oft before him come A girl as sweet as she was beautiful; Full soon they learned that both in head andjieart Each was to each the very counterpart.

" ' There is in every soul of finer grain A soul which is in self a soul apart, Which to itself doth oft deep hid remain, But leaps to life when Love awakes the heart. Then as a vapour rises with the sun, And blends with it, two souls pass into one.

" ' And so it came that he would sometimes kiss Her lovely face, nor seemed it much to prove That they in anything had done amiss. Until, one night, there came the kiss of Love, 1 Disguised in friendly seeming like the rest— Alas ! he drove an arrow to her breast.

" ' Then came the glow of passion—new to both— The honeymoon of utter recklessness, When the most righteous casts away his oath, And all is lost in sweet forgetfulness, And life is steeped in joy, without, within, And rapture seems the sweeter for the sin.

" ' Then came in its due course the sad awaking To life and its grim claims, and all around They found, in cold grim truth, without mistaking, These claims for them did terribly abound ; And the poor priest was brought into despair To find at every turn a foe was there.

" ' To know our love is pure though passionate, And have it judged as if both foul and base, Doth seem to us the bitterness of fate ; Yet in the world it is the usual case. By it all priests are judged—yea, every one— Never as Jesus would Himself have done.

" Da qualche bacio Vi chascha il vero bacio d'amor."

— Original.

" ' Because the noblest love with passion rings, Therefore men cry 'tis a!! mere sexual sense, As if the rose and the dirt from which it springs Were one because of the same elements : Therefore 'tis true that, of all sins accurst, Is Gossip, for it always tells the worst.

" ' So Gossip did its worst for these poor souls. The bishop made the priest appear before him, And, as a power who destiny controls, Informed him clearly he had hell before him, And if he would preserve the priestly stole, 1 Must leave his woman—or else lose his soul 1

" ' Now had this man had money, or if he, Like many of his calling, had been bold With worldly air, then all this misery Might have been 'scaped as one escapes the cold By putting on a sheepskin, warm and fine; But then hypocrisy was not his line.

"'His love was now a mother, and the truth Woke in him such a deep and earnest love, That he would not have left her though in sooth He had been summoned by the Power above; And so the interdict was soon applied, But on that day both child and mother died.

"'She, poor weak thing, could not endure the strain, So flickered out, and all within a day; And then the priest, without apparent pain, Began mysteriously to waste away, And, shadow-like and silent as a mouse, Men saw him steal into, or from, the house.

"'And thinner still and paler yet he grew,

With every day some life from him seemed gone, And all aghast, though living, men still knew He had become a literal skeleton; And so he died—in some world less severe Than this to join the one he held so dear. 2

"'Yet no one knew when 'twas he passed away

Out of that shadowy form and 'scaped life's power, For still 'twas seen beneath the moon's pale ray, Or gliding through the court at twilight hour. But there it still is seen—and so it came The Via del Scheletro got its name.'"

1 " Altrimenti

L'avrebbero levato il collare."— Original.

" In una altra stella Per raggiungere la sua bella."— Original.

There is not a word of all this which is "Protestant invention," for though I have poetised or written up a very rude text, the narrative is strictly as I received it. There is one point in it worth noticing, that it is a matter of very general conviction in Italy that in such matters of Church discipline as are involved in this story, it is the small flies who are caught in the web, while the great ones burst buzzing through it without harm, or that the weak and poor (who are very often those with the best hearts and principles) are most cruelly punished, where a bold, sensual, vulgar frate makes light of and easily escapes all accusations.

There is something sadly and strangely affecting in the conception of a simply good and loving nature borne down by the crush of the world and misapplied morality—or clerical celibacy—into total wretchedness—a diamond dissolved to air. One in reading this seems to hear the sad words of one who thought his own name was written in water:

" I am a shadow now, alas! alas! Upon the skirts of human nature dwelling Alone. I chant alone the holy mass, While little signs of life are round me kneeling, And glossy bees at noon do fieldward pass, And many a chapel bell the hour is telling, Paining me through: those sounds grow strange to me, And thou art distant in Humanity!"

THE MYSTERIOUS FIG-TREE

A LEGEND OF THE VIA DEL FICO

" In every plant lie marvellous mysteries, In every flower there is a dream divine; The fig-tree bears the measure of a life, And, as it leaves or fruits, our lives do pass, And all things in each other subtly blend."

" Ha chiappato il fao—ficum capit." — Old Proverbs.

" Quidam itidem medium digitum ostendunt, idque in Hispania adhuc dicitur fieri, et FICA appellatur, hie illudendi actus, de quo Eryc. Puteanus, loc. cit., p. 70."— Curiosus Amuletorum Spectator, D. Wolf, 1692.

THE following tale is, for reasons which I will subsequently explain, one of the most remarkable which I have collected:

LA VIA DEL FICO.

" There stood formerly in the Via del Fico a very ancient palace with a garden, in which there grew a fig-tree which was said to have grown of itself, or without ever having been planted.

This tree bore much fruit of great beauty.

" But however proud the owner of the tree was of its beauty, or however much he might desire to have its fruit, something always strangely occurred to prevent its being enjoyed. For when any one was about to pluck it, there suddenly appeared a great black dog, who, seizing men or women by their garments, dragged them away, beginning to howl and bay. 1 And then they hurried away and let the figs alone, in order to make the dog cease his terrible unearthly baying ; for it is believed to be an omen of death when a dog utters such sounds, it being

1 Faceva il verso del lupo, the deep baying which is a subject of superstition in all countries.

such a presage of disaster as when a civetta or small owl hoots on the roof.

" However, it sometimes happened that the dog did not come, but those who took and ate the figs fared just as badly all the same. For they soon began to feel ill and suffer dire pains, and when they had gone into their bedrooms and laid down, there always entered a beautiful girl clad in white, who began to whirl round (a girarst) or spin, making all the time a great buzzing sound, until horror came over them, which when she perceived, she vanished.

" And many tried also to lop off boughs from the fig-tree, but they were found the second night replaced by a perfect new growth with fully ripe fruit. And it was not the least marvel of the tree that it was always in full leaf, with abundance of ripe figs on it, even in winter, when there was snow on the ground.

" One day men digging in the garden found a tablet of stone or metal on which was inscribed :

" ' Il fico rispettate E non la toccate, E non cercate Neppure mangiarne.'

" ' Respect the tree, and let it be,

From branch to root, nor touch its fruit! Of itself the tree did grow, From a dog who long ago, Enchanted by the fairies' power, Was buried here in mystic hour ; Therefore we bid you let it stand, And if you follow the command You will be happy all your days, But woe to him who disobeys !'

" Now, the owner of the palazzo and garden was a man who had no faith in old legends, or love for such mysteries as these, and so he said, ' It is time to put an end to all this superstition, and I am determined to at once see whether all my prosperity depends on a fig-tree; so do you cut it down and tear it up, root and branch, utterly.'

" This was at once done by the labourers, but, while doing so, they heard sounds as of wailing and great lamenting in the earth beneath them. And when they, astonished, asked the signore to listen to the voices, he replied, ' Away with your superstitions ; we will see this time whether the tree will grow or return again.'

" Truly it did not return, but passed away for ever, and with it all the property and prosperity of the lord. For in time he had to sell all he had, and, losing what he got, died in poverty. Then those who had to go in the street where his palace had been would say, ' Andiamo nella Via del Ficoj just as they say, ' Andar per la Via </<?' Carrij but meaning to ' go in the way of what is worthless or poverty-stricken,' and so it was that the street came by its name."

This strange tale, which is evidently of great antiquity, and deeply inspired with real witch tradition, has, indeed, nothing in common with the pretty fairy stories which are so generally presented as constituting the whole of popular narrative folklore. It was not made nor intended to serve as a pleasing tale for youth, but to embody certain ideas which the witch-teacher explained to the pupil. The first of these is, that the jig-tree planted under certain circumstances became a kind of Luck of Eden Hall to its possessor. This story comes from the

Etruscan-Roman land, where traditions have been preserved with incredible fidelity. In the olden time Tarquin the Elder planted a fig-tree in a public place in Rome, and it was a matter of common faith that this tree would flourish for ever if undisturbed, and that on it depended the prosperity and preservation of the city. 1 And in India, the motherland of Greek and Roman mythology, it was believed that whenever one of certain ancient fig-trees died, that the reigning family would pass away. The opinion was widely spread that the fig-tree was above all others the one of life and destiny. In the Bagvatgeta, Krishna says of himself: " I am the spirit, the beginning, the middle, and the end of creation. I am as the Aswatha (pipal or Indian fig) among trees." Hence it came that many Christians believed that the Tree of Life in Eden was not an apple but a fig-tree. The traditions which establish the fig-tree as being above all others one on

1 Friedrich, " Symbolik der Natur."

whose existence that of individuals, families, and states depended, are extremely numerous and varied. " It was," remarks Alt, " not only a symbol of fertility, but an emblem of ever-renewed and never-extinguished vitality, and one of eternity, the resurrection, and of the transmigration of the soul." On the celebrated altar in Ghent, the Tree of Life is represented as a fig-tree (Menzel, Christliche. Symbolik, \. 277). This universal belief explains why the fig-tree determines the duration and destiny of lives and families.

It may have struck the reader as singular that those who eat of the forbidden figs are punished by the visit of a beautiful girl who whirls around with a buzzing sound till they are overcome by awe. Here be it noted first of all, that the fig, like the pear, is exactly the shape of a top, even the stem representing the peg. Now, in ancient Latin witchlore or sorcery, extraordinary magic power, or even sanctity, was attached to everything which made a humming or buzzing sound. It was supposed, when properly made, with certain incantations or instruments, to be capable of throwing people into a trance. Chief among these instruments was the top. Thus Horace begs Crattidia to stop the enchantment of the buzzing top (Ode xv. Book v.).

On this subject I find the following in Diavoli e Streghe, by Dr. A. Zangolini, 1864 :

" The rombo * is an instrument not unlike the trottola or peg-top of our boys, called in Latin turbo, and in common language also paleo. It was believed that with it in witchcraft a lover could have his head turned with passion, or that he would be turned at will while it spun. The same held true of other disks (tee-totums) of wood, iron, or copper."

This idea was extended to the hum of spinning-wheels, which aided the conception of the Fates, and the thread

1 A humming-top.

of life, to the buzzing of bees and flies, and many other variations of such sounds. Mr. Andrew Lang has in an admirable paper shown that the bull-roarer has been regarded as so sacred among certain savages that women, or the profane, were not allowed to touch it. A bull-roarer is so easily constructed, that it is remarkable how few people are familiar with it. Take a common stick, say six inches in length, tie a cord three feet long to one end, and, grasping the other, whirl it round, with the result of astonishing all to whom it is not familiar by its sound:

" First it is but a gentle hum,
Like bird-song warbling in the trees, Then like a torrent it doth foam,
And then a wild and roaring breeze."

When vigorously spun, it may be heard of a calm evening for a mile, and its effect is then indescribably— I will not say, as most novelists here would, " weird" for I do not know that it prophesies anything, but it is certainly most suggestive of something mysterious.

Therefore the bayadere, with her spinning pas seul and buzzing romore, who appears to the eater of the figs, is the magic top in person, her form being taken from the fig. The connection of the enchanted dog with the tree is not so clear, but it may be observed that there is a vast mass of tradition which makes the black dog a chthonic, that is, a subterranean or under-earthly symbol, and that in this story he comes out of the earth. This animal was a special favourite of Hecate-Diana of the world below, the queen of all the witches.

There is a vast quantity of folklore in reference to the fig as an emblem of fertility, reproduction, and sensual affinity, and, on the other side, of its being an emblem often used in proverbs to express the very contrary, or trifling value, worthlessness, and poverty. Thus, the barren fig-tree of the New Testament had a deep signification to all who were familiar with these poetic and

o

mystic "correspondences." The reader has probably observed that in this story there is, as in a parable, a strong intimation of symbolism, or as if more were meant than meets the ear.

" Remains to be said," that the putting the thumb between the index and middle finger, which was regarded with awe by the Romans as driving away evil spirits, was called " making the fig," or far la castagna, to make the chestnut—in Latin, medium ostendere digitum. The same sign as the fig to drive away devils became a deadly insult when made at any one, as if he were a wizard and accursed. It had also a jeering and indecent meaning. It has been said that the fig, as a synonym for anything worthless, originated from the great abundance and cheapness of the fruit in Greece, but this is very unsatisfactory, since it would apply as well to olives or grain.

" This tale doth teach," notes the learned Flaxius, " as regards the folklore of the black dog, that in this life most things are good or bad, as we take them. For the black dog, Monsieur, of Cornelius Agrippa (like that in Faust) was a demon, albeit his pupil, Wierus, records that he himself knew the animal well, but never supposed there was aught of the goblin in it. And this same Wierus has mentioned (loc. at., p. m. 325), that one of the things which most terrify the devil and all his gang is the blood of a black dog splashed on the wall. So in ancient symbolism death meant life, the two being correlative, and in witchcraft the spell of the frog and many more are meant to do deadly harm, or great good, according to the way in which they are worked. Wherein lies an immense moral lesson for ye all. Remember, children—

" ' There is no passion, vice, or crime,

Which truly, closely understood, Does not, in the full course of time,

Do far less harm than good."

SHOWING HOW IT GOT ITS NAME FROM A FAIRY

" Ah me! what perils do environ The man who meddles with cold iron ! Thus sang great Butler long ago, In Hudibras, as all men know ; But in this story you will see How Iron was sold by irony."

ONE of the most picturesque mediaeval palaces in Florence is that of the Feroni, and its architectural beauty is greatly enhanced by its fine situation at the head of the Torna-buoni on the Piazza della Trinita, with the magnificent column of the Medicis just before its gate. According to Italian authority, " this palace may be called, after those of the Praetorio (i.e., Bargello) and the Signoria, the most characteristic building of its epoch in Florence. It is said to have been built by Arnolfo di Cambio. It once belonged to the Spini, from whom it passed to the Feroni." When I was in Florence in 1846-47, this palace was the best hotel in Florence, and the one in which I lived. There have been great " restorations " in the city since that time, but very few which have not been most discreditably and foolishly conducted, even to the utter destruction of all that was truly interesting in them; as, for instance, " the house of Dante, torn down within a few years to be rebuilt, so that now not one stone rests upon another of the original; " and " Santa Maria Novella, where the usual monkish hatred of everything not rococo and trashy has shown itself by destroying beautiful work of earlier times, or selling it to the Kensington Museum,

setting up a barbarously gilt gingerbread high altar, and daubing the handsome Gothic sacristy with gaudy colours." To which the author of Murray's " Guide-Book for Central Italy " adds, that " perhaps on the whole list of ecclesiastical restorations there does not exist a more deplorable instance of monastic vandalism than has been perpetrated here by the architect Romoli"—a remark which falls unfortunately very far short of the truth. Such ruin is wrought everywhere at present; witness the beautiful Fonte Gaja, " the masterpiece of Jacopo della Quercia in Siena (1402), which, since the change of Government, was not ' restored/ but totally destroyed and carted away, a miserable modern copy having been recently set up in its place " (Hare, " Cities of Central Italy "), all of which was probably done to " make a job " for a favoured builder. " But what can you expect," adds a friend, " in a country where it is common to cover a beautiful dry stone wall with plaster, and then paint it over to resemble the original stone," because, as I was naively told, " the rough stone itself looks too cheap " ? Anybody who has lived long in Italy can add infinitely to such instances. The Palazzo Feroni has, however, suffered so little, for a wonder, from restoration, and still really looks so genuinely old, that it deserves special mention, and may serve as an excuse for my remarks on the manner in which ancient works are destroyed so con amore by monks and modern municipalities. I may here note that this building is, in a sense, the common rendezvous for all the visitors to Florence, chiefly English and Americans, since in it are the very large circulating library and reading-rooms of Vieusseux. 1 There is, of course, a legend attached to the Palazzo Feroni, and it is as follows:

1 The Philological Society (Circolo), has also its rooms in this building.

IL PALAZZO FERONI.

"The Signore Pietro, who afterwards received the name Feroni, was a very rich man, and yet hated by the poor, on whom he bestowed nothing, and not much liked by his equals, though he gave them costly entertainments; for there was in all the man and in his character something inconsistent and contradictory, or of coma contra croce —' the horns against the cross,' as the proverb hath it, which made it so that one never knew where to have him :

" ' Un, al monte, e l'altro al pian, Quel che, e oggi, non e doman.'

" ' On the hill in joy, in the dale in sorrow— One thing to-day, and another to-morrow.'

" For to take him at every point, there was something to count off. Thus in all the city there was no one—according to his own declaration—who was Richer or more prosperous, Or who had enjoyed a better education, Or who had such remarkable general knowledge of everything taking place, Or more of a distinguished courtier, Or one with such a train of dependants, and people of

all kinds running after him, Or more generally accomplished, Or better looking—

" And finally, no one so physically strong, as he was accustomed to boast to everybody on first acquaintance, and give them proofs of it—he having heard somewhere that ' physical force makes a deeper impression than courtesy.' But all these fine gifts failed to inspire respect (and here was another puzzle in his nature), either because he was so tremendously vain that he looked down on all mortals as so many insects, and all pretty much alike as compared to himself, or else from a foolish carelessness and want of respect, he made himself quite as familiar with trivial people as with anybody. 1

" One evening the Signore Pietro gave a grand ball in his palace, and as the guests came in—the beauty and grace and

1 Perche si rendeva alle persone troppo triviale—A graphic sketch of a character who would be peculiarly offensive in a highly patrician community.

courtly style of all Italy in its golden time—he half closed his eyes, lazily looking at the brilliant swarm of human butterflies and walking flowers, despising while admiring them, though if he had been asked to give a reason for his contempt he would have been puzzled, not having any great amount of self-respect for himself. And they spun round and round in the dance. . . .

" When all at once he saw among the guests a lady, unknown to him, of such striking and singular appearance as to rouse him promptly from his idle thought. She was indeed wonderfully beautiful, but what was very noticeable was her absolutely ivory white complexion, which hardly seemed human, her profuse black silken hair; and most of all her unearthly large jet-black eyes, of incredible brilliancy, with such a strange expression as neither the Signore Pietro nor any one else present had ever seen before. There was a power in them, a kind of basilisk-fascination allied to angelic sweetness—fire and ice . . . ostra e tramontan —a hot and cold wind.

" The Signore Pietro, with his prompt tact, made the lady's paleness a pretence for addressing her. ' Did she feel ill— everything in the house was at her disposition—

" ' Servants, carpets, chairs and tables, Kitchen, pantry, hall and stables, Everything above or under ; All my present earthly plunder, All too small for such a wonder.'

" The lady, with a smile and a glance in which there was not the slightest trace of being startled or abashed, replied :

" ' 'Tis not worth while your house to rifle, 0 mio Signer, for such a trifle. 'Tis but a slight indisposition, For which I'll rest, by your permission.'

" The Signore Pietro, as an improvisatore, was delighted with such a ready answer, and remarking that he was something of a doctor, begged permission to bring a soothing cordial, admirable for the nerves, which he hoped to have the honour of placing directly in that fairy-like hand. . . . The Signore vanished to seek the calmante.

" The guests had begun by this time to notice this lady, and from her extremely strange appearance they gathered round her, expecting at first to have some sport in listening to,

or quizzing, an eccentric or a character. But they changed their mind as they came to consider her—some feeling an awe as if she were a fata, and all being finally convinced that whoever she was she had come there to sell somebody amazingly cheap, nor did they feel quite assured that they themselves were not included in the bargain.

"The Signore Pietro returned with the soothing cordial; he had evidently not drunk any of it himself while on the errand, for there was a massive chased iron table inlaid with gold and silver in his way, and the mighty lord with an angry blow from his giant arm, like one from a blacksmith's No. i hammer, broke it, adding an artisan-like oath, and knocked it over. Flirtation had begun.

" ' Did you hurt yourself, Signore ?' asked the lady amiably.

" ' Not I, indeed,' he replied proudly. ' A Stone is my name, but it ought to have been Iron, lady, for I am hard as nails, a regular Ferrone or big man of iron, and all my ancestors were Ferroni too; ah! we are a strong lot—at your service !' Saying this he handed the cup to the lady, who drank the potion, and then, instead of giving the goblet back to the Signore Pietro, as he expected, meaning to gallantly drink off les doux restes, she beckoned with her finger and an upward scoop of her hand to the table, which was lying disconsolately on its back with its legs upwards, like a trussed chicken waiting to be carved, when lo ! at the signal it jumped up and came walking to her like a Christian, its legs moving most humanly, and yet all present were appalled at the sight, and the Signore gasped—

"'I believe the devil's in it!'

"The lady composedly placed the draught on the table and smiled benevolently. There was something in that angelic smile which made the Signore feel as if he had been made game of. In a rage he rushed at the table, which reared up on its hind legs and showed fight with its forepaws, on which there were massy round iron balls, as on the other extremities. Truly it was a desperate battle, and both combatants covered themselves with dust and glory. Now the table would put a ball well in, and the Signore would counter, or, as I may say, cannon or cannon-ball it off; and then they would grapple and roll over and over till the Signora called them to time. At last the lord wrenched all the cannon-balls off from the table, which first, making a jump to the ceiling, came down in its usual position, while the balls began dancing on it like mad.

"At such a sight all present roared with laughter, and it was observed that the lady, no longer pale, flushed with merriment like a rose. As for Signore Pietro he was red as a beet, and heaved out that he had been canzonato or quizzed.

"'Truly yes,' replied the lady; 'but henceforth you shall have a name, for to do you justice you are as hard as iron, and Iron you shall be called—Big Iron Ferrone—and cannon-balls shall be your coat-of-arms, in sczcula s<zculorum. By edict of the Queen of the Fairies!'

"Now at this all the love in the Signore Pietro concentrated itself in his heart, passed into his tongue, and caused him to burst forth in song in the following ottava, while the music accompanied:

"'Quando vedo le femmine rammone, Mi sento andare il cuore in convulsione, Hanno certe facette vispe e sane, Da fare entrare in sen la tentazione, Oh donnina! Non siate disumana! Di Pietro abbiate compassione! Scusante la modestia se l'e troppo Di questi personal! non sene poppo.'

"'When I behold thy all too lovely features, I feel my heart in soft convulsions heaving, Thou art the most entrancing of all creatures, I tell you so in sooth, without deceiving, In fact there is no beauty which can beat yours; And Pietro loves you, lady, past believing; In breasts like cannon-balls there's naught to blame; But oh! I hope your heart's not like the same!'

"But as this exquisite poem concluded with an immense sigh, there appeared before them a golden and pearl car, in which the fairy entered, and rising sailed away through a great hole in the ceiling, which opened before and closed behind her, Signore Pietro remaining a bocca aperta, gaping with opened jaws, till all was o'er.

"'Well!' exclaimed the master, 'she gave me the slip, but we have had a jolly evening of it, and I'm the first man who ever fought an iron table, and I've got a good idea. My name is now Feroni—the Big Iron Man—ladies and gentlemen, please remember, and cannon-balls are in my coat-of-arms!'

I have naturally taken some liberty as regards mere text in translating this tale, in order to render the

better the spirit of the original; but not so much as may be supposed, and spirit and words are, on the whole, accurately rendered.

The reader is not to suppose that there are any traces of true history in this fairy tale. I am very greatly indebted to Miss Wyndham of Florence (who has herself made collections in folk-lore), for investigating this subject of the Feroni family, with the following result —it being premised that it had occurred to the lady that the "cannon-balls" or Medicean pills, or pawnbroker's sign, whatever it was, had been attributed by mistake to the Feroni. Miss Wyndham, after consulting with authority, found that the Feroni themselves had not the balls, but, owing probably to transfer of property, there is found on their palaces the Alessandri shield, on which the upper half and lower left quarter contain the Medici spheres. She also sent me this extract from the old work, Marietta di Ricci:

11 The Feroni family, originally named from Balducci da Vinci, and of peasant origin, owes its fortune to Francesco, son of Baldo di Paolo di Ferone, a dyer of Empoli. Going as a merchant to Holland, he accumulated a large fortune. Made known to Cosimo III. (just called to the Grand Duchy) by his travels, he was called to Florence. In 1673 he was made citizen of Florence, in 1674 he was elected senator, and in 1681 appointed Marquis of Bellavista. He left a colossal fortune, which has been kept up by his heirs to the present day. His grandson Guiseppe was made cardinal in 1753.

" Their arms are an arm mailed in iron, holding a sword, and above it a golden lily in a blue field."

This extract is interesting, as showing how a family could rise by industry and wealth, even in one generation, by the work of a single man, to the highest honours in Florence. And it is very remarkable that some impression of the origin of this vigorous artisan and merchant, of peasant stock, is evident in the tale. He is there clever

and strong, but vulgar and familiar, so that he was not personally liked. He remains standing open-mouthed, like a comic actor, when the fairy vanishes. In fact the whole tale suggests the elements of a humorous melodrama or operetta, a bourgeois gentilhomme.

" And should it come to pass that any read This tale in Viesseux, his library, In the Feroni palace, let them think That, even in the rooms where they do read, The things which I have told once came to pass— Even so the echo ever haunts the shrine !"

LA VIA DELLE BELLE DONNE

"The church of San Gaetano, on the left of the Via Tornabuoni, faces the Palazzo Antinori, built by Giuliano di San Gallo. Opposite is the Via delle Belle Donne, a name, says Leigh Hunt, which it is a sort of tune to pronounce."— HARE, Cities of Central Italy.

THE name of this place is suggestive of a story of some kind, but it was a long time before I obtained the following relative to the Street of Pretty Women :

" In the Via delle Belle Donne there was a very large old house in which were many lodgers, male and female, who, according to their slender means, had two rooms for a family. Among these were many very pretty girls, some of them seamstresses, others corset-makers, some milliners, all employed in shops, who worked all day and then went out in the evening to carry their sewing to the maggazini. And it was from them that the street got its name, for it became so much the fashion to go and look at them that young men would say, ' Andiamo nella Via delle Belle Donne] —' Let us go to the Street of the Pretty Women;' so it has been so-called to this day.

"And when they sallied forth they were at once surrounded or joined by young men, who sought their company with views more or less honourable, as is usual. Among these there was a very handsome and wealthy signore named Adolfo, who was so much admired that he might have had his choice of all these belles, but he had fixed his mind on one, a beautiful blonde, who was, indeed, the fairest among them all. She had large black eyes, with quick glances, beautiful light hair in masses, and was always dressed simply, yet with natural elegance. She had long avoided making acquaintance among men, and she now shunned Adolfo; but at last he succeeded, after many difficulties, in becoming acquainted, and finally won her heart—the end of it all being the old story of a poor girl ruined by a gay and great signor, left a mother, and then abandoned.

" For four years she lived alone, by her work, with her child, who grew up to be a very beautiful boy. Then he, noting that other children had parents, asked her continually,' Mamma, where is my papa ?'

" He gave her no rest, and at last she went to Adolfo and asked him what he would do for their child.

" He laughed at her, and said, ' Nothing. That folly is all over. Begone !'

"Then, in a wild passion of rage at seeing her child so despised, she stabbed him to the heart, and escaped unseen and undiscovered.

" Then, when the boy asked her again :

" ' Cara madre, cara madre, Dove e lo mio padre ?'

' Mother dear, tell to me Where may my father be ? '

" She replied:

" ' Darling son, thy sire is dead, Lying in an earthen bed ; Dead he ever will remain, By my dagger he was slain. Had he but been kind to thee, Living still he yet would be ; Other sorrows I forgave, With my dirk I dug his grave. 1

This is but a commonplace story, yet it is such as finds more currency among the people, and particularly among girls, than many a better one. There is a strong touch of nature, and especially of Italian nature, in the concluding lines.

1 " Col mio pugnale ammazato, Col pugnale e sotterato."

THE WIZARD WITH RED TEETH

" And dost thou fear to greet The Dead with me. They graced our wedding sweet."

— MOORE, The Veiled Prophet of Khorassan.

THE following ballad may be classed as Florentine, since it was in Florence that I heard it sung, but it is not attached to any particular place. It is one of those compositions which are either sung or simply recited, and quite as often intoned in a manner which is neither singing nor speaking. In such chant, when a rhyme happens to fall in by chance, the utmost is made of it by dwelling on the word or drawling it out. Sometimes, as in the following, there are verses of four lines each, but only the concluding line of every verse rhymes, i.e., with the preceding last line of the previous stanza :

IL STREGHONE coi DENTI Rossi.

" C'era un gran signore Che una bella figlia aveva, Far la felice lo credeva, Col far la maritar.

" ' Babbo, no'voglio marito, Prendo uno soltanto, Se si uomo coi dente rossi, Di famelo trovar.'

" ' Figlia, non e possibile A me mi strazzi il cuor Avanti di morire Vo farti tranquillo il cuor.'

" Un giorno allor comparvi, Un giovane assai bello, E denti rossi li teneva, La sua figlia, Amelia, ' Mi dica dove ella.'

" ' Io lo vo sposare, E con me la vo' portare.' ' Dimmi dove la porti, Giovane sconosciuto, La mia figlia no ti rifiuto, Coi denti rossi lo vuol sposar ?'

" Sposa la siora Amelia, E se la porta via. La casa dove sia, Questo poi non lo sa.

" La porta in una capanna, Di foglie, legno, e fieno, ' Ortello fa sapere, Se vuoi saper chi sono.

" ' Io sono un' streghone, Te'l giuro in verita, La notte a mezzanotte Io ti faccio levar.

" ' Ti porto al camposanto, A sotterar i morti; E se tu vuoi mangiar, Quel sangue, bella mia, Tu l'ai da succiar.'

" La giovana disperata, Piange, grida e si dispera, Ma rimedio piu non v'era Anche lei una Strega, Toccava diventar."

TRANSLATION.

" There was a grand signore Who had a daughter fair ; He longed to see her happy, And wished that she were wed.

" * Oh, father ! I would not marry, I have vowed to have for my husband One with teeth as red as coral. Oh ! find him for me,' she said.

" ' My daughter, it is not possible, You wring and pain my heart. Ere I die and pass away I would fain be at peace,' said he.

" One day there appeared before her A knight of goodly seeming, His teeth were red as coral. Said the beautiful Amelia, ' There is the spouse for me.'

" ' I will marry her,' said the knight, ' And bear her with me away.' ' Tell me where wilt thou take her, Thou strange and unknown man. I do not refuse her to thee, But whither wilt thou roam ?'

" He married fair Amelia, And carried her far away. 4 Where is the house thou dwell'st in ? And say where is thy home ?'

" He took her to a cabin, All leaves and sticks and hay, ' My true name is Ortello. To-night, at the hour of midnight, I will carry thee away.

" ' I will bear thee to the graveyard To dig up the newly dead; Then if thou hast thirst or hunger Thou mayst suck the blood of the corpses,' To her the Sorcerer said.

" She wept in desperate sorrow, She wrung her lily hand, But she was lost for ever, And in the witches' band."

This was, and is, a very rude ballad ; its moral appears to be that feminine caprice and disregard of parental love must be punished. It is very remarkable as having to perfection that Northern or German element which Goethe detected in a Neapolitan witch-song given in his Italian journey. 1 It has also in spirit, and somewhat strangely in form, that which characterises one of Heine's most singular songs. It impresses me, as I was only yesterday impressed in the Duomo of Siena at finding, among the wood-carvings in the choir, Lombard grotesques which were markedly Teutonic, having in them no trace of anything Italian.

" Quaint mysteries of goblins and strange things, We scarce know what—half animal half vine, And beauteous face upon a toad, from which Outshoots a serpent's tail—the Manicore, A mixture grim of all things odd and wild, The fairy-witch-like song of German eld."

1 Since writing the foregoing, I have found in Am Urquelle, vol. vi. 3, May 1895, a legend credited to a book by A. Bondeson, Historic Giilbar pa Dal (Stockholm, 1886), or a story entitled "The Lover with a Green Beard," which is much the same in incident as this. The editor, H. Feil-berg, notices the affinity of this and other tales to the Vampyre and Burger's " Leonora."

ORPHEUS AND EURYDICE

" Wherever beauty dwells, In gulf or aerie mountains or deep dells, Thou pointest out the way, and straight 'tis won, Thou leddest Orpheus through the gleams of death."

— KEATS.

" Silvestres homines sacer interpres que Deorum Csedibus et victu deterruit ORPHEUS. Dictus ob hoc lenire tigres, rabidosque Leones."

— HORACE.

IT may have happened to the reader, in his travels, to trace in some majestic mountain-land, amid rocky ravines, that which was, perhaps, in prehistoric times a terrible torrent or a roaring river. I mean, indeed, such a furious flood as is now unknown on earth, one which tore away the highest hills like trifles, melting them in a minute to broad alluvials, and ground up the grandest granite cliffs to gravel-dust, even as a mighty mill grates grain to flour.

You trace the course of the ancient river which when young vaulted the valley, which it had made, on either side with overhanging precipices, which now bend like silent mourners over its grave. And it seems to be dead and buried for ever.

Yet it may chance that, looking more deeply into its course to see if, perhaps, some flakes of antique gold are not to be found in the bed of the old water-course, you hear deep in some rocky crevice far below, and out of sight, the merry gurgle or voice-like murmur of a spring or unseen rivulet which indicates that the river of ancient

days is not quite lost in the land. Unsuspected, like the

sapphire serpent of Eastern legend, that diamond-clear rivulet has wound its mysterious course deep in the earth for ages, and, following its sound, you may come to some place where it again leaps forth into sunlight—little, indeed, yet ever beautiful. It is almost touching to see that diminished rill creeping timidly round the feet of giant boulders which it once rent in sport from the mighty rocks, and rolled into what were for it in its whilom power, mere marbles. It is small now, and very obscure, yet it lives and is ever beautiful.

Such a stream, which I traced yesterday in an ancient gorge in the heart of the Apennines, where the grey tower of Rocca looks down on the mysterious Ponte del Diavolo of the twelfth century—the most picturesque bridge in Italy—forcibly reminds me of the human stream of old tradition which once, as marvellous mythology or grand religion, roared and often raged over all this region, driving before it, and rending away, all the mighty rocks of human will, now tearing down and anon forming stupendous cliffs of observances, and vast monoliths of legend and faith. Such were the Etruscan and early Roman cults, which drove before them and engulfed irresistibly all the institutions of their time, and then disappeared so utterly that men now believe that the only remaining record of their existence is in their tombs or rocky relics of strange monuments.

But by bending low to earth, or seeking among the people, we may hear the murmur of a hidden stream of legend and song which, small and shrunken as it may be, is still the veritable river of the olden time. Many such streams are running in many lands, and that full openly on the earth's surface, but this to which I specially refer is strangely occult and deeply hidden, for to find it we must seek among the strege and stregoni, or witches and sorcerers, who retain as dark secrets of their own, marvellous relics of the myths of the early ages. These are,

in many cases, so strangely quaint and beautiful that they would seem to have kept something of an original perfume which has utterly perished in the dried flowers of tradition preserved in books, or even by poets.

This seems to me to be the case with the incantation to Orpheus, which is now before me, written in rude dialect, which indicates, so to speak, the depth of the earth from which it was taken. I had asked the woman who gave it to me whether she knew such a name as that of Orpheus or Orfeo, as connected with music. This was the reply which I received:

ORFEO.

Scongiurazione a Orfeo per snonare bene uno Zuffolo. This is the invocation to Orpheus for him who would fain become a good player on the shepherd's pipe. [1]

SCONGIURAZIONE.

" Ogni giorno io mi metto Questo zuffolo a suonare, Per poterlo bene inparare, E a preso dei maestri Per potermi fare insegnare, Ma non so come mi fare, Nella testa non mi vuole entrare, A che partito mi devo apigliare : Io non so come mi fare; Ma tu Orfeo che siei tanto chapace Per Io zuffolo, e il violino, Suoni bene pur Io organino, La chitarra e il mandolino, La gran cassa, il trombone, Suoni bene Io clarino, E non 'ce uno strumento Che tu Orfeo tu non sia

1 Zufolo —a rude flageolet, such as is still commonly played by the shepherds all over Italy.

    Chapace di bene suonare,
    Per la musicha siei molto bravo,
    E tu ai ogni potenza,
    Che da diavoli siei protetto,
    Dunque insegnami come fare,
    Questo zuffolo va scongiurare,
    Per poter bene suonare,
    Questo zuffolo lo prendo,
    Sotto terra io lo metto,
    E tre giorni ce lo fo stare,
    A fine che tu Orfeo,
    Bene tu me lo facci a suonare;
    Che tanto siei amante
    Di suonare sarai amante,
    Pur d'insegnare per quanto
    Ai soferto la tua Auradice,
    Dal inferno non potere levare,
    Ma vollo lei a preghare,
    Che ti aiuti questo zuffolo volere suonare,
    E tu che sempre e di musicha,
    Siei chapace che fino
    Le bestie ti vengono ascoltare,
    Orfeo ! Orfeo ! ti prego;
    Orfeo ! volermi insegnare
    Questo zuffolo bene suonare,
    E appena suonero,
    Il maestro musicho Orfeo ringraziero,
    E a tutti sempre faro,
    Sapere a chi mi a dato,
    Questo talento che le stato,
    Orfeo dal inferno lo scongiurato,
    E per la musicha o tanto,
    Pasione al mio zuffolo a dato,
    Lezione e lo zuffolo e un strumento
    Che ne son tanto inamorato
    Che dai miei vecchi era molto ramentato,
    E sempre mi dicevano,
    Se dinparar lo non siei chapace,
    Orfeo devi scongiurare ;
    E cosi io faro,
    E Orfeo preghero !"
TRANSLATION.

" Every day I try, and yet
I cannot play the flageolet;
Many masters I have sought,
Naught I learned from all they taught;
I am dull, 'tis very true,
And I know not what to do
In this strait, unless it be,
Great Orpheus, to come to thee;
Thou who the greatest skill didst win,
On flageolet and violin,
Who play'st the organ, pealing far,
The mandolin and the guitar,
Thou wak'st the clarion's stirring tone,
The rattling drum and loud trombone;
On earth there is no instrument,
Whate'er it be, to mortals sent,
Enchanting every sense away,
Which thou, O Orpheus ! canst not play ;
Great must thy skill in music be,
Since even the demons favour thee ; And since on this my heart is set,
Enchant, I pray, this flageolet,
And that its tones may sweetly sound,
I bury it beneath the ground;
Three days shall it lie hidden thus,
Till thou, O mighty Orpheus !
Shalt wake in it by magic spell
The music which thou lov'st so well.
I conjure thee by all the woe
Which grieved thy soul so long ago !
And pain, when thy Auradice
From the dark realm thou couldst not free,
To grant me of thy mighty will
That I may play this pipe with skill,
Even as thou hast played before ;
For, as the story runs, of yore,
Whenever thou didst wake its sound,
The forest beasts came raptured round.
Orpheus ! Orpheus ! I pray,
Orpheus ! teach me how to play !

And when sweet music forth I bring, On every chord thy name shall ring, And every air which charms shall be A hymn of thanks, great lord, to thee ! And unto all I'll make it known, I owe it all to thee alone, And of the wondrous skill I'll tell, Which mighty Orpheus won from hell. And by the music, and the power, Of passion in me, from this hour Henceforth in this sweet instrument I shall be ever well content ; For now, I do remember well, What 'twas my father oft would tell, That all who would learn music thus Must conjure mighty Orpheus, Even as I have done to-day, So I to him will ever pray."

To which the manuscript adds in prose:

" Thus the peasants do when they do not succeed in playing the shepherd's pipe, which they esteem beyond any other instrument."

To any one who fully feels and understands what is meant to be conveyed by this incantation—and a great deal is expressed by passionate singing and a deep thrilling intonation which the text does not give—my translation will appear to be quite accurate. But, in any case, no scholar or poet can deny that there is in it a strange depth of classic feeling, or of old Roman romance, not strained at second-hand through books, but evidently drawn from rude antiquity, which is as fresh in its ring as it is marvellous.

It may be observed as exquisitely curious that in this incantation the peasant who wishes to become a skilled performer on the flageolet buries it for three days in the ground, invoking Orpheus by what the spirit suffered in losing Eurydice, and subsequently distinctly declaring

that he won or conjured his great musical power from Hades, which means that by the penance and loss, and his braving the terrors of the Inferno, he gained skill. This is a mighty element of the myth in all its forms, in all ages, in every country. The burying the instrument for three days probably typifies the three days during which Orpheus was in hell.

It may be observed that Eurydice has become Auradice in the incantation, in which there is probably an intimation of Aura, a light wind or zephyr. Air is so naturally associated with music. This, by a very singular coincidence, yet certainly due to mere chance, recalls the invocation to the Spirit of the Air, given by Bulwer in " The Last Days of Pompeii" :

" Spectre of the viewless air, Hear the blind Thessalian's prayer, By Erichtho's art that shed Dews of life when life was fled, By lone Ithaca's wise king, Who could wake the crystal spring To the voice of prophecy By the lost Eurydice ! Summoned from the shadowy throng, At the muse-son's magic song : Come, wild Demon of the Air, Answer to thy votary's prayer."

It is indeed very remarkable that in the call to the God of Music, who is in certain wise a spirit of the air, as in that to the Spirit of the Air himself, both are invoked :

"By the lost Eurydice!"

If it could be shown that Bulwer owed this poem and allusion to any ancient work or tradition, I should be tempted to believe that the popular invocation was derived from some source in common with the latter. There is indeed a quaint naï've drollery in the word Auradice — " Air-tell! " or " Air-declare ! " which adapts it better to the spirit of Bulwer's poem, in which the air is begged to

tell something, than to the Orphean or Orphic spell. It may be that the Orphic oracles were heard in the voice of the wind, apropos of which latter there is a strange Italian legend and an incantation to be addressed to all such mystic voices of the night, which almost seems reechoed in " Lucia " :

" Verrano a te sull' aure, I miei sospiri ardenti, Udrai nell mar che mormora L'eco de miei lamenti ! "

It is worth observing that this tradition, though derived from the Romagna, was given to me in Florence, and that one of the sculptures on the Campanile represents Orpheus playing the pipe to wild beasts. It is said that in the Middle Ages the walls of churches were the picture-books of the people, where they learned all they knew of Bible legends, but not unfrequently gathered many strange tales from other sources. The sculptors frequently chose of. their own will scenes or subjects which were well known to the multitude, who would naturally be pleased with the picturing what they liked, and it may be that Orpheus was familiar then to all. In any case, the finding him in a witch incantation is singularly in accordance with the bas-relief of the Cathedral of Florence, which again fits in marvellously well with Byron's verse:

" Florence ! whom I will love as well As ever yet was said or sung, Since Orpheus sang his spouse from hell, Whilst thou art fair and I am young.

" Sweet Florence ! those were pleasant times, When worlds were staked for ladies' eyes. Had bards as many realms as rhymes, Thy charms might raise new Antonies ! "

True it is that this Florence seems to have had dazzling eyes and ringlets curled; and it is on the other hand not true that Orpheus sang his spouse from hell—he only

tried to do it. And it is worth noting that one of the commonest halfpenny pamphlets sold in Florence, which is to be found at every public stand, is a poem called " Orpheus and Eurydice." This fact alone renders it less singular that such classical incantations should exist.

The early Christians, notwithstanding their antipathy to heathen symbols, retained with love that of Orpheus. Orpheus was represented as a gentle youth, charming wild beasts with the music of the pipe, or as surrounded by them and sheep; hence he was, like the Good Shepherd, the favourite type of Christ. He had also gone down into shadowy Hades, and returned to be sacrificed by the heathen, unto whose rites he would not conform.

Miss Roma Lister found traces of Orpheus among the peasantry about Rome, in a pretty tradition. They say that there is a spirit who, when he plays the zufolo or flageolet to flocks, attracts them by his music and keeps them quiet.

" Now there were certain shepherd families and their flocks together in a place, and it was agreed that every night by turns, each family should guard the flocks of all the rest. But it was observed that one mysterious family all turned in and went to sleep when their turn came to watch, and yet every morning every sheep was in its place. Then it was found that this family had a spirit who played the zufolo, and herded the flock by means of his music."

The name is wanting, but Orpheus was there. The survival of the soul of Orpheus in the zufolo or pipe, and in the sprite, reveals the mystic legend which indicates his existing to other times. In this it is said that his head after death predicted to Cyrus the Persian monarch that he too would be killed by a woman (Consule Leonic, de var. htstor., lib. i. cap. 17; de Orphei Tiimulo in monte Olympo, &.C., cited by Kornmann de Miracnlis Mortn-orum, cap. 19). The legend of Orpheus, or of a living wife returning from another world to visit an afflicted

husband, passed to other lands, as may be seen in a book by Georgius Sabinus, in Notts ad Metamorp. Ovidii, lib. x. de descensu Orphei ad Inferos, in which he tells how a Bavarian lady, after being buried, was so moved by her husband's grief that she came to life again, and lived with him for many years, semper tamen fuisse tris-tem acpallidem —but was always sad and pale. However, they got on very well together for a long time, till one evenrngpostvesperipottiJii —after he had taken his evening drink—being somewhat angry at the housemaid, he scolded her with unseemly words. Now it was the condition of his wife's coming back to life and remaining with him that he was never to utter an improper expression (ut que deinceps ipse abstineret blasphemis conviciandi ver-bis). And when the wife heard her husband swear, she disappeared, soul and body, and that in such a hurry that her dress (which was certainly of fine old stiff brocade) was found standing up, and her shoes under it. A similar legend, equally authentic, may be found in the " Breitmann Ballads," a work, I believe, by an American author. On which subject the learned Flaxius remarks that " if all the men who swear after their evening refreshments were to lose their wives, widowers would become a drug in the market."

Of the connection between aura as air, and as an air in music, I have something curious to note. Since the foregoing was written I bought in Florence a large wooden cup, it may be of the eleventh century or earlier, known as a misnra, or measure for grain, formerly called a modio, in Latin modus, which word has the double meaning of measure for objects solid or liquid, and also for music. Therefore there are on the wooden measure four female figures, each holding a musical instrument, and all with their garments blowing in one direction, as in a high wind, doubtless to signify aura, Italian aria, air or melody. These madonnas of the four modes are rudely but very gracefully sketched by a bold master-hand. They represent, in fact, Eurydice quadrupled.

There is a spirit known in the Toscana Romagna as Turdbug. He is the guardian of the reeds or canes, or belongs to them like the ancient Syrinx. There is a curious ceremony and two invocations referring to him. Ivy and rue are specially sacred to him. One of these two invocations is solely in reference to playing the znfolo, partly that the applicant may be inspired to play well, and secondly, because the spirit is supposed to be attracted by the sound of the instrument. The very ancient and beautiful idea that divinities are invoked or attracted by music, is still found in the use of the organ in churches.

A large portion of the foregoing on Orpheus formed, with " Intialo," the subject of a paper by me in Italian, which was read in the Collegio Romana at Rome at the first meeting of the Italian Societa Nazionale per le Tradi-zioni Popolari Italiani, in November 1893. Of which society I may here mention that it is under the special patronage of her Majesty Margherita the Queen of Italy, who is herself a zealous and accomplished folklorist and collector—" special patronage " meaning here not being a mere figurehead, but first officer—and that the president is Count Angelo de Gubernatis.

I believe that the establishment of this society will contribute vastly to shake in Italy the old-fashioned belief that to be a person of the most respectable learning it is quite sufficient to be thoroughly acquainted with a few " classic " writers, be they Latin, French, or Italian, and that it is almost a crime to read anything which does not directly serve as a model or a copy whereby to " refine our style." As regards which the whole world is now entering on a new renaissance, the conflict between the stylists and the more liberally enlightened having already begun.

But Orpheus, with the ecclesiastical witch-doctors, was soon turned into a diabolical sorcerer; and Leloyer writes of him : " He was the greatest wizard who ever lived, and his writings boil over with praises of devils and filthy loves of gods and mortals, . . . who were all only devils and witches."

That Eve brought death and sin into the world by eating one apple, or a fig, or orange, or Chinese nectarine, or the fruit of the banana tree, or a pear, a peach, or everything pomological, if we are to believe all translators of the Bible, coincides strongly with the fact that Eury-dice was lost for tasting a pomegranate. " Of the precise graft of the espalier of Eden," says the author of the ' Ingoldsby Legends,' " Sanchoniathon, Manetho, and Berosus are undecided; the best informed Talmudists have, however . . . pronounced it a Ribstone pippin," Eve being a rib. The ancients were happy in being certain that their apple was one of Granada.

" Hcec fabula docet" writes our Flaxius, "that mysteries abound in every myth. Now, whether Orpheus was literally the first man who ever went to hell for a woman I know not, but well I ween that he was not the last, as the majority of French novelists of the present day are chiefly busy in proving, very little, as it seems to me, either to the credit of their country or of themselves. But there are others who read in this tale a dark and mysterious forewarning to the effect that ladies a la mode who fall in love with Italian musicians or music-masters, and especially those who let themselves and their fortunes be sifflees (especially the fortunes), should not be astonished when the fate of Eurydice befalls them. Pass on, beloved, to another tale !

"'Walk on, amid these mysteries strange and old, The strangest of them all is yet to come!'"

INTIA\LO

THE SPIRIT OF THE HAUNTING SHADOW

" O ombra che dalla luce siei uscita, Misuri il passo al Sole, all'uom la vita."

" Umbram suam metuere."

" Badate. La vostra ombra vi avra fatto paura."

— Filippo Pananti.

" There is a feeling which, perhaps, all have felt at times ; ... it is a strong and shuddering impression which Coleridge has embodied in his own dark and supernatural verse that Something not of earth is behind us —that if we turned our gaze backward we should behold that which would make the heart as a bolt of ice, and the eye shrivel and parch within its socket. And so intense is the fancy, that when we turn, and all is void, from that very void we could shape a spectre as fearful as the image our terror had foredrawn."— BULWER, The Disowned.

THE resemblance and the relation of the shadow to the body is so strangely like that of the body to the soul, that it is very possible that it first suggested the latter. It is born of light, yet is in itself a portion of the mystery of darkness; it is the facsimile of man in every outline, but in outline alone; filled in with uniform sombre tint, it imitates our every action as if in mockery, which of itself suggests a goblin or sprite, while in it all there is something of self, darkling and dream-like, yet never leaving us. It is only evident in brightest hours, like a skeleton at an Egyptian feast, and it has neither more nor less resemblance to man than the latter. Hence it came that the strange " dwellers by the Nile " actually loved both shade and death by association, and so it happened that

" Full many a time

They seemed half in love with easeful Death ; Called him soft names in many a mused rhyme,"

while they made of the cool shadow a portion of the soul itself, or rather one of the seven or eight entities of which man consisted, these being— Khat, a body; Ba, the spirit; Khon, the intelligence; KJiaibit, tJic shadow; Ren, the name ; Ka, eternal vitality; Ab, the heart; and Sakn, the mask or mummy.

It is extremely interesting to consider, in connection with this Egyptian doctrine, the fact, illustrated by every writer on Etruscan antiquity, that these ancient dwellers in Italy, when they represented the departed, or the dead, as living again on a tomb, added to the name of the deceased the word Hinthial. This I once believed meant simply a ghost or spirit. I had no other association with the name.

I inquired for a long time if there was any such name as Hintial for a ghost among the people, and could not find it. At last my chief agent succeeded in getting from sources to me unknown, but, as in all cases, partly from natives of the Toscana Romagna, or Volterra, and at different times, very full information regarding this mysterious being, which I combine as follows :

INTIALO.

" This is a spirit in human form who shows himself in any shadow, 1 and diverts himself by inspiring terror in a sorcerer, or in any one who has committed a crime. He causes a fearful shadow to be ever present to the man, and addresses him thus :

suo spirito lo fa presentare qualunque ombra, that is, in any or varied shadow ; a haunting shade, and not strictly the mere shadow of the one who is haunted. demone al Stregone.

" Vile—tu non potrai Avere mai bene — avrai Sempre la mia ombra In tua presenza, e saro Vendicato . . .

" Tu non potrai giammai Essere solo, che l'ombra Mia ovunque andrai Ti seguira : tu non potrai Essere mai solo, tu sarai Sempre in mio potere !

" Al mio incantesimo non avrai Ne pace ne bene, al mio Incanto tu tremerai, Te e tutta la casa dove ti troverai, Se sei in mezzo alia strada, Tu tremerai— Te e tutta la terra !

" Al mio volere tu andrai Come cane alia pagliaio, Alia voce del suo maestro; Tu me vorrai Vedere, e non mi vedrai, Mi sentirai— Vedrai sola la tua ombra.

" Tu sei cattivo e scelerato, Tu sei avelenato, Nel cuore e nell anima, E piu bene non avrai, Sei avelenato nel cuore, E nell anima, vai, Tu siei maladetto ; E il spirito sempre ti seguira Ovunque tu vada ! "

That which here follows of the invocation was obtained subsequently by my agent, I think, from another source. What precedes is evidently only a fragment.

TRANSLATION. The Demon to the Sorcerer.

" Wretch ! long lost in wickedness, Thou shalt ne'er have happiness ; Though to distant lands thou'lt flee, Still my shadow thou shalt see, And I will revenged be.

" Solitude thou ne'er shalt know, Where thou goest my shade shall go, And wherever thou mayst fly Still the shadow will be by-Ne'er alone at any hour, And for ever in my power.

" By my spell thou ne'er shalt know Peace or joy on earth below, At my charm a deadly fear Shall seize on all men standing near; Thou shalt tremble in thy home, Or if thou abroad shouldst roam, Shivering with fear thou'lt be, And the earth shall shake with thee.

' At my bidding thou must stir, And hasten as the vilest cur Must hasten when his master calls, And leave his straw amid the stalls; And if thou wouldst gaze on me, Still my form thou shalt not see ; Thou shalt feel when I am here, Feel me in thy deadly fear, Yet only see thy shadow near.

" Thou art vile and wicked too, Thou art poisoned through and through In thy heart and in thy soul, Cursedness is in the whole,

In thy soul and in thy heart, Poison steeped in every part. Cursed ever ! now, depart! Yet wherever thou shalt flee I will ever follow thee !

" Then this man will be in terror, and he will ever see the shadow before him by day and by night, and thus he will have no peace, and yet this is all the time the spirit of Intialo.

" Now, when he is thus tormented for some past misdeed, and he feels himself haunted, as it were, by the shadow of the one whom he has wronged, when he finds at last that he is not pursued, indeed, by it, but by Intialo, then he shall repeat the Exorcism:

Scongiurazione di Intialo.

" Intialo ! Intialo ! che quando Una persona ai preso, O per seguitare le ingombri Le ingombri sempre la cammina.

" Intialo ! Intialo ! se libero II passo mi lascerai meglio Per te sara, se non mi verrai Lasciare ti faccio sapere Tu sarai sempre in mio potere.

" Intialo ! Intialo ! ti faccio sapere, Se metto in opera La mia scongiurazione, Non ti lasciero piu bene avere, E ogni mi a chiamata Ti faro correre Come chane al pagliaio,

" Intialo ! Intialo ! Ti faccio sapere Che tu pensi a fare II tuo dovere,

Se ancora mi viene a tormentare Muso di porco tu possa diventare.

" Intialo ! Intialo ! Tu siei furbo e maligno, Ma io me ne infischio, Perche io sono di te, Molto piu maligno.

" Intialo ! Intialo ! ti prego Di non mi piu tormentare Se vuoi aver bene, Se no ti acquisterai Delle pene— e questo sara II tuo guadagno.

" Intialo ! Intialo ! Con tutta la tua furberia, Non sai ancora Che io son protetto Da una bella stregha Che mi adora.

" Intialo ! Intialo ! Se piu ne vuoi sapere Vieni sta sera, Vieni a mezza notte, Viene di dove sei, Te Io faro vedere, Vieno sotto 'quel noce E tu Io vedrai.

" Intialo ! Intialo ! La mezza notte in punto, Noi l'abbiamo, E ti vedo (vedro) appogiato Al noce che credi di vedere, Vedere l'ombra mia, E vedi l'ombra tua stessa !

" Intialo ! Intialo ! Dentro al mio seno Quattro cose tengo, Che mi fanno vedere, E non son veduto, Ellera, pane, Sale e ruta, E la mia buona fortuna.

" Intialo ! Intialo ! Non ti voglio dire, Perche io voglio Andare a dormire; Ma solo ti ho fatto Ti ho fatto vedere Che non son' in poter tuo, Ma tu siei in mio potere."

The Exorcism of Intialo.

" Intialo ! it is known When thou followest any one, Be the victim whom he may, Thou art ever in his way.

" Intialo—hear! if free Thou wilt leave the road to me, Better for thee shall it be; If thou wilt not, from this hour I will hold thee in my power.

" Intialo ! thou shalt learn That I'm wizard in my turn; All the power of sorcery So about thee I will throw— All around, above, below— That thou shalt accursed be, Held in fear and agony, And as a dog shalt follow me.

" Intialo ! thou shalt know What thou art ere thou canst go; If thou comest here again To torment or give me pain, As thou'dst make a dog of me, I will make a swine of thee.

" Intialo ! sorry cheat, Filled with hate from head to feet, Be malignant if you will, I am more malignant still.

" Intialo ! for thy sake I pray thee no more trouble take To torment me, for thy gain Will only be thy greater pain, For so cursed thou shalt be That I needs must pity thee.

" Intialo ! now, confess That with all thy craftiness Thou didst not know what now I tell, That I am protected well By a lovely witch, and she Is mightier far, O fiend ! than thee.

" Intialo ! ere we go, If thou more of me wouldst know, Come at midnight—I shall be 'Neath the witches' walnut tree, And what I shall make thee see I trow will be enough for thee.

" Intialo ! in that hour Thou shalt truly feel my power, And when thou at last shalt ween That on the witches' tree I lean, Then to thee it shall be known That my shadow is thine own.

" Intialo ! everywhere With me magic charms I bear, Ivy, bread and salt and rue, And with them my fortune too.

" Intialo ! hence away, Unto thee no more I'll say ; Now I fain would go to sleep, See that thou this warning keep. I am not in power of thine, But thou truly art in mine."

I had the belief, derived from several writers, that HintJiial in Etruscan meant simply a ghost or revenant — the apparition of some one dead. But on mentioning my discovery of this legend to Professor Milani, the Director of the Archaeological Museum in Florence, and the first of Etruscan scholars, he astonished me by declaring that he believed the word signified a shadow, and that its real meaning in its full significance had apparently been marvellously preserved in this witch-tradition. Too little is known as yet of the old Etruscan language to decide with certainty as to anything in it, but should this opinion of Professor Milani be sustained, it will appear that at least one word of the mysterious tongue has existed till now in popular tradition.

There will be very few of my readers who will not be struck, as I was, with the remarkable resemblance of the terrible curse uttered by Intialo to the invocation in Byron's tragedy of " Manfred." It is like it in form, spirit, and, in many places, even in the very words. That there was, however, no knowledge of the English poem by the Italian witch-poet, and therefore no imitation, is plain from intrinsic evidence. As the question is interesting, I will here give the Incantation from " Manfred " :

INCANTATION.

" When the moon is on the wave, And the glow-worm in the grass,

And the meteor on the grave, And the wisp on the morass ;

When the falling stars are shooting,

And the answered owls are hooting,

And the silent leaves are still

In the shadow of the hill,

Shall my soul be upon thine
With a power and with a sign.

" Though thy slumber may be deep, Yet thy spirit shall not sleep ; There are shades which shall not vanish, There are thoughts thou canst not banish ;

By a power to thee unknown Thou canst never be alone ; Thou art wrapt as with a shroud, Thou art gathered in a cloud, And for ever shall thou dwell In the spirit of this spell.

" Though thou see'st me not pass by, Thou shalt feel me with thine eye, As a thing that, though unseen, Must be near thee, and hath been; And when in that secret dread Thou hast turned around thy head, Thou shalt marvel I am not As thy shadow on the spot, And the power which thou dost feel Shall be what thou must conceal.

" And a magic voice and verse Hath baptized thee with a curse, And a spirit of the air Hath begirt thee with a snare ; In the wind there is a voice Shall forbid thee to rejoice ; And to thee shall night deny All the quiet of her sky; And the day shall have a sun Which shall make thee wish it done.

" From thy false tears I did distil An essence which hath strength to kill; From thy own heart I then did wring The black blood in its blackest spring; From thy own smile I snatched the snake, For there it coiled as in a brake ; From thy own lip I drew the charm Which gave all these their chiefest harm; In proving every poison known, I found the strongest was thine own.

" By thy cold breast and serpent smile, By thy unfathomed depths of guile, By that most seeming virtuous eye, By thy shut soul's hypocrisy,

By the perfection of thine art,
Which passed for human thine own heart;
By thy delight in others' pain,
And by thy brotherhood of Cain,
I call upon thee, and compel
Thyself to be thy proper hell!

" And on thy head I pour the vial Which doth devote thee to this trial; Not to slumber, nor to die, Shall be in thy destiny, Though thy death shall still seem near To thy wish, but as a fear ; Lo ! the spell now works around thee, And the clankless chain hath bound thee : O'er thy heart and brain together Hath the word been passed—now wither ! "

The Italian poem forms, in its first and second parts, a drama as complete as that of " Manfred," and, as I hope to render clear, one more consistent to the leading idea, or, as critics were wont to say, " more coherent in the unities." This idea in the one, as in the other, is that of a powerful sorcerer assailed by a fiend in the form of remorse, and that with the most aggravating and insulting terms of contempt. In " Manfred " the persecutor tells his victim that he shall be his own hell, for that of all poisons his own evil heart is the worst. The Italian, more direct and less metaphysical still, alludes, in the accusation by the spirit, to no other punishment save that of conscience, and declares the magician to be poisoned through and through in himself:

" Tu sei cattivo e scelerato, Tu sei avvelenato Nel cuore enell anima,"

and bids him go forth to be for ever pursued by the avenger.

Byron's poem is entirely based on sorcery, and is intended to set forth the tremendous mental struggles of a

mind which has risen above mankind with supernatural power, which assails him with remorse. In the first place he simply goes to sleep; in the grand finale he resists, like Don Juan, or, as the saying is, " dies game "— " only this, and nothing more "—leaving all idea of an end, object, moral, or system, entirely in the dark. " Manfred " is merely dramatic for the sake of stage effect, and only excellent in impressing us with the artistic skill of the author. Its key is art for the sake of art, and effect on anybody, no matter who. Within this limit it is most admirable.

In both the Italian and English poems the one persecuted makes his strong point of departure from the discovery or knowledge that the persecuted is not one whom he has injured, but simply a mocking and tormenting sprite. Thus the former text declares that when he finds he is pursued simply by Intialo, the shadow, which we may here translate "his own imagination," he rallies with a tremendous counter-curse in which far more is meant than meets the eye. The grand mission of the magus or sorcerer in all the occult lore of all antiquity, whether he appear as Buddha or any other man of men, is to conquer all enemies by tremendous power won by penance or by iron will. A favourite means of tormenting the enemy or fiend is to awaken the conscience of the magician, or, what is the same thing, to tempt him to sin, as Satan did Christ. But even conscience loses its power when we feel that the foe is exaggerating our sins, and only urging them for torment's sake, and especially when these sins are of a kind which from a certain standpoint or code, are not sins at all.

And here we are brought to a subject so strange and witch-like that it is difficult to discuss or make clear. It is evident enough in "Manfred" that the great crime was the hero's forbidden love for his sister Astarte. This it is which crushes him. But it does not appear from the

Italian (save to those deeply learned in the darker secrets of sorcery) why or how it is that the one persecuted so suddenly revives and defies the spirit, turning, as it were, his own power against him. In explaining this, I do not in the least conjecture, guess, or infer anything; I give the explanation as it was understood by the narrator, and as confirmed by other legends and traditions. It is this :

Michelet, in La Sorci/rc, which amid much lunacy or folly contains many truths and ingenious perceptions, has explained that the witchcraft of the Middle Ages was a kind of mad despairing revolt against the wrongs of society, of feudalism, and the Church. It was in very truth the precursor of Protestantism. Under the name of religion conscience had been abused, and artificial sins, dooming to hell, been created out of every trifle, and out of almost every form of natural instincts. The reaction from this (which was a kind of nihilism or anarchy), was to declare the antithetic excess of free will. One of the forms of this revolt was the belief that the greatest sorcerers were born (ex filio et matre) from the nearest relations, and that to dare and violate all such ties was to conquer by daring will the greatest power. It was the strongest defiance of the morality taught by the Church, therefore one of the highest qualifications for an iron-willed magician. It is specially pointed out in the legend of Diana that she began by such a sin, and so came to be queen of the witches; and the same idea of entire emancipation or illumination, or freedom from all ties, is the first step to the absolute free will which constitutes the very basis of all magic. This, which is repugnant to humanity, was actually exalted by the Persian Magi to a duty or religious principle, and it was the same in Egypt as regarded "first families." The sorcerer pursued by Intialo bases all his power to resist on the mere fact that he is beloved by a beautiful witch. This is the Astarte of the

Italian drama, or a sister—the terrible tie which shows that a man is above conscience, and free from all fear of the powers that be, whether of earth or air. By it his triumph is complete. He surmounts the accusation of being without morals by utterly denying their existence from a higher or illuminated point of view. The magus claims to rank with the gods, and if a divinity creates mankind as his children, and then has a child by a woman, he is in the same state as the sorcerer, according to wizards.

If any reproach attaches to the employment of such an element in poetry, then Byron and

Shelley are far more to blame than the Italian witch-poet, who veiled his allusion with much greater care than they did, and who had the vast excuse of sincere belief, while their highest aim was mere art. The wizard-poet has his heart in this faith, as in a religion, and he is one with his hero. Manfred is at best only a broken-down magician who presents a few boldly dramatic daring traits—the Italian sorcerer, who is far more defiant and fearless, conquers. " I am more malignant than thou art," is a terrible utterance; so is the tone of affected pity for the baffled tormentor, in which we detect a shade of sarcasm based on overwhelming triumph. This feeling, be it observed, progresses, crescendo forte, gradually and very artistically, from the first verse to the last. Intialo has threatened to make the victim a sorry cur who comes at a call; the sorcerer replies that he will make " a swine's snout" of Intialo. Finally, he dares the fiend to meet him at midnight at the great Witches' Sabbat, at the dread walnut-tree of Benevento. Here the threats reach an ingenious and terrible climax, though the form in which they are expressed is only quite clear to the initiated. The sorcerer says, " When thou thinkest that thou see'st my shadow thou wilt behold thine own," or in other words, " You who have sought to torment me by a sliadow shall

yourself be mocked by finding that you are only mine." This climax of daring the fiend to meet him at Benevento, at the tremendous and terrible rendezvous of all the devils, witches, and sorcerers, and then and there trying conclusions with him in delusion and magic, or a strife of shadows, while leaning against the awful tree itself, which is the central point of the Italian Domdaniel, is magnificently imagined.

In Goethe's " Faust," as in Byron's " Manfred," the hero is a magician, but he is not in either true to the name or character. The great magus of early ages, even like the black Voodoo of America, had it clearly before him all the time that his mission or business, above all things, was to develop an indomitable will superior to that of men or spirits. Every point is gained by force, or by will and penance. In real sorcery there is no such thing as a pact with a devil, and becoming his slave after a time. This is a purely later-Roman invention, a result of the adoption of the mixture of Jewish monotheism and Persian dualism, which formed the Catholic Church. In Goethe's " Faust " we have the greatest weakness, and an extreme confusion of character. The conclusion of the tale is contradictory or absurd, and the difficulty is solved with the aid of a Deus ex machina. The hero is a sorcerer, and there is not a trace of true sorcery or magianism or tremendous ^vill and work in the ivJiole drama. Beautiful things are said and done, but, take it for all in all, it is a grand promenade which leads to nothing. 1

In the Italian legend, brief and rude as it is, there appears a tremendous power worked out with great consistency. The demon or spirit, intent on causing remorse or despair (ad affrctare il riniorso), threatens the sorcerer with terrible maledictions. And these words, if we regard

1 The concluding portion of this chapter is taken from the Italian original paper read by me at the first meeting of the Italian Folklore Society in the Collegio Romano, Rome, November 20, 1894.

their real meaning and spirit, have never been surpassed in any poem.

And we should note here that the Italian sorcerer who subdues the devil by simple will and pluck is no Manfred or Faust drawn from the religious spirit of the Middle Ages. He belongs to the Etruscan age, or to that of the ancient Magi; he meets malediction with malediction, spell with spell, curse with curse, injury with injury, sarcasm and jeer with the same; he insults the devil, calling him his slave :

" Perche io sono di te — molto piu maligno."

Until in the end they change parts, and the demon becomes the one tormented. Therefore there is in this legend, with all its rudeness, a conception which is so grand, as regards setting forth the possible power of man, and the critis sicut dens of modern science, that it is in unity and fulness far beyond any variant of the same subject.

That this is of great antiquity is clear, for out of this enchanted forest of Italian witchcraft and mystical sorcery there never yet came anything, great or small, which was not at least of the bronze, if not of the neolithic age.

Truly, when the chief character in a tradition of the old Etruscan land bears an Etruscan name, or that of a shadow called a shadow, we may well conclude that it is not of yesterday. So all things rise and bloom and pass away here on this earth to winter and decay, and are as phantoms which

" Come like shadows, so depart."

For a last word, " Manfred " and " Faust " are only works of art, intended to "interest " or amuse or charm the reader, and as such they are great. They are simply dramas or show-pieces, which also give a high idea of the artistic skill of their writers. " Intialo " sets forth the great idea of the true sorcerer, in which they both fail, and carries

it out logically to a tremendous triumph. It is the very quintessence of all heresies, and of the first great heresy, eritis sicut deus.

There will not be wanting one or two critics of the low kind who take their hints from the disavowals of the author to declare that his book is just what it is not, who will write that I think I have discovered a better poet than Keats in Marietta Pery, and a far greater than Goethe or Byron in the unknown author of the invocation to " Intialo." But all that I truly mean is that the former is nearer to old tradition, and more succinct than the English bard— " only this and nothing more "—while in " Intialo " we have given, as no one ever expressed it, the true ideal of the magician who, overcoming all qualms of conscience, whether innate or suggested, and trampling under foot all moral human conventions, rises to will, and victory over all enemies, especially the demons of the threshold. As a poem, I no more claim special merit for it than I would for Marietta's; x indeed, to the very considerable number of " highly cultivated " people who only perceive poetry in form and style, and cannot find it in the grandest conceptions unless they are elegantly expressed, what I have given in this connection will not appear as poetry at all.

1 These references to Marietta Pery are in regard to a certain Italian poetess, of whose work I originally intended to give specimens in this book, but which were omitted as want of space did not permit their insertion. I hope to include them in another volume of legends. — C. G. LELAND.

CAIN AND HIS WORSHIPPERS

THE SPELL OF THE MIRROR—THE INVOCATION TO CAIN—THE WITCH-HISTORY OF CAIN AND ABEL

" Rusticus in Luna Quern sarcina deprimit una, Monstrat per spinas Nulli prodesse rapinas."

—ALEXANDER NECKHAM, A.D. 1157.

THIS is, for reasons which I will explain anon, one of the most curious traditions which have been preserved by the Tuscan peasantry. I had made inquiry whether any conjuring by the aid of a mirror existed—" only this and nothing more"—when, some time after, I received the following:

LA SCONGIURAZIONE DELLO SPECCHIO.

When one wishes to enchant a lover.

" Go at midnight when there is a fine full moon, and take a small mirror, which must be kept in a box of a fine red colour, and at each of the four corners of the box put a candle with a pin, or with a pin in its point, and observe that two of the pins must have red heads, and two black, and form a cross, and note that every candle must have two tassels hanging from it, one red and one black.

" And within the box first of all put a good layer of coarse salt, and form on the salt a ring or wreath of incense, and in the middle of this a cross of cummin, and above all put the small mirror. Then take the photograph of your lover, but not the real photograph but the negative, because it must be on a plate of glass (lastra di vetro). Then take some hairs of

the lover and join them to the photograph (sono uniti da/la parte del quore), and then take a fine sprig of rue.

" And with all this nicely arranged in the box, take a boat and sail out to sea; and if a woman works the spell she must take three men with her only, and if a man three women and no other person. And they must go forth at an instant when the moon shines brightly (risplende bene) on the mirror. Then hold the left hand over the mirror, and hold up the rue with the right. Then repeat the following: x

INCANTESIMO.

" Luna ! Luna ! Luna ! Tu che siei tanto bella! E nel tuo cerchio rachiude Un si pessimo sogetto Rachiude Chaino che per gelosia Uccise il proprio fratello.

" Ed io che per la gelosia Del mio amante non ho potuto Ne bere e ne mangiare, Ne colle amiche Non posso conversare,

10 l'amo tanto, tanto,

E non sono corrisposta, Quanto Io vorrei e per la sua La sua fredezza io ne sono Tanto gelosa non so qual' malarono Quale malarono io commetterei, Vado a letto non passo riposare, Mi viene visioni che

11 mio amante mi debba ingannare.

" Luna, Luna, mia bella Luna ! Che tanto bella siei e ben' risplende, Ti prego volere pregare per me Chaino che per gelosia

1 Such incantations are intoned or chanted in a very peculiar style, so that those who can only hear the sound know that it is a magic spell. Therefore they must be expressed very accurately to the letter. It may be observed that there is a contradiction in the original MS., which here speaks of three companions, and subsequently of two. I believe the latter to be correct.

V

Uccise il proprio fratello,
Ed io vorrei punire il mio amante,
Ma non farlo morire
Ma pero farlo soffrire,
Che non abbia mai bene
Ne giorno, ne notte,
Non possa ne bene ne mangiare.
E la notte non possa riposare,
E Chaino col suo fascio,
Suo fascio, di pruini,
Il mio amante dal su'letto
Puo le fare, alzare
E alla casa mia
Farlo presto ritornare !

"Chaino! Chaino! Chaino! Per tre volte io ti chiamo. Ti chiamo ad alta voce, In un punto dove si trova, Soltanto che cielo e aqua, E le due mie compagne.

" Chaino ! per la gelosia Che provarti tu per il tuo fratello ! Provo io per il mio amante, E vorrei a me farlo ritornare, Per non allontanarsi mai piu.

" Tu che dal alto del cielo Tutto vedi—questa scatola E bene preparata e tutte e quattro Le candele o accese, tu puoi guardare, Puoi guardare questo specchio, E se tre parole pronunzierai Tutti i pruini che ai Nell' fascio delle legne che adosso, Sempre porti potrai, Potrai farli passare Nel corpo, e nel cuore Del mio amante, Che non possa dormire e sia Costretto a vestirsi, E venire a casa mia, Per non andarsene mai piu.

" Con questo ramo di ruta Lo bagno nel mare, E bagno le mie due compagne Che pronunzierrano queste parole Tale [secondo il nome] colla ai uta Di Chaino vai dalla tua amante Per non lasciarla mai piu.

" Se questa grazia mi fai Fai alzare un forte vento, E poi spengere le candele. Chaino ! Chaino ! Chaino ! "

THE INVOCATION.

" Moon ! O moon ! O moon ! Thou who art always fair, Yet holdest in thy ring One of such evil name, Because thou holdest Cain; Cain who from jealousy His own born brother slew.

" I too through jealousy Of one whom I still love Can neither drink nor eat, Nor even talk with friends, I love so much—so much-Yet am not loved again As I would fain be loved. Through his indifference I So jealous have become, I do not know what sin I would not now commit; I cannot sleep at night For dreams in which I see Him faithless unto me.

" Moon, moon, O beauteous moon ! As thou art fair and bright, I pray thee, pray for me ; Cain who from jealousy

R

Slew his own brother born, As I would punish well The one whom I yet love, Yet would not cause his death, So may he suffer thus : May suffering be his lot By day as in the night, May he not eat or drink, Nor may he sleep at night.!

" May Cain who bears the bunch Upon his back, of thorns, Stand by my lover's bed, And make him rise from sleep And hasten to my home.

" O Cain ! O Cain ! O Cain ! Three times I call to thee, Call with my loudest voice, Just as I find myself Between the sea and sky, And my two friends with me.

" Cain, by the jealousy Which once thy brother caused, And which I now endure, For him whom still I love, Make love return to me And never leave me more.

" Thou who from heaven on high Seest all things, here behold This casket well prepared ! The mystic tapers four All lighted, look on them ! Then in this mirror look. Then if thou wilt but speak Three words —then all the thorns Which on thy back thou bear'st, All in a bundle bound, Will pass into the life, The body and the heart Of him whom yet I love, So that he sleep no more,

And be compelled to rise, Compelled to clothe himself, And hasten to my home, Never to leave me more.

" Now, with this branch of rue, Which I dip in the sea, I sprinkle both my friends, That they may speak these words :

That by the aid

Of Cain shalt seek thy love, And never leave her more.

" If thou wilt grant me this, Cause a high wind to blow, Extinguishing the lights. O Cain ! O Cain ! O Cain !"

Before proceeding further, I would explain that the use of a photograph, which must be a negative on glass, instead of being, as was suggested to me, a modern interpolation, is, strangely enough, a proof of the antiquity of the rite. In the old time, a picture or portrait painted in transparent colour on glass was held up to the moon that its rays might pass through it and enchant the subject. And among the Romans, when one had a portrait of any one cut on diaphanous stone, it was used in the same way. I had in my possession once such a portrait-gem, 2 and a fine needle-hole had been bored through the right eye so as to blind the original of the likeness. And I had a friend who lived in Russia, who discovered that a person who hated him had obtained his photograph, and pricked holes with a very fine needle in the eyes to blind him. The negative of a photograph on glass would very naturally occur as a substitute for a picture. But what is most important is that this mention of the translucent negative proves fully that the whole ceremony, in its

1 Here the name of the lover is pronounced by the friends.

2 Now in possession of Mrs. January of St. Louis, Missouri.

minutest detail, has actually been preserved to this da\'7d', and that the incantation, long as it is, exists as I have given it, since every line in it corresponds to the rite. And as I know that it was gathered by a witch and fortune-teller among others, and carefully compared and collated, I am sure that it is authentic and traditional.

Fifty pages are devoted by the Rev. T. Harley in his " Moon Lore " to the subject of the Man in the Moon, and since the book appeared in 1885 there have been great additions to the subject. This human being is declared by myths found in India, and especially among the Oriental gypsies, in Ireland, Borneo, Greenland, and South America, to be a man who is punished by imprisonment above for incest with his sister the sun. As he wanders for ever over the heavens, just as gypsies wander on earth, they claim him for their ancestor, and declare that Zin-gan (or gypsy) is derived from two words meaning sun and moon. Kam \'7d the sun, has been varied to kan t and in gypsy the moon is called ckone, which is also t-chen, chin, or sin. But the point lies in this, that Cain was condemned to be a " a fugitive and a vagabond in the earth," which gives much apparent strength to the idea that Cain, whether Shemitic or Aryan, was, for a great crime, or as chief of sinners, imprisoned in the moon.

This sufferer, in different legends, has been represented as a Sabbath-breaker, as Judas Iscariot, as Isaac, and many more transgressors, almost always with a bunch or bush of thorns, for which there has been literally no real explanation whatever. This I will now investigate, and, I think, clearly explain.

Dante in two places speaks of the Man in the Moon as Cain, and as if it were a very popular legend (-ferno, xx. 123):

" Ma vienne omai che gia tiene '1 confine

D'ambedue gli emisperi, e tocca 1'onda Sotlo Sibilia, Caino e le spine E gia iernolle fu la Luna toncla."

" But now he comes who doth the borders hold Of the two hemispheres, and drive the waves Under the sibyl, Cain, with many thorns. And yesternight the moon was round and full ; Take care that it may never do thee harm At any time when in the gloomy wood."

This twentieth canto is devoted to the sorcerers in hell, and ends with allusion to the full moon, the sibyl, and Cain, as allied to witchcraft, prediction, and sin. When the moon is full it is also " high tides " with the witches, now as of yore :

" Full moon, high sea, Great man shall thou be : Red dawning, cloudy sky, Bloody death shall thou die."

Dante again mentions Cain in the moon, in the Paradiso,

50:

" Ma ditemi, che con li segni lui Dio questo corpo, che laggiuso in terra Fan di Cain favoleggiare altrui?"

" But tell me now what are the gloomy marks Upon this body, which down there on earth Make people tell so many tales of Cain ? "

To which Beatrice replies by a mysterious physical explanation of the phenomenon, advising him to take three mirrors and observe how the moon is reflected from one to the other, and that in this manner formal principle, or first creative power, passes from light to darkness. The reader will here remember that with the witches the mirror is specially devoted to conjuring Cain.

It is worth noting that a speckietto, or small looking-glass, was specially (Barretti) " a little mirror placed at the bottom of a jewel casket."

I would now note that the thorns which Cain carries signify, not only in modern Italian, but in old Roman sorcery, the sting of hatred and of jealousy. It is a most apparent and natural simile, and is found from the crown of thorns on Christ to the Voodoo sorcery in Western America. Miss Mary Owen knew a black girl in Missouri who, as a proof of being Christianised, threw away the thorn which she kept as a fetish to injure an enemy. But in early times the thorn was universally known as symbolical of sin, just as Cain was regarded as the first real sinner. Therefore the two were united. Menzel tells us in his Christliche Syinbolik (Part I. p. 206) that it is a legend that " there were no thorns before the Fall; they first grew with sin, therefore thorns are a symbol of the sorrow or pain which came from sin." Of all of which there is a mass of old German myths and legends, which I spare the reader, for I have endeavoured in this comment to avoid useless myth-mongering in order to clearly set forth the connection between Cain, his thorns, and the moon.

That the conjuring the moon with a mirror is very ancient indeed appears from the legend drawn from classic sources, which is thus set forth in " A Pleasant Comedie called Summer's Last Will and Testament. Written by Thomas Nash. London, 1600" :

" In laying thus the blame upon the Moone Thou imitat'st subtill Pythagoras, Who what he would the People should beleeve, The same he wrote with blood upon a Glasse, And turned it opposite 'gainst the New Moone, Whose Beames, reflecting on it with full force, Shew'd all those lines to them that stood behinde, Most pleynly writ in circle of the Moone, And then he said : ' Not I, but the newe Moone Fair Cynthia persuades you this and that.' '

In the " Clouds " of Aristophanes the same idea is made into a jest, in which Strepsiades thus addresses Socrates:

" Strepsiades. If I were to buy a Thessalian witch, and then draw down the moon by night, and then shut her up in a round helmet-case like a mirror, and then keep watching her—

Socrates. What good would that do you, then ?

Strepsiades. What ! If the moon were not to rise any more anywhere, I should not pay the interest.

Socrates. Because what ?

Strepsiades. Because the money is lent on interest." *

" Moon Lore," p. 152.

These instances could be multiplied. What I have given are enough to show the antiquity of the conjuration ; and I also venture to declare that any Italian scholar who is familiar with these formulas of sorcery will admit that, making all due allowance for transmission among peasants, the language, or words, or turns of expression in this incantation denote great antiquity.

The next paper or tradition on the subject of Cain, which, as every phrase in it indicates, was taken down from an old dame who at first slowly recalled forgotten sentences, will be to many more interesting, and to all much more amusing than the first. It once happened that an old gypsy in England began to tell me the story of the ghostly baker of Stonehenge and the seven loaves, but, suddenly pausing, he said : " What's the use of telling that to you who have read it all in the Bible ? " There is, however, this trifling difference, that I am not sure that my Italian witch friends knew that Cain and Abel are in the Bible at all. The Red Indian doctor, whose knowledge of the Old Testament was limited to its being good to cure neuralgia, was far beyond the contadini as regards familiarity with "the efficacy of the Scripture."

This is the witch-tale as written word by word:

ABELE E CHAINO.

"They were two brothers. Abel greatly loved Cain, but Cain did not love so much the brother Abel.

" Cain had no great will to work.

"Abel, however, on the contrary, was greatly disposed (si ingegnava) to labour, because he had found it profitable. He was industrious in all, and at last became a grazier (mercante di manzf).

"And Cain also, being moved by jealousy (per astia\ wished to become a grazier, but the wheel did not turn for him as it did for Abel.

"And Cain also was a good man, and set himself contentedly to work, believing that he could become as rich as his brother, but he did not succeed in this, for which reason he became so envious of Abel that it resulted in tremendous hate, and he swore to be revenged.

" Cain often visited his brother, and once said to him, ' Abel, thou art rich and I am poor ; give me the half of thy wealth, since thou wishest me so well!'

" Then Abel replied : ' If I give thee a sum which thou thyself couldst gain by industry, thou shouldst still labour as I do, and I will give thee nothing, since, if thou wilt work as I do, thou wilt become as rich.'

" One day there were together Cain, Abel, and a merchant, whose name I forget. And one told that he had seen in a dream seven fat oxen and seven lean. And the merchant, who was an astrologer or wizard, explained that the seven fat oxen meant seven years of abundance, and the seven lean as many years of famine.

" And so it came to pass as he foretold—seven years of plenty and seven of famine.

" And Cain, hearing this, thought: ' During the seven years of plenty Abel will lay by a great store, and then I will slay him, and possess myself of all his goods, and thus I will take care of myself, and my brother will be dead.'

" Now, Cain greatly loved God ; he was good towards God, more so than Abel, because Abel, having become rich, never spoke more unto the Lord; and Abel would gladly have become a wizard himself.

" Then Cain began to think how he could slay Abel and become a merchant in his place, and so went forth to cut wood.

" One day he called his brother Abel, and said to him : ' Thou art so rich, while I am poor, and all my work avails me little.' And with that he gave Abel a blow with a knife, and dressed himself in his garments, and took a bundle of thorns on his back, and thus clad he took Abel's place as merchant, believing that no one would recognise him as Cain.

"And while thus buying and selling he met the merchant-wizard who had foretold the seven years of famine and of abundance. And he said, ' Oh, good day, Abel,' to make Cain believe that he was not discovered. But the oxen who were present all began to chant in chorus :

" ' Non chiamate questo, Abele ! E Chaino, non lo vedete, Per la gola della monete II fratello ammazato, E del suoi panni e vestito. O Chaino or siei chiamato Alia presenza del gran Dio, Che a morte ti 'a condannato Che di richezza eri assetato.'

" ' Do not call that person Abel; It is Cain, do you not see it? Cain who, for the greed of money, Treacherously slew his brother, And then clad him in his garments. Now, O Cain 1 thou wilt be summoned Speedily unto the presence Of the Lord, who has condemned thee Unto death for thy great avarice.'

" Cain came before God.

" ' O gran Dio di clemenza Voi che siete grande, buono, Velo chiedo a voi perdone, Per il bene vi ho valuto, Un instante vi ho dimenticato Ma ne sono molto pentito, Di aver ammazato Abele il fratello mio.'

" ' O great God of endless mercy, Thou who art so good and mighty, Grant, I pray thee, grant me pardon For the good I did while living ! Truly once, but for an instant, I forgot myself, but deeply I since then have long repented That I slew my brother Abel.'

" But God replied : a

" A punishment thou shalt have because thou didst slay thy brother from a desire to become rich. Likewise thou didst meddle with witchcraft and sorceries, as did thy brother. And Abel made much money and was very rich, because he did not love God, but sorcerers. Albeit, ever good he never

I have no doubt that originally all the spoken parts of this narrative were sung.

did evil things, and many good, wherefore God pardoned him. But thou shalt not be pardoned because thou didst imbrue thy hands in human blood, and, what is worse, in thy own brother's blood.

" The punishment which I inflict is this :

" The thorns l which thou didst put upon thy brother are now for thee.

" Thou shalt be imprisoned in the moon, and from that place shalt behold the good and the evil of all mankind.

"And the bundle of thorns shall never leave thee, and every time when any one shall conjure thee, the thorns shall sting thee cruelly; they shall draw thy blood.

" P nd thus shalt thou be compelled to do that which shall be required of thee by the sorcerers or by conjuring, and if they ask of thee that which thou wilt not give, then the thorns shall goad thee until the sorceries shall cease."

v — This is clearly enough no common popular nursery tale, such as make up collections of Tuscan tales or popular legends, gathered from pious or picturesque peasants. Through it all runs a deep current of dark heresy, the deliberate contravention of accepted Scripture, and chiefly the spell of sorcery and deadly witchcraft. It is a perfect and curious specimen of a kind of forbidden literature which was common during the Middle Ages, and which is now extremely rare. This literature or lore was the predecessor of Protestantism, and was the rock on which it was based.

There have always been in the world since time began certain good people whose taste or fate it was to be invariably on the wrong side, or in the opposition; like the Irishman just landed from a ship in America, who, being asked how he would vote, replied, "Against the Government, of course, whatever it is," they are always at war with the powers that be. With Jupiter they would have opposed the Titans; with Prometheus, Jupiter ;

1 Thorns here plainly mean suffering, Fasio di pritini che ai tnesso al luo Jratello.

as early Christians they would have rebelled against the Pagans, and as heretics, Orientalised Templars, Vaudois, illuminati, sorcerers, and witches, they would have undermined the Church, never perceiving that its system or doctrine was, an fond, fetish, like their own. Among these rebels it was long the rule to regard those gods or men who were specially reviled by their foes or oppressors as calumniated. Even Satan was to them " the puir deil; " according to the Taborites, an oppressed elder brother of Christ, or a kind of Man in an Iron Mask kept out of his rights by Jehovah the XIV. These discontented ones deified all who had been devilled, found out that Jezebel had been a femme incouiprise, and the Scarlet Woman only an interesting highly-coloured variant of the ancient hoary myth of Mademoiselle or Miss Salina the Innocent. When Judas was mentioned, they solemnly remarked that there was a great deal to be said on both sides of that question ; while others believed that Ananias and Sapphira had been badly sat upon, and deserved to be worshipped as saints of appropriation—a cult, by the way, the secret observance of which has by no means died out at the present day—several great men being regarded in Paris as its last great high priests.

The Cainites, as known by that name to the Church, were a Gnostic sect of the second century, and are first mentioned by Irenaeus, who connects them with the Val-entinians, of whom I thought but yesterday when I saw in a church a sarcophagus warranted to contain the corpse of St. Valentine. They believed that Cain derived his existence from the supreme power, but Abel from the inferior, and that in this respect he was the first of a line which included Esau, Korah, the dwellers in Sodom and Gomorrah, the worshippers of Ashtoreth-Mylitta, or the boundless sensualists, the sorcerers, and witches.

Considering what human nature is, and its instincts to opposition, we can see that there must have been natu-

rally a sect who regarded Cain as a misjudged martyr. Abel appeared to them as the prosperous well-to-do bourgeois, high in favour with the Lord, a man with flocks, while Cain was a tiller of the ground, a poor peasant out of favour. It must be admitted that in the Book of Genesis, in the history of the first murder, we are much reminded of the high priest Chalcas in La Belle Helene, where he exclaims, " Trap de fleurs ! " and expresses a preference for cattle. It is the old story of the socialists and anarchists, which is ever new.

The witches and sorcerers of early times were a widely spread class who had retained the beliefs and traditions of heathenism with all its license and romance and charm of the forbidden. At their head were the Promethean Templars, at their tail all the ignorance and superstition of the time, and in their ranks every one who was oppressed or injured either by the nobility or the Church. They were treated with indescribable cruelty, in most cases worse than beasts of burden, for they were outraged in all their feelings, not at intervals for punishment, but habitually by custom, and they revenged themselves by secret orgies and fancied devil-worship, and occult ties, and stupendous sins, or what they fancied were such. I can seriously conceive—what no writer seems to have considered— that there must have been an immense satisfaction in selling or giving one's self to the devil, or to any power which was at war with their oppressors. So they went by night, at the full moon, and sacrificed to Diana, or " later on " to Satan, and danced and rebelled. It is very well worth noting that we have all our accounts of sorcerers and heretics from Catholic priests, who had every earthly reason for misrepresenting them, and did so. In the vast amount of ancient witchcraft still surviving in Italy there is not much anti-Christianity, but a great deal of early heathenism. Diana, not Satan, is still the real head of the witches. The Italian witch, as the priest Grillandus said,

stole oil to make a love-charm. 1 But she did not, and does not say, as he declared, in doing so, " I renounce Christ." There the priest plainly lied. The whole history of the witch mania is an ecclesiastical falsehood, in which such lies were subtly grafted on the truth. But in due time the Church, and the Protestants with them, created a Satanic witchcraft of their own, and it is this aftergrowth which is now regarded as witchcraft in truth.

Cain-worshippers and witches seem to have been all in the same boat. I think it very likely that in these two traditions which I have given we have a remnant of the actual literature of the Cainites, that Gnostic-revived and mystical sect of the Middle Ages. But I doubt not that its true origin is far older than Christianity, and lost in earliest time.

One last remark. We are told in the tale that Abel, having Become rich, " cut" the Lord, or would speak to him no longer. I suppose that he dropped the synagogue and Yom kippur, and became a Reformirter, and his children in due time Goyim. Also that he wanted to become a wizard, which may be a hint that he was " no conjuror." But it is seriously a proof of the naivete, and consequent probable antiquity of the tale, that these details are not "wrote sarcastic," nor intended for humour. And it is also interesting to observe how impartially the narrator declares that Cain was "a good man," and how he, in pleading his own cause before the Lord, insists that in killing Abel he only inadvertently forgot himself for an instant. One almost expects to hear him promise that he will not do it again.

It is a striking proof of the antiquity of this tradition

1 It is amusing that this stealing oil wherewith to make love-charms, which was denounced so bitterly as damnable sorcery at one time, and frequently punished by death, i.e., by burning alive, is now tacitly encouraged by the priests. There are churches about Rome in which the oil is placed where it may be stolen or taken, it being understood that a soldo or two shall be left to pay for it.

of Cain, as I have given it, that the witch or wizard sympathy for the first murderer is in it unmistakable. The sending Cain to the moon, instead of hell, is understood to be a mitigation of his sentence. In his work on magicians and witches, A.D. 1707, Gold-schmidt devotes many pages to set forth what was believed by all the learned of his time, that Cain was the father of all the wizards, and his children, the Cainites, the creators of the Gaber, fire-idolators, Cabiri, magic soothsaying, and so forth. So the tradition lived on, utterly forgotten by all good people, and yet it is to me so quaint as to be almost touching to find it still existing, a fragment of an old creed outworn here among poor witches in Florence.

"Sacher Masoch," a Galician novelist, informs us in a romance, "The Legacy of Cain," that the Cainites still exist in Russia, and that their religion is represented by the following charming creed :

" Satan is the master of the world ; therefore it is a sin to belong to Church or State, and marriage is also a capital sin. Six things constitute the legacy of Cain : Love, Property, Government, War, and Death. Such was the legacy of Cain, who was condemned to be a wanderer and a fugitive on earth."

I have another apparently very ancient conjuration of a mirror, in two parts. It is of the blackest witchcraft, of the most secret kind, and is only intended to injure an enemy.

From an article in La Rivista delle Tradizione Popolare of July 1894, by F. Montuori, I learn that in a little work by San Prato on " Cain and the Thorns according to Dante and Popular Tradition," Ancona, iSSi, which I have not seen, the history of Cain is given much as told by Maddalena. What is chiefly interesting in the version of Maddalena is, however, wanting in all the folklore on the subject collected by others; it is the manifest trace of Cainism, of sympathy with the first murder, and in its heresy. This opens for us a far wider field of research and valuable historical information than the rather trivial fact that Cain is simply the Man in the Moon.

Merk in Die Sitten und GebrducJie der Deutsclien, gives (p. 644), from Wolf, a strange legend which is nearly allied to Moon worship by witches, and the mirror :

" There was a man in Kortryk who was called Klare Mone (bright moon), and he got his name from this. One night when sleeping on his balcony he heard many women's voices sweetly singing. They held goblets [there is some confusion here with gliiserne Pfannen or glass panes in the roof from which the man looked ; I infer that the witches drank from " glass pans," i.e., metallic mirrors], and as they drank they sang :

" ' We are drinking the sweetest of earthly wine, For we drink of the clear and bright moonshine.'

" But as the man approached them, ' with a club to beat or kill them, all vanished."

"Which fable teaches," as the wise Flaxius notes, " what indeed this whole book tends to show—that few people know or heed what witches ever really were. Now, that this boor wished to slay the sorceresses with a club, for drinking moonshine, is only what the whole world is doing to all who have different ideas from ours as to what constitutes enjoyment. So in all history, under all creeds, even unto this day, people have been clubbed, hung, tortured, and baked alive, or sent to Coventry for the crime of drinking moonshine ! "

And so this volume ends, oh reader mine!

" So the visions flee, So the dreams depart; And the sad reality, Now must act its part." Ite, lector benevole, lie, mis so. est.

THE END

Printed in Great Britain
by Amazon